Remember This

Remember This

STEVE ADAMS

THE UNIVERSITY OF WISCONSIN PRESS

The University of Wisconsin Press
728 State Street, Suite 443
Madison, Wisconsin 53706
uwpress.wisc.edu

Gray's Inn House, 127 Clerkenwell Road
London EC1R 5DB, United Kingdom
eurospanbookstore.com

Printed in the United States of America
This book may be available in a digital edition.

Library of Congress Cataloging-in-Publication Data
Names: Adams, Steve (Writer and editor), author.
Title: Remember this / Steve Adams.
Description: Madison, Wisconsin : The University of Wisconsin Press, [2022]
Identifiers: LCCN 2021060198 | ISBN 9780299339241 (paperback)
Subjects: LCGFT: Romance fiction. | Fiction. | Novels.
Classification: LCC PS3601.D3965 R46 2022 | DDC 813/.6—dc23/eng/20220204
LC record available at https://lccn.loc.gov/2021060198

To the city

Remember This

1

New York City, 1988

It was a Saturday night, it was summer, and I rode the subway to meet her, not thinking it through. If anything, doing my best to not think it through. I was actually irritated at losing most of a precious Saturday night. My downtown 6 train stopped at Union Square, where I stepped off to switch to the express. Couples going out on dates and clutches of young people waited on the platform laughing, looking forward to the evening. Two black kids beat rhythms with drumsticks on white plastic tubs turned upside down, and the cadence reverberated off the concrete walls. Everyone moved to it whether they knew it or not. An uptown 6 local screeched into the station on the opposite platform. Nearby, a Middle Eastern man in a gray suit dropped a quarter into a payphone and began yelling over the noise into the receiver.

My right heel tapped against the floor. I was wound up, though I told myself there was no reason to be. She and I were friends. I was doing her a favor. Jeremy had no doubt stopped by to see her too, probably more than once. We'd watch the movie, then I'd leave. I looked down the tunnel and spotted the headlights of an approaching downtown 4 express. A moment later it barreled in front of me, pulling with it a wall of wind and heat. A stream of white kids poured out its doors, and I squeezed past them and sat. Most of the riders remaining in the car were black or Latino, and like me, headed to Brooklyn. I was white with long dark hair, slightly built, twenty-eight, from Texas, and on my way to watch a movie with my boss, my friend, after she'd gotten stuck at home with her baby. The yellowing walls of the car were scarred with graffiti and street iconography, slashes and streaks of Krylon spray paint.

We pulled from the station and into the tunnel, rattling, shaking down the line. It would've been better if we'd met at Union Square like we'd planned and caught a film there. Two hours and maybe a drink and I would've done my bit. But here I was, on work duty on a Saturday night with no pay. The train squealed to a stop at Brooklyn Bridge, where more people boarded, then the metal doors closed and we were off again to Fulton Street, then Wall Street, and the last stop in Manhattan, Bowling Green. The doors opened. A few late-shift workers straggled in.

She'd been going stir crazy alone with the baby all these days, she told me, and just wanted to have a night out, but would feel self-conscious sitting in a movie theater by herself. And we were friends, after all, had worked together three years at this point, so what's the big deal of meeting for a movie in the city? More than anything she just wanted to have a normal conversation with a grownup. Have a drink. But her sitter canceled at the last moment. When she'd phoned to tell me, she'd sounded so disappointed. She had hesitated. A moment hung between us, then I told her I had no other plans and if she wanted I could rent a video. I'd bring it over. It wouldn't be the same as going out, but at least she could talk to a grownup. "You really wouldn't mind?" she asked.

But taking the subway all the way out to Brooklyn, getting back . . . my night would be shot. Maybe I could take a cab back to Manhattan, hit a bar along the way. My fingernails tapped the plastic seat beside me, rat-a-tat-tat, tat-a-tat-tat-tat. I noticed this. Noted it. Pulled my hand into my lap and held it still. I needed to settle down. Instead of asking myself why, I stared through the marred windows of the car. The station walls were painted red-orange with black trim against a cream background. The colors shone starkly. All the stations I passed and had passed each day on the subway must have had their own specific color themes. I'd failed to notice until now, until this night.

The train pulled away and we went down, we went under the water, under the deep mud of the Hudson toward Brooklyn and hurtled through the straight dark pass. The subway conductor thought he was a cowboy, gunning it, and the clatter was deafening as the wind gyrated through the open windows. A couple of Latina girls wearing electric colors stood at the back of the car clutching silver handrails, grinned as they were jerked back and forth like dolls on strings. The lights went out and I sat in the darkness and racket. Then they flashed on again. Then off, then on, and finally the conductor cut the speed and we slowed, rising to the other side. My stomach fluttered from the shift in pace, from a rush of anxiousness at arriving in Brooklyn when there should be nothing to be anxious about. Except that she and I worked together. And she was my boss, though somehow she never made us think of her like that. We loved her for it, did our jobs as well as we could so she never had to remind us and break the spell.

There was nothing to be anxious about, I told myself. The boundaries were established long ago. Though she got to me at first. It wasn't easy to shake off. I thought about the movie I'd chosen—Louis Malle's *Atlantic City*. I'd seen it before. It's a beautiful film. But there's that scene where Susan Sarandon takes off her shirt and washes herself with lemon juice over her sink not knowing Burt Lancaster's watching her from across the way. It was too sexy. I'd made a mistake. She'd get the wrong idea. I'd . . . I'd what? I'd tell her. I'd explain. The movie was great but the director's French and maybe she had another video to watch instead because this one might be inappropriate. I loved it but I wasn't thinking. I'd apologize and she'd let it go. She'd probably even want to watch it more then, but I would've diffused any misunderstandings. It wouldn't mean anything and we could laugh about it and watch the movie like grownups. Then I'd take a taxi and salvage an hour of Saturday night before going home.

That's how it would go. My fingers tapped the seat beside me again and I pulled them back into my lap. It would've been better if we'd met in the city. My hand found its way to my belly and I breathed into it. It would all be fine. She had a baby and a husband.

I turned my attention to the station walls, those incredible old city walls that were even dirtier, buried under even more layers of soot, than Manhattan's. But the color themes were still prominent, and I spotted insignias on the wall for each station we passed: Borough Hall with a taupe *B-H* in an old serif font inside an indigo box; Nevins, with a simple white *N* for a logo; Atlantic Station with a black *A* in a white circle with gold filigree; Bergen, a white *B* on violet in a pale green frame. They were stunning, hidden under grime. What would it have been like to ride the subway in 1904 when the system opened?

The train stopped at Grand Army Plaza, and I stepped off. When it pulled away it revealed the insignia hidden behind it—a mustard *P* against a charcoal background. I was a designer, a typographer by avocation if not by profession. I stared at this icon, at these walls, and realized, once again,

I was still only waking in this city. Scratch a surface and god knew what you'd find. Two trains reeled in and out of the station behind me. My nerves jangled, and my adrenaline increased. Finally I turned, walked up the concrete steps and into the night.

Down the long slope of Flatbush Avenue the old Williamsburg Savings Bank Building and its narrow clocktower rose, dark and taller than everything around it, a few of its office windows lit. Below, car lights twinkled, flashed red and white as the string of traffic lights above them rippled from green to yellow to red. I walked downhill, turned right at the first corner, and continued up a dark, quiet, tree-lined street toward a red brick structure at 223 Sterling Avenue. A small courtyard separated two wings of the building, and through the glass a single vase of purple irises stood against a beige wall on a vacated doorman's desk.

Inside the first set of doors I examined the list of names on a small silver panel to find "Marino, 7-C." I hesitated at pressing the black square button beside it, feeling as if two, three, four, god knew how many parts of myself were watching. As each began to clarify, to take on traits, specifics, I worked harder to ignore them: The feline one, the canine, the one waiting in shadows, the one laughing at how dense I could be. One was female, her head tilted and her eyes slit expectantly. One was a child blinking in the light while stronger, surer hands led it forward.

~

"Sorry I'm late," I told her softly so as not to wake her child, and stepped into her apartment. "Did you know there are color themes throughout the subway system? Every station has its own color motif and logo. They're actual mosaics. I never noticed before. It's so beautiful. Even under years, maybe decades of soot."

I followed her to a plush gray couch where I sat beside her. She wore a simple white terrycloth bathrobe, and no makeup, not even lipstick. I'd never seen her with no makeup. She'd stripped it all off. The lines of her body were long. They swept, fixed in sudden and striking angles. As always, every gesture carried import, caught the eye.

"Can I get you something to drink?" she asked. "I only have orange juice though. Or water."

It seemed odd that's all she had. Her long dark hair tumbled down her back. Her face was Mediterranean—almond eyes, straight nose, high

6

cheekbones, a wide, full mouth. She was from Italy but had lived in New York since she was fourteen. Her family traced their lineage to ancient Crete, the land of the bull jumpers. She'd seemed so pleased when I'd asked her about them three years earlier, just after I'd started. No American ever had before. I'd discovered them in a book in the library. I'd looked up Crete. "Water would be great," I said.

She rose barefoot. I watched the orange-pink bottoms of her feet as she step-step-stepped across her plush white carpet and disappeared into her kitchen. I distracted myself by thinking of the subway hurtling underground, its squeals rising through the metal sidewalk grating at its passage. And all the people inside the subway cars, the many faces, races, the partyers, the homeless, the workers on the late shift.

In her absence, the couch and its one matching chair seemed lost in the vast living room. A dark wooden dining table with four chairs sat in front of an air conditioner churning in a section of the window spanning the north wall. Through the glass I saw the Brooklyn Clock Tower again, its round clock face at its top. To the left of the window was a narrow hallway with a closed door. Baby's room, I guessed. At the other end of the apartment a doorway opened into a dark room. The bedroom. The TV was blank in front of me, its screen dusty. Unplugged. I thought of the tape I rented, *Atlantic City*, still in my backpack. Susan Sarandon. Burt Lancaster. She entered the room carrying a small glass of water, the skirt of her white robe bouncing lightly against her knees. I considered her mouth, the fullness of its contours, its shade blood-rose, even without lipstick. I replaced the thought again with the subway beneath us, the 4 train on the green line heading north. She placed the glass on the coffee table and sat beside me. I picked up the glass and took a sip. She shifted and my eyes fixed where her bathrobe briefly separated, revealing a length of thigh that quickly disappeared under terrycloth. I raised my eyes to hers. She was watching me.

I knew what would follow even as I pushed it from my mind. The ethical mistake of it. The moral mistake. Who I might put at risk. Yet I'd come here whether or not I'd been conscious of the real reason. Which was her. But there was more involved, of course. There's always more.

I looked back at my glass, took another sip.

"John," she said, and my hand was in hers. She was leading me to her bedroom. It had to be her decision. I went easily, as if toward home.

The moment we crossed the boundary into the dark room we banged against each other, our teeth, our knuckles and fingers and elbows hitting. And yes, of course, she was naked and freshly scrubbed beneath her bathrobe and it fell from her shoulders in an instant, and I somehow managed out of my clothes faster than I could've hoped and had her in my hands, my arms, finally, after these three long years and thinking it hopeless, impossible, accepting that. She fell and opened beneath me where I pressed her to her husband's broad bed, where I entered that place, that cleft, that dark heart of hers. I plunged and came and came and came.

My breath heaved and caught in my chest in a sudden choked sob. And it had ended that quickly. She held my head motionless by a twist of hair she'd captured in her hand. She slowly released it, then her fingers trailed down my jawline. I began to tremble. As I slipped out of her she gasped. I looked down into her eyes.

"Are you okay?" she whispered.

"No," I said. A moment passed, then we both laughed abruptly. I rolled off of her. I looked up. I had no words, but felt an urge to speak. I said her name. "Alena."

She angled her leg across me and melded into my side, then put her mouth to my ear and took away my ability to say more. Sounds came from her lips, some soft clacking, coaxing of another tongue, and as I lay there watching the light from streetlamps dance across the ceiling, that quickly my blood coursed toward my center. And with it I felt the darker, truer parts of myself stepping to the fore again.

2

The day after our encounter Alena ignored me at the office, was pointedly abrupt and cold, and I wasn't prepared for it. I sat at my cubicle alongside the word processors—Esmy, Tanya, Jin, and Berne Mason from the day shift, Marjorie who worked with Jeremy and me on the swing—trying to manage my responses. It ate me up, her passing back and forth in front of me like I'd been erased. I had no idea where I stood, if she hated me, if she was glad it happened, if my job was now in jeopardy because of it. When she openly flirted with a dark-haired exec and he turned to leave, an image flashed in my mind of springing on him. I was gripping a sharpened pencil in my hand. I set it down, headed to the bathroom, and washed my face in the sink. I looked in the mirror and told myself to get a grip. Back at my desk Alena scolded me. Someone in Legal had complained about a few typos that turned up in a document I'd apparently worked on. Heads turned her way at the remonstrance. She felt the eyes on her, calmed instantly, and walked away.

Later when she was alone I stepped into her glass office. She looked up. "Yes?" she said.

"We should talk."

She looked at me impatiently. "About what?"

I paused. "My future with the company. The bull jumpers. The Mets. Pick a topic."

She looked past me out the glass windows toward the open air, the other skyscrapers. Whatever it was she was looking at, or for, it appeared to have little to do with either me or her husband. Her husband was gone, on a business trip in Italy for two months. The whole office knew it.

"Just tell me if it's over," I said.

She turned her eyes back to me. "Do you want it to be over?"

My pulse sped up. Her face flushed. She leaned toward me, a touch of anger lighting her expression.

"Well?" she asked.

"You're kidding, right?"

"Tomorrow," she mouthed. "Eleven. Call from the street."

~

Three years earlier I'd sat across from her at that same desk when she'd interviewed me. She wore a violet dress with thin shoulder straps exposing her throat, the subtle muscularity of her shoulders, her long neck, long arms. Her hands swept over her desk as she spoke, withdrew, reappeared, the plum-colored nail polish on her fingernails flashing, then receding.

She explained the job—typing on a computer for SR&G, an investment bank that had their hands in technology, media, healthcare, you name it. Much of the work consisted of reports written up by analysts from Equity Research, but our department had to be ready for anything, she told me, printing nametags, table tents, text for prospectuses, and mail-merging hundreds of letters to recruits at top business schools every spring. The work came to her as supervisor, and she doled it out. My interest in design was a plus, she said. They had a few designers on staff who hand-drew charts and simple drawings for presentations. There were no openings along those lines now, but rumor was there'd be more of that kind of work in the future.

Her eyes were confident, curious, dark, focused. She provoked me on sight beyond my understanding. My hands wanted to move to her. Nothing seemed more natural or right than crossing her desk. I could not stop looking at her mouth. I pulled my gaze away and tried to root it elsewhere, even as words having nothing to do with my reaction streamed from between my teeth. I had no idea if they made any sense, distracted as I was by the armies of warring impulses rioting in my brain. They galloped this way and that, hurled themselves against walls and over cliffs. I thought at the time if I gave away any intimation of the effect she had on me, of the impulses her subtlest gesture fired off in my brain, then I'd be looking for employment elsewhere. After a year of shit jobs in New York I was broke, almost out of time to find work that would sustain me, and going home was not an option.

Her body shifted forward. Her head tilted. I raised my eyes to hers, said something—I have no idea what—and she laughed. The sound of which saved me, made the battling factions in my mind stop their careening, tumbling, and infighting. They dropped their flags and weapons, looked up into the sky, and cheered.

She settled back into her chair. With my next words I purposely let a trace of my Texas accent slip and saw her face register satisfaction at having caught one of my secrets. She told me how she'd come over from Italy at age fourteen and lived with relatives to establish citizenship. She'd worked in her uncle's restaurant in Queens from the time she got off the plane until she graduated from CUNY. She'd been at SR&G ever since.

"We're both immigrants," she said.

"It's different here."

"Very."

Abruptly there was no more to say. I glanced at her left hand and spotted the wedding ring, the diamond at its center. She blinked and smiled, then stretched her other arm across her desk and shook my hand. I tried not to react when my skin met hers. I wouldn't touch her again until a year from the coming fall, in her office, one member of a small group standing around her, when she guided my hand to her growing belly, and I felt the tiny, emphatic kick of her child, Carina.

A hand settled on my shoulder, snapping me back. I looked up from my desk and met Jeremy's eyes.

"Where were you?" he asked. "Back in Texas?"

"Of course. Where else?"

He was a good six inches taller than me and towered over me. He had a subtle smirk that reached his blue eyes. He patted my shoulder twice, then moved down the aisle to his desk two cubicles back. What was that about?

I turned around, but he wouldn't meet my eyes. Odd. Funny, I thought. He was the first to touch me since last night, since Alena. I looked through the glass in Alena's office and saw her on the phone. I wondered if she saw us. Silly as it was, would she feel a touch of jealousy in spite of herself? Or would she approve? Jeremy, her dearest friend in the office, his hand on my shoulder. I used to think I was dear to her. I didn't know what I was to her anymore. But I'd be seeing her again tomorrow night.

I remembered Jeremy holding her daughter, Carina, then only five months old, the first time Alena brought her to the office. The baby reached for him as if she'd expected to be presented to him, had been waiting for him to appear in her life. When Alena took her away, the child continued to look back toward him even as her mother carried her through our department to each one of us.

Alena's husband stood outside the door waiting. I saw the tip of his shoe. I saw the edge of his charcoal gray suit behind the doorframe. The company had thrown their summer children's party for parents and their kids. The father had made an appearance at the party but hung back outside our door, wouldn't step into our room where his wife was boss.

"We need to go, Alena," he said in a tone I found condescending. I figured he'd squeezed her party into his lunch hour. When several of the guys from the copy room came in to see Carina, I noticed his arm rise slowly as he made a point of looking at the watch on his wrist. The wrist lowered, then lifted again a moment later when his wife presented her child to me, when she smiled and said, "Carina, this is John."

Carina couldn't care less about me, but I was almost as taken with her I was by Alena holding her. Even if Alena looked a bit tired, her eyes a little red as they tended to be then from lack of sleep and managing a new baby, she was buoyed by the child in her arms and who they were together. Being seen together where she worked, for the first time. They looked timeless. "She's beautiful," I said. "She looks like you."

Alena blinked once, then focused on me. "Thank you," she said.

An exhausted, pointed sigh rolled in from the hallway. It seemed unforgivable. Alena's body stiffened with embarrassment. I smiled and nodded in an attempt to cue her a graceful exit. She nodded in return, then walked toward where he stood—out in the hallway, behind the door, checking his watch—the man whose bedroom I would a year later violate.

Carina stared back over her mother's shoulder at Jeremy. Tall, blond Jeremy, who was hired the same day I was, who trained alongside me, who I'd disliked on sight. Who, by all appearances, she'd traveled across time to meet.

~

Past Astor Place, past Bleeker, past Bowery. Past the tip of Manhattan and under the water toward Brooklyn, I rode the subway to meet her. I stepped off at Borough Hall in Brooklyn. I called her from the street, the corner of Flatbush Avenue and Sterling, taxis and cars shooting down the hill under the hazed night, the temperature in the mid-eighties.

"I'm here," I said into the payphone when she picked up.

"The door's unlocked."

As I approached her building a man and a woman exited through the front doors. I instinctively kept walking past. They turned to their right behind me toward Flatbush. I stopped at the next corner, then doubled back. I hesitated outside, realizing at any moment someone could step out of the elevator who knew her, who could see me coming in and remember me. I hurried on, punched the square black button, and she buzzed me in. I walked to the left around the desk and its vase of irises toward the single beige elevator beyond it, out of sight from the street. The door opened, and I stepped in and pushed 7.

Her hall was empty. Her door was unlocked. I twisted the doorknob and entered her dark apartment. She met me in her hallway.

"Did I hurt your feelings yesterday?" she asked with a slight smile. She was in her bathrobe again. She reached for my hand but I pulled it back. Her smile vanished. "Second thoughts?"

"Second thoughts are part of the landscape."

"But you are here."

Her bathrobe opened at the knees as she shifted, then it closed again. The gesture was subtle enough that I could question if it was intentional. But she was playing me, of course. She knew I wasn't going anywhere; I'd arrived at my destination. "We have to watch ourselves," I told her. She softened, stepped toward me. "I insist on it."

She stopped at my tone, then nodded.

～

I lay on my back staring up at the ceiling while she rested on her side against me, her leg stretched over me. She trailed her fingers over my chest. "I was just playing with you at work."

"It hurts."

"I don't want to hurt you . . . much." She raised up on an elbow and looked down at me. "If I show favoritism I'll arouse suspicion."

"If you *don't* show favoritism you'll arouse suspicion. We've been friends for some time. Suddenly you bark at me. Heads turn. They don't know what's going on, but clearly *something* is."

She shrugged. "I dunno. I was angry."

"Why?"

13

"Because."

I waited for more, but there was none. "Just don't work against me. We need to be really clear and not misunderstand one another."

"Okay."

"We keep whatever happens between us here."

"Sometimes part of me wants to . . . you know . . . burn it all down."

I hesitated. "Just try to not hurt me publicly. I'm not exactly rational about this. I don't want to overreact."

She put her head beside mine again. "John," she said. "How is it you know how to do this?"

"What?"

"Have an affair."

"It's pretty basic. You reduce risk wherever possible." I turned my head toward her. "Why wouldn't I want to protect you?"

"But I mean, you've done this before. Haven't you."

"No." I turned away. "I mean, not like this. Not with a married woman. With a child."

She rolled onto her back and looked up at the ceiling. "There's something I haven't told you. Well. No one's seen you, right?"

"Here? At your apartment complex? No."

"Good."

"You're memorable. It occurred to me people on your floor would notice your comings and goings."

"My husband is an owner of the building."

"An owner?"

"With another guy. A business partner."

Everyone in the building would know them, watch them, talk about them. Talk about *her*. "Where does this other guy live?" I asked.

"Connecticut."

"Well. That's good, at least."

"Sometimes people slip rent checks under our door."

"Yeah, then. Alright. Something else to keep in mind."

3

New Braunfels, Texas, 1965

I've lost Amanda's brush. I pull the big square cushions off the couch then stick my hands down the back and feel for the wooden handle, the stiff black bristles, but only touch soft fabric and lint. My sisters are dressing upstairs. I put the cushions back on the couch, then walk through the kitchen and out onto our screened-in back porch. Outside it's October. The cool wind blows through the screen, and the trees hum from it. It seemed the brush would be here, on the wooden rocker, on top of the white table next to it. On the painted white floor where it was dropped. I can't think why, except it would be a good place for a girl to brush her hair. The chair rocks a little from the wind.

"John?" Amanda calls from upstairs.

Running back across the wooden floor, my foot hits the rug at the bottom of the stairs and it flies out from under me. I go down hard, hitting my face, my cheekbone against the first wooden step. Tears start to press against my eyes and my mouth starts to open. I press my fists to my eyes and sit up. I will not cry. The brush is gone. The throw rug is tumbled up at my feet. The staircase looks huge, like a giant. I grab the handrail and pull myself up the first step, then the next. My knee hurts. My hand slips over the smooth wooden handrail, grabs and pulls, till I'm at the top. I open the door to Amanda's room. My sisters sit on stools in front of Amanda's white vanity with its long mirror. They are so beautiful it's sometimes hard to look at them. Like now, when they're trying to be brave.

"Did you find it?" Amanda asks.

"No."

I am five. She is fifteen. Her hair is long and dark. Sometimes she picks me up and carries me and I wrap my arms around her neck.

"John, what's wrong with your face?" Catherine asks. She is thirteen and has long dark hair too, though hers is more brown. She sits next to Amanda, in the middle.

Amanda turns on her stool to look closer at me. "Joujou," she says, coming for me. She bends down to touch my cheekbone with her finger. Her fingernail is red with nail polish. "You're going to have a black eye."

"I'm okay," I say. Kari begins crying. She has blond hair and is eleven. She is thin. She's staring at her face and her mouth twists. She reads to me when our sisters are gone. They all read to me, but Kari reads to me the most. "It's okay," I tell her.

Amanda goes to hold Kari. My sisters are dressed in white slips. Their dark dresses are hanging on the door. Catherine's hair is rolled up. Amanda is wearing red lipstick. "John," Amanda whispers. I know what to do. I take Kari's hand and hold it. Catherine strokes Kari's hair. "We've still got each other," Amanda says.

Then the door opens and my mother stands in the hallway. Kari stops crying and her face freezes. Mother's dress is dark gray. Her eyes are tight and blue from makeup. Her face is puffy. She looks at the four of us. She starts to say something, then stops herself. "Make yourselves pretty," she tells my sisters, then closes the door.

~

I sit in the church up front on the soft red seat. My cheekbone hurts. My legs stick out from the cushions. I'm small for my age, people say. The hard black shoes on my feet are like two beetles. Kari will not let go of my hand. Her legs don't stick out like mine. They bend but don't touch the floor. Catherine sits with her hands in her lap, just like Amanda beside her. My mother is on the other side of Amanda. The preacher talks. He talks and talks. I don't like his voice. I don't care what he's trying to say. He says this, "Blah blah blah." He says this, "Moo moo moo." I start to giggle and bite my lip, but it gets worse. I'm shaking and the giggle is growing. It will become a laugh if I let it and I won't be able to stop it. So I think of the brush and I don't want to laugh anymore.

When the preacher stops talking the organ begins to play, and we stand and follow our mother down the aisle toward the long dark box with flowers all around it. The flowers are every color, every shape. Part of the top of the box is open and my mother looks down into it. I want her to hurry. I want to go home. Finally she moves away and Amanda looks into the box. Then Catherine. The box is higher than my head. Amanda and Catherine look at me. They want to know if they should lift me so I can see. I shake my head no. I don't want to look. It's not really Daddy. Then it's Kari's turn, and she's on her tiptoes looking inside. Her mouth twists again, like it doesn't know what to do. She steps back, turns to all the flowers. She reaches for one and I pull her hand. "Kari," I say. She's not coming. Amanda steps toward us and says her name softly. Kari turns and comes with me away from the box.

At my house there's food everywhere and too many people. I duck below their hands. I get fried chicken and pie and put it on a paper plate. But someone takes my plate from me and sets it down. It's Aunt Phyllis. She hugs me. She is big and soft and smells like milk turned sour. She's crying and pulls me into her and I can't breathe. Her tears drip down the back of my neck. I try to wriggle loose. I push back. I push and push. Then she suddenly lets go and I see Catherine hugging her. Aunt Phyllis looks surprised, but hugs Catherine and begins crying again. I grab my plate of chicken and pie and hurry to where Amanda stands by the fireplace. Where Kari stands beside her. Amanda whispers to Kari. Kari takes my hand and leads me away. In my other hand I carry my plate and hold it real careful so it doesn't spill. She leads me out the back door onto the screened porch, then across the yellow grass toward our swing set beside the big oak tree, and three gray birds fly out of the branches and away. Kari takes my plate and tells me to sit on the swing. She hands me my plate and I eat my food. I rock back and forth. The wind is cool and the sun is warm. Kari sits beside me. She watches me.

~

It's late. I'm downstairs in my pajamas in the dark with my flashlight. I get down on the floor by the couch, lift up the fabric, and click on my light. I see dust balls and a shiny magazine. In bed I couldn't sleep and thought the brush might be here under the couch. I turn off the light and sit on the floor. The wind blows outside, and the house creaks. I get up to make sure the front door is locked like Daddy would at the end of the night, then walk through the kitchen to check the back. It's my job now. I walk down my mother's hallway and stand in front of her closed door.

When I pass my sisters' doors they're crying, one after the other, each in her own room. It is almost a kind of singing, like wolves calling to each other from far away. My bedroom is the smallest one at the corner of the house beside Amanda's. I close my door and crawl into bed. I can still hear my sisters.

Soon I dream. There is a different car for each of us. Red for Amanda, orange for Catherine, yellow for Kari, blue for me. We all drive away, one after the other.

4

New York City

Under the river, headed toward Brooklyn, the subway car suddenly went dark, then lights from the tunnel walls whipped across the faces of the riders. I wondered if Jeremy knew about us, if Alena told him, if that's why he put his hand on my shoulder yesterday. Jeremy, who I sensed in the background of what has happened.

We began work the same week, were both struck by the same woman and competed for her attention in our different ways. His hope of an eventual career in photography paralleled my hope to be a poster designer. A little over a year ago we were the first from our department to be trained on the new graphics-based Xerox computers that would replace the hand-drawn charts the designers sketched and taped and photocopied in the back room. I'm sure Alena had something to do with that. Still, we were clearly the two most talented graphically. We had to interview for the position with Alena's boss, and by extension, mine, David Rohmer. I sat outside the door waiting for Jeremy to finish his interview, and when he left he winked at me, whether to encourage me or throw me off, I didn't know. Probably it was neither; he was just playing me for a reaction, as usual. I entered David's office and sat across from him and Alena. An antique oak coffee table separated us. The window behind them looked out on Rockefeller Center. Below, skaters would be skating, and soon an enormous Christmas tree would be set above the rink like I'd seen year after year on television back in Texas. I fought off an urge to walk to the window and look down on it all.

David was a tall, soft-spoken man with thinning brown hair who'd worked his way up through the secretarial pool. I'd brought one of my posters to show him that I had an eye for visuals. Through Billy Harmon, a friend from Austin who worked in theater, I'd managed to score a few design gigs for small theater companies. This poster was in sepia and black and showed a man from the chest up strapped to an electric chair, his head wedged into its wired metal helmet, his mouth gaping, enormous and black inside. In the black mouth I'd scratched out the words "Killer's Head" in white.

"Jeez," David said.

"It's for a Sam Shepard play," I told them. "It's a one-act where this guy is strapped into an electric chair and says all this random stuff having nothing to do with his situation. He's the only one in the play."

"What happens at the end?" Alena asked.

"Bzzt," David told her. Alena and I glanced at each other, surprised he knew. "I love one-acts," he said as he leaned forward for a closer look. "Why haven't I seen any of your art at your desk, John? Most people would be plastering their cubicle with it."

"It's not what I do here."

"John flies under the radar," Alena told him.

He turned to Alena, his eyebrows raised at her comment. She maintained a trace of a smile as he turned back to the poster. "How did you do the lettering?" he asked, pointing to the mouth.

"I found a photo in the library of a guy in an electric chair, photocopied it, then projected it onto a sheet of paper taped to my bedroom wall. I traced over the image. I'm not a paint-and-brush artist, but I can manipulate an image. I cut across the head at the mouth and separated the page. Then to expand the mouth for distortion, and also so the title would stand out, I taped the pieces onto a larger piece of paper and drew the mouth back together, which made it much larger, and filled it in with black crayon. Then I scratched the letters away with a razor blade to get this distressed effect."

"Smart," he said.

"Then a simple band across the top with 'An Evening of Sam Shepard Plays,' and the performance details on the band across the bottom. Sans serif."

"Because . . ."

"Serif is more formal and can have a busy look. It works great for pages filled with text. It's very readable, but when you make a sign you generally don't want to pull attention from the image. I used Helvetica for simplicity, neutrality, and to contrast with the distressed text in the mouth. Throw a rock in this town you'll hit something in Helvetica, but there's good reason for that."

"Talk to him about typography, John. Explain it to him like you explained it to me."

"You mean my speech?"

"Yes."

Once when I'd attempted to explain to Alena my fascination with type, a string of words had fallen out and she'd told me to memorize them. I cleared my throat, then a little self-consciously began, "The strokes and gestures, the arcs, angles, gaps, and implied movement of letters, words, can give a poem weight, presence before you've read a word, make you choose one band over another on a Saturday night, persuade you to try a different bottle of wine." My voice sounded distant. I paused, then continued. "Type acts on you like a touch of breeze, and you turn your head because of it and decide to walk in a different direction, not knowing exactly why."

They stared at me. I felt a bit odd and exposed. David leaned back in his chair, glanced at Alena, then back at me. "John," he said, "this goes to a whole other place."

I looked down at the poster, worried I'd blown the interview. "Everything isn't this edgy," I said. "I have other work. Stuff that's more straitlaced."

"You don't understand. What you're showing us is *advanced*. It's *personal*. Take this as a compliment."

"I don't get the job?"

He looked at me like I was crazy. "It's yours if you want it. But graphically it won't be challenging."

"It'll be more challenging than word processing."

"I just want you to understand this going in."

I turned from him to Alena, who was smiling, then back to him. "Thanks for letting me know, David. It won't be a problem."

～

I stepped off the subway. I rose to the street. I called her from the corner and she said the door was unlocked. Soon I was fucking her. I would use another word, but there was none better for what we were doing. It's a word she would've used. It's a word she would have enjoyed using. I held myself over her body, her eyes closed, her head hanging over the edge of the bed, rocking from each pulse where my center met hers. I sustained a steady rhythm, paused, then drove into her with force, paused, did it again. She cried out each time. I loved her cries, I adored them. I was filled with a touch of meanness that was serving me well, the idea that there was a well-heeled guy out in the world, some guy with money who felt satisfied with himself and didn't bother much to understand his exceptional, if occasionally cruel wife, and deserved what he was getting. Or rather, what he wasn't. Something in me a degree merciless. Giving it to this married woman, my boss, my friend, this way.

I slipped my hand under her head as a cradle as she began to come. Her neck arched. Her mouth opened.

Afterward I lay on top of her, breathing deeply, covered in a thin layer of sweat. Her skin felt as if it had been dusted in powder. I was thinking of how easily we slid over each other's bodies, when from far away I heard what I thought at first was a siren. Alena's eyes opened.

"What?" I said.

"Get off," she told me. She pushed me away, rolled off the bed, and headed for the bedroom door. As she pulled it open the sound increased, clarified into that of an eighteen-month-old child crying. It filled me with terror; no, horror. Alena stepped through the doorway and was gone. I lay alone on her husband's bed, naked, staring at the ceiling as the child's cry pulsed in the air around me. I'd wronged a man I did not know, and now his child was crying. The sound changed everything. I couldn't bear it.

It took effort to begin dressing myself. As I pulled my T-shirt over my head the child went silent. I tied my shoes and stood. Alena appeared at the door carrying Carina asleep against her shoulder. Both were naked. They seemed too beautiful, as if I was not meant to see such beauty, as if my eyes had violated the image by witnessing it and some punishment would follow. It was an image more intimate than anything she had given me in our three nights together, in our three years of friendship. I turned away ashamed. The image did not belong to me.

Alena told me that when the baby got like this she didn't stop until she was asleep with her mother. And it was okay, don't worry about it. But yes, I'd better go.

And I knew our affair had ended. At her front door I considered how disastrous it would be if we were caught now, if the elevator doors opened at the wrong moment, if a neighbor stepped out of an apartment. I put my ear to the door. Hearing nothing from outside, I told myself there was no option but to walk out into the fluorescent hallway. I took one look back at Alena and her child—I couldn't help myself—then opened the door. I hurried toward the stairwell, relieved that if I were spotted now it wouldn't matter, then charged down the seven flights of concrete steps and glaring strip lights, my footfalls clattering and echoing. Finally I reached the ground floor and pushed the bar that opened the heavy steel door and stumbled out blinking into the night. The door slammed and locked behind me. I turned back at the noise, then lowered my head and began moving down the street until I reached Flatbush Avenue. Random cars shot by. Everything seemed to be moving much too fast yet somehow not fast enough. I stepped between two parked cars into the street, hoping to wave down a cab, when a black sedan flew past inches away. At the blast of wind I leapt back onto the sidewalk, then stumbled downhill until I found an opening where I could see, and be seen, more clearly. A cab careened down Flatbush toward me. I stepped into the street and waved, swept by a sudden panic that if I missed this cab I would be lost, we would be found out. It pulled over at an angle with a squeal of brakes.

"24th and 2nd," I told him, my voice sounding strangely calm, in control. As he pulled away I began to sob. He didn't bother to look back at me, and I didn't bother to try and stop.

~

I stepped into her office the next day, steeled for what would follow. She looked up, smiled a little sadly, a little concerned. She looked tired. I shrugged. "You understand," she said quietly. "It's too complicated." I nodded and walked back to my desk where I did my best to continue my work. She left at five o'clock without saying goodnight to any of us. At seven she called me at my desk from home.

"John, I just wanted to talk to you. I know you can't really speak with Jeremy and Marjorie there, but I didn't want to wait."

"Right," I said, thinking she chose this method to control my ability to respond.

"But you know. Carina, and everything . . . it's just . . . this is a good place for us to stop. Before anybody gets hurt."

"I understand."

"It's not as if I didn't like it. I liked it. But so what? You know?" She sighed. There was a moment of silence, but I wasn't going to help her get through it. "Look," she said. "Draw me something. Make me something."

"What?"

"Anything."

So the lady wanted a souvenir. I shook my head. "Sure," I told her, trying to sound indifferent. "No problemo."

She hesitated. "Bye, John."

5

New Braunfels, Texas, 1966

I sit on my stool and watch my sisters get ready in the mirror. Kari has set a vase on the counter holding two marigolds. The cups of the flowers are so yellow they look like honey would pour out if you tipped one.

I am six. Amanda is sixteen and has a date. It is a Friday night in October and a boy is coming over to pick her up and take her to the football game. He just got his driver's license and his name is Mike. He makes good grades. My mother approves of him. Amanda says, "That's necessary." She tells us she likes him anyway. She says he wants to leave this town as much as she does.

Amanda is showing Kari how to put on lipstick. She holds her mouth wide open, touches the lipstick to her top lip, then slowly paints to her left. She touches it to the top again and paints to the right. Then slow and careful she runs it over her bottom lip. When she finishes she looks at her mouth in the mirror, then closes it, presses her lips together. She turns to Kari and opens her mouth. When she does it makes a kissing sound, and like magic her mouth has changed shape. It's red and beautiful like a flower that's blossomed and you can't look away. You want to touch it. Amanda sees me watching her in the mirror. "Hey, mister," she says, then winks. "What do you think?"

"Yes," I say.

My friends don't have sisters like mine. Nobody does. By the way Amanda smiles at me I know it's time to brush her hair. My brush is like the one I lost the day of Daddy's funeral, except it's wider and its wooden handle is brown. It does a good job on all of their hair, even Kari's, which is light and blond. I set it into Amanda's hair and run it down. Her hair smells like jasmine. She lets out a breath and looks at me in the mirror. "If you want him to fall in love with you, he will," I tell her.

"Mouse," she says.

"Man of the house," says Catherine.

I set the brush in Amanda's hair and run it down again.

"Little brother," Kari says softly.

I find a tangle, a small knot, so I grip Amanda's hair above it tightly in my free hand so the brush won't pull and hurt, and I carefully work my way through it. When I go back to brushing she smiles to herself in the mirror, picks up her eyeliner brush and begins painting the edges of her eyes, following the shape, making such a pretty line that curves over where she sees.

"I was thinking," Amanda says to my sisters. "When we get married. Who's going to walk us down the aisle?"

Catherine smiles. "John?" she says. Kari grins and nods her head.

Amanda swivels around on her stool. "Would you, baby?"

"Yes. What?"

"Give us away. It's what daddies usually do at a wedding. Otherwise we're going to have to get Uncle Larry or somebody."

"Yes!" I say, I shout. And I can see it. I'm bigger, holding their hands, taking them down the aisle to each of their husbands. Now my sisters are laughing. They can't stop and I can't either. But there's a rapping at the door.

"Come in," Amanda says.

The door opens and our mother steps through it. "Hello, girls," she says. She has her glass of Coke. Her hair is poofed up high on her head. My sisters' hair falls down their backs. Mother looks at me. "Are you helping them, John?"

"Yes." The brush is in my hand. When she sees it I wish it wasn't there.

She turns to Amanda, who has started putting on her mascara, and smiles. Her smile is tight. "He's here, Amanda," she says.

"Thank you."

"Will you be ready soon?"

"I don't know."

Mother looks at Kari in the mirror. "Good lord," she says, starting to laugh. "Try to find your mouth." And I see Kari's put on too much lipstick and it smeared around her lips. Kari's hand rises and covers her mouth.

"I'm *teaching* her, Mother," Amanda says in a way that tells her to leave Kari alone. They stare at each other in the mirror. "She's just learning," Amanda tells her. We hold our breath, wondering what will happen next. If Mother will get angry. Or sad. What if we have to put her to bed in front of the boy. What would he think about us?

But instead she shrugs and takes a swallow from her Coke. "I just want what's best for you girls."

"We know," Amanda says softer now, smoothing it over. I nod. We all nod and let out our breath.

"Daddy's money isn't going to last forever," Mother tells us.

Amanda begins painting her eyes again. "Uhm hmm," she says.

And it's all okay again. Mother takes another drink. "Pay attention to your sister," she says to Kari. "She knows what she's doing."

"Thank you," Amanda says. Kari's hand stays over her mouth.

"Alright then. Don't make that boy wait too long."

"I won't," Amanda tells her.

Mother starts to leave, then turns to me. "John," she says.

"Yes."

"Come with me now. Let your sister get ready."

"He's not bothering us," Amanda tells her, but careful, not like before.

"I need his help. Let's go, John."

Amanda's shoulders tighten and she stops painting with her eyelash brush. We watch her. Then she sighs and switches to the other eye and begins there. I set the brush on the vanity. Mother smiles and closes the door behind us as we leave. She's happy now, patting my shoulder, guiding me. "That boy, his daddy is a lawyer," she whispers. Her hands move too quickly as she talks, and her eyes are wet. In the kitchen she opens a bottle of Dr Pepper and pours it over ice. She smiles while it fizzes and pops and the brown bubbles rise and fall in the clear glass. Daddy was the pretty one, my sisters say. They say he's the one we take after. But I think my mother was pretty once. I see it in the shape of her face, even if it is too skinny. Even if she's holding her smile too tight.

She turns to me, but then stops, holding the drink, looking in my eyes like she doesn't understand. "John?" she says. "Why are you looking at me like that?"

"You're so pretty," I tell her. And that works. And her smile is real now. She leans down and hands me the glass. She kisses me on my cheek. Her makeup is cracking around the corners of her mouth. "Take it to him," she whispers, and her whisper smells like what she pours into her Coke. I carry the Dr Pepper toward the boy. And I think if I walk my sisters down the aisle I'll be taking them to men like this one. Maybe even this one. I see him sitting on the couch. His name is Mike. He has brown hair and looks younger than Amanda. His eyes stare at his hands in his lap, then he looks up the stairs, then goes back to his hands. He's nervous. He doesn't see me until I can almost touch him, then he jumps a little.

"Hey, little man," he says.

"Hi," I say. He looks happy to see me. He looks relieved. I like him. If I didn't like him, if he wasn't nice to me, I could tell Amanda and she would be done with him.

"Dr Pepper?" I say.

He takes the Dr Pepper from me, sips it, then sets it on the coffee table. "You must be John." He stretches out his hand and we shake. "That's a good handshake," he tells me.

"I know."

He laughs. "I'm Mike," he says. "I've heard a lot about you."

"I've heard you make good grades."

He looks at me like he's thinking about what I said. "Do you play base-ball?" he asks.

"No."

"Can you play catch?"

"No."

"Want me to come over and teach you sometime?"

"Okay."

"Deal," he says, and shakes my hand again. I grip his big hand, feel the muscles. Then he looks up the stairs. Amanda's at the top watching us. She's smiling and he smiles back. She begins walking down. She's wearing a blue skirt and a white shirt and white socks and white tennis shoes. It's the high school colors. Mike is standing now and watching her. "Amanda," he says.

"What are you two planning?" she asks. I see Catherine and Kari watching from around the corner upstairs, and they're smiling too.

"John and I were just talking about playing a little catch." She stops and looks down at us. She tilts her head.

"Some weekend," he says. He can't stop grinning. "I'll come over," he tells her. "Right, John?" He pats me on the shoulder. "I've got a glove that'll fit you. We'll cover the basics. Throw the ball a little."

She's looking at him in a way I've never seen her look at anyone, like there's no one else in the world but him and her. And I know he's in love with her. How could he be anything else?

~

I sit in the dark at my window looking out at the street. At the corner a streetlight shines like moonlight on our Ford parked in front of the house. The wind blows through the big elm tree in the front yard, and its leaves move, and the cool air comes in through my screen. My mother is watching TV downstairs and waiting for Amanda. Amanda is supposed to be home by eleven. I look at the clock. She only has eighteen minutes. What will Mother do if she's late?

A car turns down our street and lights the dark pavement. It slows and pulls over at our curb, makes a crunching sound, then stops. It's Mike's dark green Chevy, and Amanda is on time. The car is low and long. When he turns off the engine I hear the radio playing, buzzing like bees. Then it is silent. Their voices are soft, are murmurs. When the doors open the light comes on, lighting them both, then it goes dark after they step out. Mike hurries around to catch up with Amanda. They bump, and suddenly they're holding hands. She looks taller than him. Brighter. She stands straighter. He knows he is lucky. You can see it on his face. Their legs move together, left-side, right-side. They watch the grass as they walk up the slope of our front yard. When the porch lamp lights their faces I see Amanda is smiling. Then they're on the porch and I can't see them anymore.

I wait for a long time but don't hear anything. Then the front door squeaks open and I hear his voice. "Okay, see you." The boy walks down the grass as he looks back toward our porch and Amanda. He waves, and the front door closes. He catches his toe in the grass and stumbles but keeps going toward his car. I walk to my doorway. Amanda is talking to mother downstairs. Soon the stairs are creaking with each step she takes. When she reaches the top she's smiling in a new way. She's been kissed.

"Mouse," she says. "What are you doing there in the dark?"

"Nothing," I tell her.

"Go to bed."

"Okay."

"Now."

When I run and jump into my bed I start to laugh. I crawl under the covers. The wind blows the tree outside. The shadows fly over the grass. Amanda has a boyfriend, and I approve of him. In my mind I see a book open. I see letters on the page. Kari says they're called characters because they have different personalities. Little *b* is roly-poly. *j* wants to hop away. *y* wants to know why. Capital *M* is dependable. They all join in bunches. They can't wait to speak. They say: Once upon a time there was a girl named Amanda, and she was beautiful.

6

New York City

I called my friend Jennifer. She was a painter from West Texas; I knew her from UT, a tall, long-limbed daughter of a rancher near El Paso. I told her the basic story. Alena and me. She insisted on buying me dinner the next night at the Odeon, the spacious, amber-lit, art deco restaurant in Tribeca where the beautiful art people go.

I sipped at a glass of red wine at the bar while I waited for her and stared into the long, darkened mirror over the bar, seeing myself in the carefully constructed shadows and amber light. In my dark clothing I fit in well with the others in the mirror, even though I was motionless and they were laughing, talking, gesturing with drinks and cigarettes. I felt a tug on my sleeve and turned to see Jennifer. She had dressed up for me and I appreciated it. She was striking in her somewhat rugged, West Texas way, with her white skin and her blue eyes, her wide shoulders and her straight dark hair cut short. She smiled, then took me by the hand and led me to our table. When her glass of wine arrived she lifted it, and we clinked glasses. "To love," she said.

We ordered more wine, then food, and she was doing a not terrible job of cheering me up and providing a distraction, an outlet. I told her what it was like riding the subway to meet Alena, the walk down Flatbush Avenue, then up her street. The irises on the desk. The elevator. The empty hallway. Her unlocked door. I told her of Alena's last phone call at work and her request. I told her how Alena had looked in the dark as she held Carina, how they'd looked together.

She shook her head. "It's a lot to handle," she told me. "It sounds like something that could get away from you quickly." She took a long sip of her wine. "I mean, there's a child involved. I really think it's for the best."

"I know."

"And you lived to tell the tale." She smiled. "You both did."

I shrugged. "Okay."

She glanced toward the bar and her eyes widened in surprise. I turned to see a lean scarecrow of a figure draped in something like a cape that flowed with the movement of his body. He looked to have stepped in from the streets of last-century London, gesturing, smiling, drifting through the light and shadows of the restaurant with four other men in his wake. He was using a cane, and when the light struck his face I saw it was too thin, too hollowed, frighteningly handsome.

"Mapplethorpe," she whispered. She touched my arm. "Don't stare." I turned quickly back to her. But my eyes wanted to study him. "He's got *it*," she said. "You know this, right?"

"Yeah."

"He's getting sicker. He says he's going to keep working. Remain in the public eye."

Robert Mapplethorpe was notorious for his photographs, especially his S&M shots, which were beautiful and explicit and startling. Of course he caught it. He would've gone to the bathhouses, the piers, the hard-core bars. Then again, he could've just as easily caught it from the love of his life. And I considered how Alena and I had not used a condom.

When I asked myself why, I didn't have an answer, or at least not a good one. I remembered the moment Jeremy stopped me in the hallway at work when Alena was on maternity leave. He struggled to find a place to begin.

"What?" I asked.

"Alena gave birth today."

"She did?"

"But . . . there was a complication."

"A what?"

"You know. With the pregnancy."

"Is she okay?"

"Yeah. You know the baby was late term, right? Well, something spooked the docs, so they did a C-section. But all's well that ends well. The baby's healthy."

I stared at him. "How do you know all this?"

"I've kept in touch. I visited her this morning. They're going to keep her there for a few days."

"When are visiting hours?"

"She said we didn't need to see her. She's swamped with relatives. They all talk with their hands. Honestly, I think she wants everyone to let her be. Fat chance with that crew."

"How does she look?"

"Beat up."

"I guess we should send flowers."

"I'm taking up a collection."

I nodded. "So the baby's okay?"

"Yes."

"Did you see it? What's its name?"

"Carina. It means 'dear little one.' Yeah, I saw her through the glass."

"What does she look like?"

"A newborn. She looks like a little red monkey."

"But . . ." I trailed off.

"You want me to say she looks like her mother?"

I shrugged. I was hollowed out and empty, didn't know what to feel. "But she's okay?"

"John, John," Jeremy said. He put his hands on my shoulders, looked down into my eyes, and smiled. "What is it?" He wrapped his arms around me and pulled me into his taller, broader body. I was surprised how easily I went, how well I fit. He laughed. "My god, if anyone ever needed a hug it's you," he said. He squeezed me tighter. I'd never been hugged by a gay man before. "Not to worry. Not to worry," he said. "Alena's going to be alright."

Two months later she was back looking a little tired, a little distracted, but happy. Everyone in the department seemed almost as relieved as I was to see her. As soon as I found a moment I sat across her desk from her. I told her Esmy had done a good job in her stead but she didn't have the touch Alena did. It was true. Alena handled both male and female execs and analysts with little effort. From our cubicles we'd watch her smile and charm them, and when they threw a tantrum she'd let them rant in her office as she leaned back in her chair, letting them run. Before long they'd start to calm down, then shrug and smile, as if finding themselves suddenly not wanting to look any more foolish in front of her. She kept them off guard in this way, protected herself and us.

I hesitated, then asked her about the trouble with the birth even as I apologized for such a personal question. She looked through the glass at the other typists in the department, then after a moment turned back. Quietly she told me there'd be no more babies. There would just be this one. It was too risky, the doctors thought, so for the sake of her health it had been arranged. Her words shook me. She continued to stare into my eyes.

"Well, you have your baby," I said.

She nodded. "That's right."

They made her unable to get pregnant. And now, for the first time since this plague appeared, I'd not used protection. Truth was, I knew we would never use a condom, accept any physical barrier between us, as stupid and risky as that might sound, and be. As irresponsible. It didn't matter. And now it was over. It was time to let her pull away, to allow the water to carry me, and her, elsewhere.

I raised my eyes to Jennifer's. She was watching me.

"Alena. That's a pretty name," she said. "So what are you going to make for her keepsake?"

"Her souvenir? I don't know. Maybe something that'll leave a mark."

She lifted her eyebrows. "Then just tell the truth."

I raised my glass in the amber light of the restaurant where the beautiful art people went, where Robert Mapplethorpe was publicly dying of AIDS. I wondered how many other people in this room it would kill within the year. I wondered if anyone here would catch it this night. In my wineglass the amber light had penetrated the dark red wine and hovered, in a golden parabola, at its center. It arced and trembled in my hand. "To love," I said.

"To love," she answered.

~

Sunday I sat in front of my drawing table in my apartment trying to make Alena "something," as she'd asked, but my pens wouldn't draw, my colors wouldn't flow, no shape seemed tangible. The project had taken on so much personal weight it seemed I'd be crushed by it.

When the phone rang I jumped, thinking for a moment it could be her, though I knew better. A female voice greeted me, my friend Sandra from Charleston, an actress, assistant director, and jack-of-all-trades for the Front Door Theater Company, based in Astoria. She wanted to know if I'd be interested in designing another poster for them. They couldn't afford to pay me, of course, but they'd cover expenses, which I could pad a little, she said, and I could see the show as many times as I wanted.

"There might be something extra in it for you, too." She said it with a wink, like she was joking around, though I didn't think she was. "Are you okay?" she asked.

"Why?"

"You sighed."

"I'm just . . . working through something."

"If you need somebody to talk to . . ."

"I appreciate it."

"It's a crime we can't afford to pay you, John. We know that."

I looked up at the posters I'd designed and pinned to my living room wall. A few small theater productions. Some rock-and-roll shows from Austin. "What's the play?"

"A musical version of *Waiting for Godot*." She hesitated, hearing my silence. "It's not as bad as it sounds," she told me.

"I hope not."

"I know, I know. The playwright's one of our backer's kids. We have to do it. It's a showcase."

I looked back down at the paper in front of me. "I'm just . . . in the middle of this thing."

"I hear it in your voice. Don't worry about it, honey. They told me to ask you, and now I have. We really appreciate what you've done for us. Next time I'll offer you something better."

We hung up. The thought of calling her back and asking her out for a drink played through my head for a moment, but fluttered away just as quickly. There was nothing for it to root to. Maybe later, I thought. She's good-looking, fun. But not now. Maybe not for awhile. I stared at the blank paper and wondered how I imagined that my homegrown poster art, my blunt manipulations of geometric shapes and type on a canvas . . . how I could have possibly thought that such attempts might lead to a gesture that would do Alena, and my feelings for her, justice?

In my frustration I picked up a charcoal stick and began streaking lines down the page. It was awful. It was wrong, but maybe it was a beginning. I tore the page away and tried again. The streaks were angrier now, like the slashes and graffiti on the street and subways. I tore that page loose and let it fall to the floor. Then another. And I felt the change before I acknowledged it, how the lines were no longer hard, how my hand was moving with something akin to grace. By the time I realized I was drawing the lines Alena's body made in space when she said I should leave her that night—the lines of her child in her arms, the little girl's head resting on her mother's shoulder—it was all in place. I continued, trying not to think, just passing over the lines, again and again. I swept, stroked, thickened and diminished them until they were perfect. Finally I stopped. I had no doubt this was unlike anything I'd ever done. And it was as if a small bell inside me had been struck. Its clear tone traveled through me in waves. I looked up. Outside the windows of my twelfth-floor apartment, I saw the hours had flown by and it had gone dark. I pulled myself from the drawing, covered it in sheets of tissue paper, and slid it into a large manila envelope. Good, I thought. That's that.

The next day I set it before her as she was about to leave at five o'clock. She looked up, acknowledged it with a smile. I walked back to my desk.

At 7:30 I was beginning to gather my things, thinking I might slip out ten or fifteen minutes early. I'd decided to allow myself a drinking night and planned on hitting the old bars around Times Square. Buy an old vet some drinks and get him talking about WWII, how that had all gone down. My phone rang.

"It's me," she said, her vocal pitch higher than usual, wavering. "Do you . . . do you want to come over?"

I hesitated for an instant, at a sensation I was falling. "*Want?*" I asked.

"Just promise me: you'll never ask me to leave him."

~

She buzzed me in at eleven and I took the elevator up. Her door was unlocked. I opened it and stepped inside. She was there in the dark hallway, her face wet with tears. "I thought you weren't coming," she said.

I was horrified at my mistake. "You told me never to get here earlier than eleven. You've been expecting me all this time?" She wrapped her arms around me, held me so tight I could hardly take a breath. Her breathing, jagged, sped up, then slowed and recovered as her body released into mine. I looked past her to see the drawing on the dining table. I stepped out of my shoes. She unbuckled, unzipped me, took my hand and led me toward a bed she'd made of sheets and blankets on her living room carpet. Her bathrobe fell away. She lowered herself to her hands and knees, facing away from me toward the window and the clocktower in the distance. "Okay," she whispered, as if resigned. "Okay," she said again, louder, anger edging her voice.

This was how it was going to be. This is who we were together. I dropped down behind her and grasped her long dark hair in my hand. I twisted her head to the side so I might see in her face what I did to her, who I was to her, and I knew, I knew, I would never recover.

7

New Braunfels, Texas, 1968

I am eight. Kari reads to me in her bed. She always reads to me while my sisters are out on their dates. The book is *Catcher in the Rye*. The book is *To Kill a Mockingbird*. The book is *Animal Farm*. The book is *Wuthering Heights*. I follow the words, look at the letters. I could read aloud too, but I like hearing Kari. Like me, she is still small for her age. Her voice never trembles when she reads.

We're propped up on pillows and my head rests against her shoulder. Our legs are under the sheets. Her leg touches my leg. My mother opens the door without knocking. "Aren't you two peas in a pod," she says. She looks at us with her glass of Coke in her hand. "John, I need some help in the kitchen."

I uncover my legs and follow her down the stairs. Amanda says Mother's becoming more manageable. So long as she has her bottle and her TV and nobody starts a fight, she mostly leaves us alone. Though, Amanda says, sometimes it's hard to not start a fight. When Mother gets really angry she breaks plates and glasses, then she cries and goes into her room and falls asleep. We clean up the glass. When she comes out later we apologize. We tell her how much we love her.

In the kitchen I lift the paper bag out of the garbage. It's so heavy I have to lean back to pull it out. She walks by and pats my head, and I feel where her hand touched me even after she goes back into the living room.

I carry the bag out the back door onto the porch, then down the steps. The trees are green with leaves. New dandelions have popped up. They're white and open and I want to blow on one and see the little seeds fly away like soldiers with parachutes. I put the bag down to pick one, but the bag hits too hard and splits open. Something pokes through that is dark and wooden, and I know what it is. My heart is beating fast and the wind rushes through the trees. I'm scared my mother saw what happened and I look back at the porch, but she's not there. I grab the bag and pull it around the house toward the trash cans. A soda bottle falls out on the grass, some paper towels, but I don't stop until I'm at the cans where I reach down, grab the dark handle, and pull it out. There's food in it. There's hair. It's Mother's hair. But it is the brush. The brush I lost the day of Daddy's funeral, that's been gone all this time.

~

It's dark in my room and I sit at my window watching for Amanda and Mike. At the end of summer they'll leave to go to the University of Washington in Seattle. Amanda can't wait. None of us can wait.

His car pulls up. The engine stops. They're talking inside. The talking gets faster and louder. Then Amanda yells something. She opens the door and gets out, then slams the door shut behind her. She holds her hand over her mouth, crying as she hurries up the slope. Mike stands in the street at his open door. "Amanda," he says, but she doesn't turn. The inside of his car is lit and empty. "Amanda," he says quieter. The door to the house opens, then closes.

I watch Mike stare after her. He has broken her heart. He doesn't know what he has let happen. He gets back in his car and drives away.

Amanda's footsteps come up the stairs, creak after creak. Her bedroom door opens, then shuts. The wind blows through the tree outside. I don't know what to do. I walk out into the dark hallway and stand in front of Amanda's door. A thin bar of light shines along its bottom. I push the door open a crack. Inside Amanda stares into her mirror. Her face is wet and red, and her mascara has run. She looks like she doesn't know who she is, who I am, who any of us are. I'm scared to make a sound. Then I remember the brush. I run to my room and click on my flashlight, then crawl into my closet toward the very back where I've hidden the baseball glove Mike gave me. I reach inside it, grab the wooden handle, and pull it out.

I push Amanda's door open. She's still staring at her face and doesn't even look at me. I walk toward her. "He won't leave with me," she says. "He wants to stay here in New Braunfels. He's decided to go to Texas State. He didn't even tell me he applied there."

Mike always looked younger than Amanda. I approved, but they never looked like they belonged together. "Amanda," I say.

"He already found another girlfriend."

At first I can't believe it, but then it makes sense. "It's someone who doesn't shine so much brighter than him," I tell her.

Her mouth makes a small *o*, then tears run down her cheeks. "Mouse," she says.

I hold up the brush. "Look."

"Is that . . . ?"

She recognizes it. "It was in the trash," I tell her. "Mother's had it all this time. Why would she keep it? Her hair was even in it, so she used it to brush her hair. I cleaned and washed it."

I reach up and begin stroking her hair with it. Amanda takes a deep breath, then another. "She was always jealous," she says. "We're the real family now. The four of us. The five of us, before Daddy died. Do you remember?"

"A little bit."

"She was jealous of him too. There's been no air here since he left."

"But Amanda. *We* love each other."

"Of course, sweetheart." She watches me in the mirror. Her hair smells like cigarette smoke and jasmine. I could brush her hair all night. I could brush it forever. "We'll look out for each other," she tells me, "because god knows Mother will be no use. Then we'll make our own families."

"Yes." The brush feels right in my hand, like it's home. "She shouldn't have taken it," I say.

"Where will you hide it?"

"In the baseball glove that Mike—" Amanda shuts her eyes when I say his name, and I stop brushing. I shouldn't have said his name.

"Don't stop," she says. I begin again. She nods. "You're right, John. Maybe he wasn't the right guy. Maybe I even knew it, in my heart, but I guess I thought he was right enough." She looks at me again, takes a deep breath. "Maybe it's better this way."

"It is."

"I'll be free. And . . . well . . . there are other boys."

"Better boys," I tell her. "Better for you."

~

Amanda carries her big sky-blue suitcase toward her car. I carry her little matching suitcase. I have to tilt to my side to carry it down the grass. Catherine and Kari wait on the sidewalk, and Kari's hand rests on Amanda's red Ford. I set the bag beside them. Catherine's hand is on my shoulder now, squeezing it. We're all talking, laughing. We sound like birds. Amanda is crying and smiling. She hugs Catherine, then Kari, then she picks me up and holds me. "Joujou," she says.

We put the bags in her trunk. Amanda waves to Mother watching from the porch, and for a second I feel sorry for her standing up there alone. She takes a step toward us, then stops herself. Part of me wants her to come down and join us, but part of me doesn't, is glad she stopped. Amanda hugs us one more time, then she takes my head in her hands, tilts my face up toward hers, and kisses my forehead. She touches her fingers to my cheek, then gets in her car. The motor starts. "Good luck," we yell. "Have fun." As she takes off I push the car from behind, then I hit the trunk as it pulls away. I run as fast as I can after her down the street, my feet slapping against the hard asphalt.

~

That night Catherine knocks on my door and opens it. The light from the hallway falls across my bed where I'm sitting at its edge at my window. "Joujou," she says. "What are you doing in the dark?"

"Watching the tree and the street."

She closes the door and comes around the side of the bed, then leans over, gathers me, and holds me to her chest. She squeezes me tight and I wrap my arms around her neck. They feel good there. They feel right. She kisses me on my cheek, then leans back and smiles. Her cheeks are wet. She bounces me in her arms. "We're going to be fine, aren't we?"

"Yes."

"And you can brush my hair, and Kari's, and make sure we're pretty like you did for Amanda."

"Then you'll get to leave too. Then Kari."

"Then you."

"Then me. One after the next. We'll make our escape."

She laughs and sets me back down on my bed, then sits beside me and puts her arm around me. We watch the elm tree outside, the leaves and limbs moving from the wind. She leans into me, and along my side I can feel where her waist curves in. I can feel her breathe. "Little brother," she says. "My little man."

"Catherine?"

"Yeah, baby?"

"Why did Daddy die?"

"The doctors said his heart was too big. And that's why it went out on him."

I nod like I understand, but really I don't. I can hardly remember what he looked like.

~

Catherine moves into Amanda's room. Kari moves into Catherine's old room. I stay put, in the boy's room, the one at the corner with the most windows. Amanda is in Seattle. She called on Sunday and said she's in the dorm and misses us, but it's exciting and beautiful there and she's happy. We should come visit.

It's late, and so I walk down the stairs with my flashlight to check the house. There's a blue light on downstairs. The TV's still on. The Indian head sign-off is on the screen, and the screen is hissing. I walk toward it and when I see her in the chair I nearly scream. Mother, asleep. I try to take a breath. My heart won't slow down. I thought she was someone else. I thought she was a body. I don't know what I thought she was. But it's only my mother. Her Coke is on the table beside her half full. Her arm dangles over the side. I reach over and push her shoulder but she doesn't wake. I push again, harder. She jerks her head up, and it startles me. "What what?" she says.

"It's me," I tell her. "It's John."

"John?"

"You fell asleep. You should go to bed."

"John."

I grab her arm and help her get to her feet. The TV shines its blue light on her. She looks old in the light, like a stranger.

"I'm sorry," she says. "I fell asleep."

"It's okay."

I hold her elbow and walk her down the hallway and into her room. "You're such a good boy," she says. She falls on her bed and rolls onto her side. I cover her with a blanket. I leave her room and close the door behind

42

me, then turn off the TV. The Indian's head sizzles into a tiny star and blinks off. I'm in the dark again. My eyes adjust, and I can see things on the walls and the floor. I don't need the flashlight to see, but I like to shine it. I shine it on the front door to make sure it's locked, then the back, then sit on my couch in the living room. A car drives by on our street. I peek out the window and it slows down. It is Mike's green Chevy. It is Mike. He looks at our house as he passes. And is he haunted now? Is he a ghost?

8

New York City

At 5th Avenue and 50th Street, just down from Rockefeller Center, the revolving doorway propelled me into the pink granite lobby of the building where I worked. The ceiling stood at least three stories tall, and the spacious interior housed a number of small shops—an upscale clothing store for men, a shoe store for women, a small art and print gallery—all of which were usually empty. Carefully tended trees grew inside near the outer glass walls. There was the murmur of voices, the dim echo of footsteps, the faint ding of the elevator chime, the chirping of a few sparrows who had somehow entered the space and bonded into a small flock. Near the coffee stand, an elegant white-haired man in a tux who'd look much more at home at the Algonquin played "Autumn in New York" on a grand piano atop a white platform. He was always playing when I came in for my shift. He stayed true to the songs, though I heard traces of jazz in his flourishes. I suspected he was a New York City lifer, had played in jazz bands going back to the fifties. He probably jammed with friends in clubs into the wee hours, then made rent money here.

The escalator carried me to the second floor where I crossed in front of the security desk to the tenants' elevators. Two women waited beside me. We glanced at one another via our reflections on the elevator doors. An elevator opened, a chime rang, we stepped inside and began to rise. The lighting inside was golden, flattering. One of the women was my height and a little older than me, but not much. She looked type-A, a degree too lean, her face and body cut a bit harshly. My guess was she ran marathons, drank wheat grass and inordinate amounts of coffee. She probably worked sixty hours or more a week and made a fortune.

The other woman had rounder lines, a softer shape. She was my age or a bit younger with light brown hair. She showed more cleavage than the other, carried more color on her face. They glanced at each other. I suspected they'd gone out for an errand, or maybe coffee and gossip. I figured the one I liked best, the softer one, was smarter than her job. I read it in her eyes, her air of relaxed confidence. She typed, or was a personal assistant, and outside of work was maybe a painter, an actor, a writer. She lived in Brooklyn or Queens or, like me, subleased a place in the city. Something was passing between them, information in subtle glances that appeared related to me. The type-A drifted behind me so I could no longer see her, then I sensed her looking me over. I felt physically exposed from behind. I looked back to meet her eyes. They were direct. They didn't turn away. They asked me what I wanted, looking at her like that, who I thought I was. I turned forward, saw the other woman had a faint smile on her lips. She glanced back at her friend, then the bell rang and we'd stopped at their floor. They stepped off, turning to acknowledge each other. Then the softer one looked back at me and held eye contact as the doors closed. And I knew their behavior was because of Alena, because of what had happened between us and how my body hummed with it.

In the document production room, Tanya, Marjorie, Jin, and Esmy sat behind their computers, while Millie keyed in messages on the teletype. There was Jeremy at the second cubicle behind mine typing away. "Hi, Jeremy," I said. He nodded to me—I couldn't read his face—then turned back to the chart on the screen in front of him. I sat and turned on my computer. Looking for a pen, I pulled open my right-hand desk drawer. Inside, a small yellow flower rested on a white tissue. The petals had begun to wither at their edges. It was a marigold. It was hard to fathom how yellow the flower was. I wanted to lift it out, to smell it, to feel the softness of the petals against my skin, to leave a trace of its pollen on my nose.

I looked to see Alena in her office on the phone smiling as she watched me. Then she let her gaze drift past me across the office. It was Tuesday, the first of the three nights we would see one another. Tuesday, Thursday, Sunday, we decided. Fridays and Saturdays would be too risky, too heavily trafficked. Three nights each week for two months, then her husband would return, and it would end. I watched a female analyst take a seat across from her. Alena leaned toward her, said something, and they both laughed. I loved to see her laugh. Already in my mind I was riding the subway. I was rattling past the grimy stations with their ancient mosaics and icons and their bright color themes. I was passing under the water.

At eleven o'clock I called her from the corner of Flatbush and Sterling. "The door's unlocked," she said. Inside her lobby the irises in the two vases had been replaced by marigolds.

~

"Tell me about the bull jumpers," she said. "Tell me what you found out." She was pressed to my side, her mouth an inch from my ear.

"You know already. You know more than I do."

"Yes, but tell me anyway. Tell me about the girl."

"On the statue?"

"Yes. The girl on the statue."

I thought of the cars and buses flying down the hill a half-block away, the subways beneath them rattling toward Manhattan, the trees shifting below us from the summer wind and their patterns of leaves playing across our ceiling, and in the distance the clocktower dominant over everything, the passage of time marked on its four faces: north, south, east, west. I thought of the island of Crete thousands of years ago and wondered at how anyone could've made an object as beautiful as the statue.

"I found a picture of a bronze statue," I said, "made by an artist in Crete, before Rome was Rome, before Greece was Greece. Some artist we'll never know. I found the picture when I was looking up Crete in the library."

"Why were you looking up Crete?"

"Because I wanted to understand you."

"Why did you want to understand me?"

"You know why."

"And the statue was . . ."

"A bull jumper. A female bull jumper and a bull."

"Female?" she asked. She knew there were female bull jumpers. She just wanted to hear it again.

"Yes," I said. "One of the public games they played in Crete was lining up their finest youth, female as well as male, and setting a charging bull upon them. The bull would pick a target. That target would run toward the charging animal, and at the last possible second leap or somersault over the creature. This was before either the Coliseum at Rome or the Olympic games."

"So who was this girl in the statue?"

"We don't know. She was just a bull jumper."

"What does she look like?"

"She's thin. She's lithe, elegant. A young woman stretched out in midair over the animal, her back to its back, the back of her head to its head, her arms held out, her body curved over it as she faces the sun. She forms a perfect arc. Like a golden crescent moon. She must have put her hands to the horns of the bull and pushed off, then flipped in the air to stretch out like that. How else could she have arrived at such a position?"

"It sounds dangerous."

"It would be."

"What's going to happen to her?"

"What does it matter? It's a complete moment. There's no future or past."

"It matters."

"Okay. She lands on her feet behind the bull. She bows to the crowd. They applaud wildly."

"What happens to the bull?"

"The bull? It's fine. It's alright."

"You're sure."

"No. But it's implied by the statue. The statue's all we've got."

～

After I dressed she followed me to the front door. She placed three brief, childlike kisses on my neck, then stepped away. Now came our most vulnerable moment. Now the risk I was exposing her to swept over me again, and for a moment I couldn't believe we'd carried it so far. We'd carried it too far. I shouldn't have drawn her image. She shouldn't have called me. I put my ear to the door, then not hearing anything outside, I turned the lock. It made a horrible metal *thunk* as its cylinder fell into place. Anyone in the hall would've heard it and turned to the sound. I pulled the door open a crack and waited, then hearing nothing, stepped outside once again. Each time it was like stepping off a high dive. You had to will yourself forward, and let go.

Then I was in the hallway, moving over the thin carpet, hearing her door lock behind me. If someone opened their door now they would not know where I'd come from. If someone stepped from the elevator I'd be another stranger. Now the metal door to the stairwell was in my grasp. I pulled it open and knew we'd made it again.

9

Jeremy sat across from her in her office. There was that pause they took, familiar to me now, a moment between words. Alena's head dropped a degree as she looked up at him, and her smile became a grin. They both burst out laughing. I couldn't help but feel a pang of jealousy. Were they talking about me? Us? Or was I not a consideration? And I recalled our first company Christmas party three years ago, held at a dance club a few blocks above the theater district. It was dark with an open bar, but the dance floor was lit. I'd just picked up an hors d'oeuvre from a young woman carrying a silver tray when someone tapped me on my shoulder. I turned around to see Jeremy dressed in a suit that fit him so well it had to be tailored. In his buttoned-up white shirt but no tie, he carried himself with the casual grace of a model. He grinned slyly and took a sip from the straw in his glass. "Have you seen her?" he asked. I smelled gin and tonic on his breath.

"Who?"

He nodded toward the dance floor. Alena stood with a man at its edge, well lit, laughing. She wore red. It seemed every other woman in the place was wearing black and attempting boldness by showing cleavage, but Alena showed none. Her dress swept up the front of her body where it curled around her throat in a thin collar. There was no telling where else it was tied, how it held itself up. When she turned to set her drink down on a table I saw the plunge of fabric and the exposed back, the long torso, the dancer's muscles. My chest seized.

"I should've brought my camera," Jeremy said. "That dress looks like it was built for her body. Sexy *and* tasteful. I promise it did not come cheap."

She and the man began dancing. "Is that her husband?" I asked.

"No. He didn't come. He's a jerk, FYI."

"How do you know?"

"I met him down in the lobby last week. Just a first impression, so maybe I'm wrong. Though I'm never wrong." He looked toward the dance floor, then back at me. "He's very handsome, of course. Not Italian, though. Italian-American." He sipped at his drink, then gave me a sideways glance. "Trust me, there's a difference."

His speaking casually of her husband sent my mind spiraling. "Handsome," Jeremy had called him, then tagged him as a jerk. One with money. Why couldn't he make his wife's Christmas party? I couldn't imagine any man letting his woman come here looking like that and not be standing beside her. How stupid was he? And now she was dancing with other men. What was he trying to tell her? Anything? Or was something else going on, something I didn't understand? Still, best case he was a total fool, money or no money. Why would she be with a fool?

Jeremy's hand passed in front of my eyes and snapped me out of my trance, then he placed that hand on my shoulder, and with weight. It wasn't just a friendly touch; it was contact, and it held me as it grounded me. He looked down into my eyes, then smiled in a manner both intimate and irritating, a smile that told me he knew. Until then I'd managed to hide my response to this woman from everyone, but with the wave of his hand my cover vanished like vapor, and I stood exposed. A wave of anger flooded me, but before I could pull away, he lifted his hand. I took a step back, sorry I hadn't done so a moment sooner when he would've felt it. He looked down at his drink, sipped at it. Alena turned to see us standing together. She looked pleased. She smiled and waved.

Jeremy waved back as broadly as if he were bringing an airplane in for landing. "I'm dancing with her tonight," he said. "You should too." He glanced back at me and suddenly laughed. "John. Your face."

"What?"

"You should see yourself. Relax. Put down that beer and grab something harder."

"I need to go," I told him. "I'm late."

"For what?"

"Another engagement."

"Another engagement?" he chortled. "Suit yourself," he called out as I walked away.

I headed to the bar, knocked back a shot of their best tequila, then slipped out the doors. I'd made an appearance. I could go now. Truthfully, I was afraid to be seen dancing or even interacting with her, worried my feelings would be as obvious to everyone as they were to Jeremy.

I walked west, then turned south down 8th Avenue, hitting one circa-1950s bar after another—Smith's, McCale's—places with old guys sipping short beers at the bar and techies from the Broadway shows knocking back a quick one during intermission. After a few drinks my edge dissipated and I began to relax. I liked these environs, the New York equivalents of the honkytonks and roadhouse bars in Austin where bands played, where posters I designed still hung on walls. I kept drinking, much more than I normally would have, and chatted with bartenders and whoever might be on the next stool, to anyone who would listen.

Walking down the avenue, past the porn shows and the live sex shows with their lewd, ridiculous posters and dim lights, I kept a check on my balance. You didn't want to stagger on these streets and make yourself a target. I'd lost track of how many drinks I'd had, but didn't feel the least bit drunk. It was odd, as if adrenaline from the party had overridden the alcohol. The wind blew strong and cold at my back. Two blocks down a tall rawboned white prostitute with black hair stood near the corner of a building, her legs exposed to the top of her thighs. "Wanna date?" she asked, as they do, but spoke distractedly, her index finger scratching patterns in the air. Hunkered in a doorway two buildings past, a second prostitute, a black woman with a blond wig, held her jacket tightly around her torso as she shivered, her legs exposed like the first. It was roughly the same uniform, likely the same pimp. She didn't bother to speak to me—she knew I'd never be interested in a working girl, which was true—but she followed me with her eyes. On impulse at the end of the block I turned into a bodega and bought a cup of hot chocolate and carried it her way. Finally she turned her face toward mine. There was no telling how old she was, but she wasn't young. She looked weary. Her front tooth was chipped.

"Merry Christmas," I said.

She stared at the cup. "Thank you." As she took it our thumbs touched, and hers was cold and rough. Unlikely, I thought, neither of us wearing gloves on such a cold night. She took a sip, looked at me and nodded, then turned away, back toward the avenue on the watch for someone from a world more familiar than mine.

As I walked away I wished we hadn't touched. It was an odd moment for me. Out of character, proof I was off-center and it was time to get off the street. There was no telling where her hand had been that night. I felt guilt at my reaction, but as soon as I got to the next bar I headed for the bathroom and washed my hands, then slipped out to make my way home. I truly couldn't comprehend this culture—johns and whores. I tried to allow for the possibility, the likelihood I just didn't understand, that there might be something more complicated than a B-movie narrative, but even so it was still hard to get past the disease any of them could carry. The one most of us try not to think about now, that shadows everything.

~

The next morning the alcohol had caught up with me. The previous night was fuzzy and unclear and it felt like I'd committed a social error I couldn't quite recall. My head pulsed, but not as strongly as it should have, considering how much I'd drunk. On Monday I arrived at work uneasy, worried I'd said or done the wrong thing. As I passed by Alena's office, she stopped me.

I stuck my head in her door. "Yes?" As soon as I saw her I remembered her in the dress, and the way Jeremy had looked at me and smiled, and his hand on my shoulder. I felt the exposure all over again and my face tingled from blushing. My situation was becoming unmanageable. If I couldn't control my reactions, I might have to find a new job.

"Did you have a good time at the party?" she asked.

"Sure."

"I hardly saw you."

"I had to leave."

"Jeremy said you had another engagement."

"That's right."

She motioned me to take the seat across from her. As I sat she started to smile. It was a smile that couldn't help itself, that would break through regardless. "Guess what?" she said.

"What?"

"Can you keep a secret?"

"Sure."

"Well . . ."

"What?"

She leaned toward me and whispered, "I'm pregnant."

I could hardly respond. Entire sections of my psyche seemed to be running into one another as they tried to rearrange themselves at this information. "How far along?" I managed to say.

"Seven weeks. I know it's early. I shouldn't be telling anyone yet."

"You can't tell. You sure couldn't tell at the party."

"You'll be able to tell soon enough."

I stood. "Well. Wow. Congratulations."

"Thank you."

I went back to my desk feeling an odd combination of relief and disorientation. As I was leaving that night, Jeremy whispered, "Did you hear Alena's pregnant?"

"Yes," I said. "She told me."

"She told me first," he said, and winked. He hesitated. "Do you think she told anyone else?"

"I dunno."

"It's awful early to go public. You think she told her boss?"

"David? Probably."

"Anyway, I guess that'll change the mood around here." He shrugged and smiled a little sadly, as if we shared something we were going to lose. "John?"

"Yeah."

"I'm sorry if I . . . at the party . . ."

"What?"

He shrugged again. "I'd drunk rather a lot. And she was so beautiful. I hope I didn't cross any boundaries."

"With me?"

He nodded. Jeremy was one of those people who turn their attention on you and you feel you matter. It's like a drug, and models and actors are the masters of dealing it. But for the first time since I met him, he'd put me in the position of power. He seemed unsure, worried I might write him off.

"It's New York," I told him.

~

The next day Alena walked past escorting a female executive who looked to be from India. She wore a gray business suit and her black hair was pulled back in a tight bun. Alena's dress was medium blue, her skirt ending just above her knees. I still couldn't see the swell, the curve holding the child. The two stood in the doorway speaking softly. Their body language and attitude came across as conspiratorial and full of secrets, knowing smiles, girl stuff that always gets to me. The woman touched a finger to Alena's belly, then both laughed briefly as the executive waved and walked away.

Alena was so proud and happy, she was apparently telling anyone who would listen. She'd never been pregnant, and I worried for her a little. That's when I realized my madness, the overwhelming drive toward her I'd been fighting, had lifted as if a wind had carried it away. I questioned myself. Had it actually passed? Was it really over? I took a deep breath as she walked past grinning and knew it was true. How odd, I thought, that this could happen so suddenly. It was the pregnancy that broke the spell. The next day Alena came to work with her hair tied back in a basic pony-tail, as if gearing up for motherhood. And though I would miss—I had to face it—my response to her, I was grateful, as if I'd come down from some drug and could now go back to my life.

I had fun outside of work. I dated a few girls. As the months went by the whole office, including myself and most definitely Jeremy, became increasingly excited by her pregnancy. Women clustered around her like relations, laughed, gave advice, asked questions. If she needed something lifted or moved, I made myself available. That's the thing with feminine beauty—it draws in everyone, male, female, gay, straight, invited, uninvited, kind, predatory. But pregnancy creates its own field of protection, and only the most sociopathic would attempt to cross it.

Now, lying beside her, I found myself looking back, searching for the moment the whole thing turned for her, turned toward me instead of someone else, because no matter how suddenly we came together, there was nothing sudden about the days and the months and the years that had led us here. So when did it shift?

Was it the moment when she took my wrist between her thumb and first two fingers and guided my hand to her belly? It was only the second time I'd touched her. She was thirty-seven weeks pregnant. Yolanda, Rachel, Marjorie, and Jeremy watched me as we stood around Alena in her office. She would be going on maternity leave the following day. The baby was being demonstrative as my fingers curved over the tight orb. I felt the whorl of her navel at my thumb and the heat seeping through her blouse as she flattened my hand against her. Her breath rose and fell. And there was the thump, the tiny thump against my hand from the child inside, breaking into the conversation between her mother and me.

"Did you feel it?" she asked. I felt a second kick.

"Yes."

Jeremy seemed to be taking a keen interest in reading my face. I tried to ignore him. Alena cast a sidelong glance at me, then as surely as she'd brought my hand to her body, she guided it away and took Marjorie's hand and placed it on the same spot.

10

It was her idea for us to wait this time, to lie on the bed of sheets on her living room floor. But we'd run out of words, which was unlike us. For the first time I felt a river of tension expanding between us, pulling her one way and me the other. If I didn't do something it could kill the night, maybe even make us doubt ourselves. And afterwards our imaginations might turn from each other. At least that was my fear. I lifted up on an elbow so we wouldn't be flat on our backs, the way I imagined she and her husband slept, and I saw it. The one part of her body I hadn't yet directly touched, a thin horizontal scar three inches below her navel, the mark of her C-section. Only a trace, but there, reflected in the secondary lights from the street outside. I reached out and brushed a finger across it.

She grabbed my hand. "Don't."

The intensity of her reaction surprised me. She gripped my hand so hard it hurt.

"It's nothing," I said. She shook her head. Her entire body had locked up. I shouldn't have touched her there, but how could I know? Yet on some level, of course I must've known. And since I wanted to touch her everywhere, every place, to leave no part of her body unaddressed, how could I not get around to this? At least she hadn't covered it yet, hadn't turned from me. I thought of her daughter.

"That's where they saved her life," I said.

She pulled my hand down to the sheet and held it to the floor. "This wasn't a good idea," she said.

"What?"

"Cuddling and talking. We should've fucked first."

"Interested in a do-over?"

I said it lightly, with a smile, but she didn't respond, just stared at the ceiling. I had no idea of the emotions warring inside her, couldn't read her face. Was she going to accept the blame for her lousy mood, then send me away? How many nights were left us? Three a week . . . for how many more weeks? I lay back down and pulled away from the thought, from the number, only wanting to know this—lying beside her as the subways beneath us trundled to Manhattan, as the old clocktower marked time. I looked past her at the Brooklyn night beyond her window. Would this be the one night we didn't make love, have sex, fuck, whatever limited term I could use for what we did? Would I remember it more clearly than any other? I couldn't bear the thought. I couldn't bear the thought of losing this night. I had to do something. *Just talk*, a voice inside me said. Calm her. You know how to do this. Tell her a story. And then I knew what to say.

"Have you ever heard about the Navajo rug weavers?"

She hesitated at the odd question. "No."

"Weaving rugs is sacred work to them, and the techniques have been passed down hundreds, probably thousands of years. The weaver works long and hard to make this object as close to perfect as possible, then consciously weaves a tiny flaw into it. There's a word for the flaw I can't remember, let alone pronounce, but it basically means spirit line or pathway. And this pathway, or portal, is what allows the weaver's spirit to leave the rug and not get trapped in it. Other cultures have similar ideas, the flaw in a work of art being a portal allowing God to enter and exit, and perfection being a kind of death. A trap. The flawed object having more value, more meaning, than the perfect one."

She continued to stare at the ceiling. "Where did you learn all this stuff?" She kept hold of my hand, but had stopped gripping it.

"Your scar . . ." I paused, wondering if I shouldn't have said *that* word, but it was too late. Maybe I needed to say it. Maybe she needed me to say it. "It makes you more beautiful because it makes you more vulnerable. It makes your beauty forgivable."

She blinked, hesitated. "My husband doesn't like it."

"It's where you were hurt." She flinched. I whispered, "It's where you're closest to God."

She turned to meet my eyes, then after a moment looked away. "This wasn't supposed to happen," she said.

"What?"

"It doesn't change anything."

"It doesn't change what?"

She shook her head. "Forget it."

I hesitated, then put my lips to her cheek. When she didn't pull away I brushed my mouth across hers once, carefully. She turned her face from me toward the window, but left her body naked and open. So I spoke there, trailing my tongue down her torso, and her fingers finally let mine go. I ran them across her skin and her body began to release. She sighed, shrugged. As I approached the scar I felt her body tighten, so I slipped to her side, curved my hand over her hips, gave her that thin line of privacy as I committed to memory the rest of her—her shape, texture, and finally reaching her center, her taste, some mix between cardamom and raw lamb.

~

Almost four in the morning, past time to go, but she was gripping my hand again, frowning at the ceiling. "Tell me how you know what you know," she said.

"What do you mean?"

"Your stories. The way you see words and colors. Did your mother read to you? Did she show you art books?"

"No."

She turned my way. "But the way you are . . . with me. I mean, did you have sisters?"

"Yes."

"How many?"

"Three."

"Did you have any brothers?"

"No."

She raised up on an elbow and looked down at me. "Tell me about your sisters."

I didn't really want to go into it. "They were older than me."

"Are you close to them?"

"Not especially. Not anymore."

"What happened?"

"We grew up."

"You can grow up without growing apart."

"How?"

She studied me. "Of course they were beautiful," she said. I closed my eyes and was surprised a tear escaped. She put her lips to it. When she pulled away tears streamed down my face like I'd been undammed.

"John, what is it?"

I sat up, wiped my face, and the tears stopped, but I was unnerved by my loss of control. "I don't know," I said. More than anything, I was confused by my reaction. "Everything, I guess."

"There's a lot going on."

"No kidding."

She leaned closer, rested her hand on my shoulder. "Listen," she said softly. "You don't have to talk about anything you don't want. But if you want, who would ever find out? Who could I tell without explaining how I knew?"

"It sounds like you've done this before, too."

"I've thought about it. I suppose everyone's thought about it."

"I suppose."

"But my husband . . ." She shook her head. "Before him there were other men, of course."

"Of course."

She smiled, guiding me back down. "So?"

I shrugged. "There's really nothing to tell. My sisters grew up and went away to college."

"Leaving you behind?"

"No," I said. "I mean, they had to. It was the right thing." She was watching me closely. "People have to leave." She lay her hand on my chest. I felt my heart beat against it. "It's really no big deal."

"Okay," she said. "Okay."

At her doorway she wrapped her arms around me and held me longer than she had yet, then rose on her feet to kiss the corner of each of my eyes before turning away. I watched her go, then put my ear to her door to listen for any sounds outside before twisting the handle and stepping into the hallway. I headed toward the stairwell, my head down, the fluorescent lights harsh and blinding.

11

New Braunfels, Texas, 1970

I am ten. Charlie's head is under the hood of his red Mustang. The engine is black and silver and smells like oil. He's poking around telling me how everything works, explaining about the gears and the pistons and the drive-shaft, about the fan belt and the sparkplugs and how you have to gap them. He has strong arms. He likes to fix things. He rises out of the hood, then slaps me on my shoulder and it leaves a black handprint on my T-shirt.

"Sorry," he says.

"I don't care," I tell him.

"Catherine's gonna kill me for that," he says, but he's grinning his crooked grin, the one that says he likes to laugh. The one that says every-thing's gonna be okay. He rubs his hands together to work the grease off. "She's always complaining about the grease."

"It's better than having the car break down along the road somewhere."

"That's what I tell her," he says. But it's what he and I tell each other when we're working on his car. I've never heard him say that to her.

Catherine opens her window upstairs and yells out, "You better wash those hands before you try putting them on me." He holds them up and waves them. She makes a face at him, then calls to me, "John?"

"Okay," I say. Charlie closes the hood, then gets a clean shirt out of the backseat. I lead him up the hill to our door. Inside he goes toward the bathroom to wash up and change, and I go up the stairs. Catherine's at the vanity, and Kari is beside her. Kari has put an iris in the vase.

"You didn't get grease on your hands, did you?" Catherine asks.

"No." I show her my hands, wiggle my fingers.

"Is that grease on your shoulder?"

"I dunno."

"From Charlie?"

"No." She frowns at me. "From his car," I say smiling. "From his engine."

She tries not to smile but can't help herself. "Go change your shirt," she tells me.

I run into my room and put on a new T-shirt. I take the baseball glove out of my closet, pull out the brush, then go back to her room where I sit on the stool and watch her. Her face is wider than Amanda's. She has a tiny dark spot, a little mole to the right and above her mouth. It's a beauty mark, she says. She's going to be bigger than Amanda. Kari will be skinnier than either of them. Someday I won't be small.

Catherine's cheekbones are high, and she's proud of how they make her face look. I watch her paint a thin white line over one, then she carefully brushes the paint down, then up, so you can't even tell it was there. But it's whitest at the top where it looks like light is hitting. She takes another brush and paints a dark brown circle on her cheek, then she fans the dark out until you can't see it either, but it makes her cheek look deep and her cheekbone look high. She turns her face side-to-side examining the difference. Kari's watching her too, but Catherine's smiling to me. "Cool, huh John?"

"Yes," I say. There are two different Catherines. One day, one night; one light, one dark.

Mother steps through the door. Catherine turns to her. "Can't you knock?" she says.

"Sorry," Mother says.

"Well, knock. You made me smear my makeup and now I'm going to have to start over."

"Well . . ." Mother looks my way. I hide the brush beside my leg.

"Mother. Do you mind?" Catherine says, standing to face her. She's bigger than Mother. I never noticed. "What do you want?" she says. No one's ever stood up to her like this.

Mother takes a sip from her Coke. She glances around like she doesn't know what to do next. Is she afraid of Catherine? "You should be more respectful," she says, but her voice is thin. She scratches her cheek and glances at me.

Catherine takes a short breath, then lets it out. "I don't mean to be disrespectful. I really don't. I'm just trying to get ready. Okay?"

"Okay." I start to relax. Mother looks over at me. "John," she begins. And I don't want to go.

"I need him," Catherine tells her.

"You *need* him?"

"He gives good advice." Catherine sits down again. "About what to wear. And you know I can always use that."

Mother looks confused. She looks at me, then takes a sip from her Coke. "Well," she says. She takes another sip. And I realize she's not going to be angry or sad. Though Charlie wouldn't care if she was. He loves Catherine that much. And Amanda was right. Mother can be managed. "That young man's all by himself down there," she says.

Catherine starts putting on mascara with her little mascara brush. "He can wait." She smiles a little to herself in the mirror. "It'll do him good." Mother stands in the door for a moment, then backs away and closes it. I'm surprised she left without me, but I'm glad she's gone. Catherine nods to me, and I walk toward her. The closer I get the more I want to brush her hair. But instead she shows me two lipsticks. "Which should I use?"

"What are you wearing?"

"The new scarlet blouse." Kari goes to the closet and pulls it out to show me. "Bring it over," Catherine tells her.

She holds it up to Catherine, then Catherine puts some of each lipstick on her lips, the lighter on the left side, the darker on the right. They don't work together. The colors fight and it's hard to look at, but one is too orange. "Use the redder one, the darker one," I tell her. "There's some orange in the shirt, but you want your lips to go toward red."

"Damnit," she says.

"You shouldn't use that orange lipstick anyway. Why did you buy it?"

"I wanted to try something different. It looked better in the store."

"Your face is too pink. Kari could use it though."

She caps it and tosses it to Kari who tries to catch it, but it tumbles from her hands.

"Is the blouse okay?" Catherine asks.

"Yes," I say. "Just use the redder lipstick."

I put my free hand under her hair to fluff it up and begin brushing down its length. It's thick like Amanda's, but not as long. It smells like lemons. It's damp and cool from her shower, and the air is cool around her hair, but her neck is warm and so is her skin. I watch the muscles on her shoulders, on her arms, and how they shift. She plays tennis and runs track. She likes to dress pretty, but in a different way than Amanda. Catherine is a jeans girl. Amanda is a dress girl.

She's watching me in the mirror. "You have Amanda's eyes," she says, and at first I think she means they're pretty like Amanda's, but then I realize she's talking about the way I see.

~

"Do you like Grandma?" Kari asks me. She's taken my hand and is pulling me toward the swing set in the backyard. She has her book in her other hand. It's called *Of Mice and Men,* and it's about two guys named Lenny and George and how they take care of each other.

"I like her okay," I say.

"Because I heard Mother talking to her on the phone." She keeps walking but stops talking. She sits on one swing and I sit on the other. Her blond hair is so light any breeze lifts it. It floats around her face.

"What did you hear?"

"She asked Grandma to come live with us." I push off the ground and start swinging. "After Catherine goes."

"We have to help her," I say as I swing past Kari. My wind makes her hair blow. She squints up at me as I zoom by.

"Grandma?"

"No. Catherine."

"I know. But Grandma's moving in."

I shoot past her again, then fall back and rise. I look down at the ground, drop toward it, then shoot up at the sky. It's cloudy. Colors are brighter on cloudy days.

"She told Grandma she should do it. She says we have so much room now, and the house is going to be empty without Catherine."

I keep swinging. I swing higher and higher, then I let go and fly. I fly and flap my arms and hit on the grass in front of the swing. The loose seat bounces around crazily behind me and Kari jumps away from it. She walks to me. Her blond hair falls forward as she looks down at me on the grass, and it frames her face against the gray sky. I notice the tiny freckles around her nose. She looks toward the house. Her mouth twists. "It's okay," I tell her. "It'll be good for Mother. She can take care of her."

"Or the other way around."

Kari looks down at the book in her hand, then walks back to her swing. I follow her. "Besides, we're going to leave," I say.

"I know."

I sit on the swing that's next to hers. She stares at her book, but I can see she's still worried. "Tell me 'bout the rabbits, George," I say in a cartoon voice.

She smiles, takes a breath, begins reading. And from her words I'm seeing mountains flaming with light from a setting sun. A water snake crossing a pool. I reach over and take her swing in my hand and pull us closer, then I put my arm through hers so we are connected, so we are linked like the chains on her swing. I lean closer to see the words. The shapes of the letters. The black marks on white paper. The story waiting for us inside of it all.

12

Catherine is leaving. She's going to the University of Wisconsin, up by the Great Lakes, up by Canada. Charlie says he hates cold weather but he's going anyway. He says the way they salt the roads up there eats the chassis out of cars. He's going to get a job as a mechanic to support her because with all that salt there's bound to be plenty of work.

He takes Catherine's smaller bag from me and puts it in the trunk. Catherine stands at the open passenger door watching him and me, watching Kari on the sidewalk. Their story is beginning. They will marry. They will never get divorced. They will never live here again.

Charlie closes the trunk and messes up my hair with his hand. Kari suddenly runs to Catherine and wraps her arms around her waist. "Hey," Catherine says. "Hey hey." Finally Kari lets go and I step up to Catherine. She sighs, then lifts me and holds me against her chest. "Take care of your sister," she whispers in my ear.

"I know," I say.

"Joujou," she says, then squeezes me so hard I can hardly take a breath. My legs dangle over the sidewalk. Then she sets me down. She looks toward the house, then at me. She stares at me.

"We need to get going, Catherine," Charlie says softly.

Charlie's right. It'll be dark soon. Catherine waves to Mother on the porch, then looks at Kari and me on the sidewalk. She shrugs, tries to smile.

"It'll be great," I say. She nods, looks down, then gets in the car and closes the door. The sky is blue with white, puffy clouds. They have a long way to drive. It'll be dark in a few hours and they need to get on the road. They need to get going. "You'll love it," I say.

Charlie looks at me and Kari. He grins that grin I like, gives us "thumbs up," then gets in the car and starts the engine. Catherine can't look at us. She looks down at her lap. Then the car starts to move and I put my hands to the trunk and push as it pulls away. "Go!" I yell running after it, hearing my shoes hitting the street. "Go go go go go!"

~

I carry Grandma's suitcase up the stairs. It is hard and plastic and heavy. It is Samsonite. Samsonite is so strong that even a gorilla can't break it. I saw this on TV. The suitcase hits against each step all the way up. The moving men have already carried the rest of her things into Kari's old room. Kari's old things have been given to Goodwill. She didn't want them. She wanted Catherine's things and Amanda's things. The vanity with the long mirror is hers now. She sits before it and looks into her face. Sometimes her mouth twists a little. Sometimes I brush her hair. What does her hair smell like? Vanilla.

~

Someone is in my room, and I'm still dreaming. I'm dreaming of cars on the road. I'm dreaming of driving, but someone, quiet and still, is in my room, and I see her, and she's pale and thin like a ghost, like she would disappear in a breeze. And is it a ghost? And what does it want? I sit up in bed so fast my heart feels like it's leaving my body.

"John?" she says. My heart's still beating too fast. Part of me knows who it is but part of me doesn't. "John," she says again, and then I know it's Kari. I see her, but she looks like a white shadow and I'm still afraid.

"Kari?"

She moves toward me, stands at the side of my bed. "It's Grandma," she tells me.

"Grandma?"

"Her sounds. I can't sleep."

I turn on my bedside lamp, and the glow illuminates her. "Are you okay?" I ask. She's trembling. "Wait here," I say. I get up and walk into the hallway toward Kari's old room, now Grandma's room. I can hear it long before I get there, rattling in the dark like chicken bones. It catches, stops, snorts, coughs, then starts again. It's awful, but it's only snoring. I don't go all the way to her door. I go into Kari's new room instead, Amanda's old room, and I close the door. I can hear it inside. It's not loud, but it's loud enough to keep Kari from sleeping. It's enough to make Kari come into my bedroom at night and scare me.

When I go back to my room, Kari's in my bed under the blanket curled up facing the window. Her pretty blond hair shines in the lamplight. "Kari?" I say. She doesn't answer. I'm not sure if I should get in the bed, but I don't know what else to do. Finally I lift the blanket and slide my legs under it. When I turn off the light Kari rolls over and looks at me.

"It's just so awful," she says.

"I think I can help," I tell her.

"Really?"

"Yes. I'll talk to Mother tomorrow."

She looks relieved, but there's something about her eyes, her face, that I haven't seen before. A change. When did this happen? She's still small like me. Skinny. But something has changed in her face. She looks so pretty in the dark. I want to look at the rest of her to see if anything else has changed.

"I hate her being here," she tells me. "I hate Catherine being gone. Amanda being gone."

"Next it's you," I say. "Then me."

I move, but she's so close my elbow accidently hits her chest. But it's more than her chest. "Ow," she says and rolls away.

"What?"

"They're sore," she whispers.

"Why?"

"Amanda and Catherine told me this would happen. Something else happened too."

"Kari. It's okay."

She shakes her head. "I didn't think it was ever going to happen. I don't know I ever wanted it to happen."

"Call Amanda. Call Catherine and tell them. Don't be afraid."

But she is afraid, and so am I. Catherine told me Kari was late. Very late. She'll be a junior when school starts. We only have two years to get her ready, and we're behind.

～

66

Mother sits in her chair in front of the TV watching *As the World Turns*, but now it's playing a commercial for Kool-Aid. The smiling red Kool-Aid pitcher is pouring a boy and a girl a drink.

"Mother?" I say.

She turns to looks at me. "Yes?"

"Kari needs a fan."

"A what? That's silly. We have central air."

"It's for the noise."

"The noise?"

"Yes." She waves for me to stop talking. *As the World Turns* is back on. "Can I watch?" I ask.

She looks at me surprised, then takes a drink from her Coke. "Why not?" she says. I sit on the couch. On the TV there is a girl and a man. The girl says the man promised he would marry her, but now he doesn't want to. Then there's a mother that's mad at her daughter because she wants to join the Peace Corps instead of going to college to be a lawyer. Then there are two men making business deals. One is old and one is young and they're both in love with the same woman. Then the show ends and there's another commercial.

"It's Grandma," I say.

"What?" She looks startled by my voice.

"The noise. She snores. Real loud."

She starts laughing. I laugh too. "You don't say."

"That's why Kari needs a fan. To drown out the sound." She laughs again, and I laugh with her. She takes a drink from her Coke. The soap opera is about to start. "So can she have one?" She looks at me and I smile.

"You take such good care of your sisters, John. You always have. Most brothers don't do that."

"I love them," I say. And they need me, but I don't tell her that.

"Lots of brothers love their sisters but would rather be playing baseball with other boys."

"I play baseball."

"I know, but . . . I mean . . ." She leans toward me. "You spend so much time making them pretty. . . . Why do you like that so much?"

She's looking at me in a funny way. I can't tell her the truth, that I'm helping them grow up and leave here, and that we're all going to follow each other out the door. I can't tell her how their hair feels in the brush, or how they move and hold me, or the way they smell. How the whole room changes when they're happy.

She's expecting an answer, and I have one. It's strange how I know what to say so she won't suspect me. It floats right in front of me. A disguise. "I just like pretty things," I tell her. "I like making things pretty."

She looks at me a moment, then shrugs. "That's fine, dear. It really is." She reaches over and pats my leg. The show is starting up. "This is my favorite soap opera," she says. "The really fun one. You'll like it."

~

The fan hums and turns on Kari's bedside table. She sits in front of the vanity and I'm behind her holding the brush. A daffodil stands in her vase. Her mouth twists.

"You're a beautiful girl," I say.

"Then why doesn't anyone like me?"

"They haven't noticed you yet." I set the brush deep into her hair and run it down. Her hair's shorter than Amanda's or Catherine's. It floats around my fingers.

"How will they ever notice me?"

She looks at me in the mirror. I feel alone with her. There's not enough of us anymore. "Don't you remember what Amanda and Catherine showed you?" I say. "How they did their makeup?"

"I never really understood."

"But . . ." I say.

"Show me, John. Help me. Please."

13

New York City

Wednesday night. I couldn't sleep. My legs twitched and my hands clenched. My body expected to be with her and refused to rest. I rolled out of bed, put on jeans and a T-shirt, and headed out. Soon I was riding the 6 downtown. The train's rocking and clatter were comforting. At the end of the car two older Asian women huddled against each other. A large black man in a blue jumpsuit slept across from them, the back of his head braced against the window and his mouth ajar. At the other end of the car a thin, scraggly, long-haired white guy cradled a bicycle and talked to himself. "My itching hands," he muttered. "My itching hands." Directly across from me a man in a pale green sweater caught my gaze. He smiled, nodding in the direction of the madman. I shrugged: *What're you gonna do?* Then I noticed how terribly thin he was. I saw he was wearing makeup. A base, in fact, that was too obvious, darker than the skin on his arms, his hands. His cheekbones were high and his cheeks sunken. His eyes were ice blue.

I drew back, then tried to mask the move by looking down the car at the man with the bicycle. When I first arrived in New York I rarely saw fullblown cases. A few of the bathhouses were still open then, and many gay men were resistant to taking "the test" for fear their HIV status would be stored in a database for later retrieval, for when the go-ahead was given to start building the camps. After ignoring the crisis for years, our president didn't even say the word "AIDS" until two years ago. Now AIDS victims have become part of the city's landscape. Only a year ago in the Village you'd still see the random, desperate, cadaver-thin man on the street trying to somehow cruise, to play the game in his late seventies leather garb or cowboy outfit. Now victims covered themselves in long coats even in the warmth of spring, of summer. You forced yourself to not shrink away as they passed, to not make them feel any more exiled. But they were all leaving us, all on their way out within a few weeks, a few months, at the end of summer perhaps, or the first cold snap.

The subway slowed to a stop at 14th Street, and I nodded goodbye to the man. I tried to look encouraging, not awkward, not afraid. More than anything else, not afraid. Without realizing it I touched my forefinger to the small, thin Celtic cross I wore around my neck, under my shirt and over my heart. He saw the gesture and returned it, thinking I'd done it for his sake. When the word "brother" formed on his lips, terror knifed through me. I could catch it. Anyone could catch it. With difficulty I forced myself to whisper the word back to him, "brother," then made my way to the door.

As his train pulled away I found myself moving quickly, pushing through the turnstiles, hurrying across the concrete floor, then taking the steps up the stairwell two at a time. I leapt above ground and landed on the sidewalk, freezing like a cat. Cars shot uptown. Dark clusters of people moved about in the dim light. Salsa music poured out of an upstairs window to the east. Somewhere a woman sang scales, stopped, then began again. The air was warm and humid, thick and dense. I glanced up at the sky, at the few stars shining through the haze. I took a deep breath and filled my lungs with the smell of it all—exhaust, heated brickwork, sweat, the Asian fruit stand beside me that was being broken down and washed, the flowers being carried inside a bodega, the garbage being carried out. It was as rich and sweet as flesh. It was fecund and living and polluted. It formed a shape in my mouth I could taste, I could swallow. I gulped it in. The city was still mine. My life was still mine. Where else would I want to be? Who else would I want to be? Especially now, because of her.

And then, of all people, I saw Jeremy across 14th Street, his camera out, in the street leaning into traffic as he took a night shot of something, maybe just 14th Street eastward and how the lights played across the dark asphalt, the shape it all made through his lens. I was surprised to see him, lifted actually. I thought I'd sneak up, trick him somehow and startle him. Maybe we'd get a drink somewhere. But then a smaller guy in black I'd not noticed stepped into the street and hooked a finger through Jeremy's belt and pulled him to the sidewalk, like he had a stake and wasn't going to let him get hit by a bus. Then I saw three other men and a woman waiting there for Jeremy. They took him by his elbows and pulled him westward, laughing.

I let them go. I let him go his way, and I went mine, wandering the East Village. I stepped over scattered crack vials at the corner of 2nd Avenue and 10th Street, keeping my eyes open for any shadows that suddenly moved. I walked past CBGB's, heard a band hammering away inside. They sounded like the last stragglers to leave a party, and I wished I'd gotten to the city a few years earlier when the scene was fresh and convulsive. I eventually found my way to Tompkins Square Park. It had become a tent city, filled with squatters, druggies, political activists trying to organize an opposition to the gentrification encroaching on the East Village. They were beating drums inside, laughing, shouting. A man staggered into one of the long benches, fell on it and curled up.

Across from the corner of the park I spotted a bar that looked like it had been there for a hundred years. I pulled open its heavy wooden door and stepped inside where bodies hunkered in shadows and ribbons of cigarette smoke hovered in the dark air. The Cramps blasted through the speakers. The worn, deeply grooved counter was built like a horseshoe so the bartender, a heavily tattooed woman with shoulder and neck muscles taut as cord, could work both sides from its center. I mounted a rickety barstool, ordered a beer, and looked out the grimy window at the tents and the bodies milling about the park. The neighborhood was conflicted about the people who'd taken it over. A lot of residents related to them because they were not much better off or different, and because the area remained extremely old-school, old-world liberal. They were worried about getting kicked out of their apartments and would welcome any political allies. But they were also worried about the crime rate in the neighborhood going even higher. Who knew what would happen? In the late 1800s a famous workers' riot erupted in Tompkins Square Park. Emma Goldman and even Trotsky held political rallies here. Things erupted and burned and spun so in this city. The thought of it all sent a buzz running up my spine. I sensed ghosts everywhere.

~

"Guess who I saw on the street," I said. We lay a few inches apart on the sheet on the floor of her living room.

"Who?"

"Jeremy. Last night. On 14th Street. He was standing in the street trying to take a photograph when one of his group pulled him to the sidewalk. I didn't see the group at first. It was odd to see him out there."

"He does have a life outside the office, you know. Outside of us. You should've said hi."

"I was going to, and then I saw these people with him. I didn't want to intrude."

"He wouldn't have minded. He's a very good photographer, you know."

"I know. I was remembering . . . maybe two years ago when we were all standing around you in your office, and you were so pregnant? Jeremy and Marjorie and Millie, a couple more of us. And . . . well, we each put our hands on your belly to feel the baby. You put my hand there and I felt her kick. I've wondered when you started wanting me. Is that when it started?"

"No," she said. "I remember it though. You were very cute. Your hand trembled against my belly. I remember that. And it was warm. Okay, maybe it happened a little bit, but really, I was all about the baby then. About being a mom. I've never felt so complete."

"You don't feel complete now?"

"You wouldn't be here if I felt complete."

Across her ceiling the shadows of the leaves fluttered and shook, the wind whipping the branches below. I wondered if Jeremy was out somewhere in the city. I wondered if a storm was coming, if I'd have trouble catching a cab.

"When did it happen, then?"

"Over time. One day I decided I wanted to make you want me."

"Why?"

She shrugged. "Because my husband stopped, I guess. And because you listened to me, was interested in what I said. Because . . . you were safe. Or so it seemed. Really, I must've known better. You're not safe at all. So did you notice?"

"A change? I couldn't trust it meant anything. But yeah, I guess I noticed."

"I was playing, I suppose. But the more I did it, the more I wanted to do it. And then I started to want you. I didn't plan on it."

"I wanted you on sight. You drove me crazy. I nearly had to quit the job, it was so bad."

"But you didn't pursue me."

"You were married. Then you had a baby. I needed the job. And it wouldn't have worked, right?"

She stretched a leg toward the ceiling, flexed and pointed her foot, then brought it back down. "Of course not," she said. She looked over at me. "So you played hard to get?"

"I just didn't play the fool. Was Jeremy involved? It feels like he was involved somehow."

"We used to sit in my office and talk about you. About what you'd be like."

"In bed?"

"Yes, in bed."

"How do I match up?"

"There's a part of you that changes. It's like a switch flips inside you. Jeremy wouldn't have expected you to be so dominant. He expected you to be sweet. You're that too. But the other part . . . there's this animal aspect. I think I must've sensed it. Sometimes when we're doing it it feels like there's not going to be anything left of me."

"Is that good?"

"We're beyond what's good. We're someplace else."

"Can I ask you a personal question?"

"You're kidding, right?"

"Your husband changed after the birth, the C-section?"

"And the *scar*? Yes, immediately. He lost interest. He got off-track."

"Maybe it wasn't the scar. Suddenly there's this life, this baby he's responsible for. Some guys see their wives differently after they become mothers."

"He shouldn't see *me* differently."

"It's not uncommon."

"Truth is, he wasn't all that special in bed before. But after Carina . . ."

"Maybe he was frightened by it all. The risk. You and Carina could've both died."

"You mean the risk of sex?" She laughed. "But John, they cut the risk out of me. I'd never even had surgery before, then they cut me open and tie my tubes and make sure I can't have any more babies. And I'm like, am I even still a woman? But I decided, yes. Yes, I still am. Maybe I can't do *that* anymore. But I can do other things. He should've taken advantage of the situation. He should've taken his pleasure and given me mine—no condom, no nothing, like you. While you, John, *are* at risk each time you see me. He has a temper, by the way. There's no telling what he would do if he found out."

I hesitated. "I guess that's to be expected."

"See? And it doesn't stop you. You come for me anyway."

"But has he ever . . ."

"What?"

"Hit you. Hurt you."

"No. He just rages. Then again, he's never caught me cheating. He has told me that if I ever left him, he'd use all his money to take Carina from me." She sighed. "Well, he told me that once. On a bad night for us both."

"You'd fight him."

"Sure. But New York's a tough state for divorce. And honestly, my salary's not that much. It's a great company, but I'm just a supervisor. There's only so high I can go and the city is so expensive, you know, especially when you have a kid. Anyway, it was a bad night."

"Why did you marry him?"

"I didn't know better. He had money and was good looking and dressed well. I was young and window shopping, trying to move up from being, you know . . ." her voice softened. "A waitress. Another Italian waitress in another Italian restaurant in Queens. Taking night courses. Getting older. All that. But actually, especially with Carina, and when I'm not . . . disrupting, he can be kind. He's not a monster. He just comes up short."

"I think he's scared."

"He is."

"Scared of you. He's overmatched." And a coward, I thought. Afraid of what people would say if they knew.

"I know," she said, then laughed briefly, as if surprised by her words. She turned my way. "But you're not, are you?"

"Which? Scared or overmatched?"

"Either."

"The only thing I'm afraid of is what it would do to you if we were found out."

The edges of her mouth curled in a slight smile. "But you're not afraid enough to stop, are you? You want to have me more than you want to protect me."

There was no denying it, however I might have wanted to. The surest way to protect her and her child would be to end it. A sense of shame flooded me. "Of course," I said.

Her smile grew as she inched closer to me. "And I'm sure you've considered this," she whispered. "There's more than my husband involved. There's a killer on the streets, in the bars and restaurants, and I don't know where you've been playing. Nor you, I. And my husband . . . God only knows." She hesitated, then took my hand. "Though I trust my intuition about you. Or at least I choose to." She turned away from me, back toward the ceiling. "The best sex is always about risk, right? Getting pregnant, or getting caught."

"Or losing your way. Or your heart."

"Something has to be at stake."

14

Monday night, too restless to fall asleep, I wandered the city again, riding the subway on the uptown 2 express to 42nd Street. I wondered if Alena was sleeping already. Or taking a bath. Or staying up to read a little after a long day. My right leg had the jitters, my heel beating the floor thump-thump-thump. I forced it to stop, then looked up to see two college-aged girls across the car watching me. They held my gaze for a moment, then turned away as the subway pulled into 42nd Street. I stepped off the car when, in an explosion of sound and sparks, colors and lines, a train covered in graffiti thundered into the station. The train's air brakes set, its doors opened. It sighed, settled, and once I realized it was going to stay put for a moment I dashed up the stairwell, across to the downtown side, down the steps, and leapt toward the nearest car. I hesitated, then put my hand to its side and felt a touch of dampness. I quickly pulled my hand back and checked to make sure no paint came away. The train had just been tagged at the yards. I felt my heart beating in my chest.

Two weeks after I arrived in New York I traveled up I-87 through Manhattan with my friend Billy. We were headed upstate where I'd signed on to help him and a small theater company by hammering and painting for a few days in the Catskills. But as we passed Manhattan we came upon the buildings of the South Bronx. They crouched, charred and hollowed out, along both sides of the highway as far as we could see, seemed to tip toward us like they might collapse over the interstate. It looked like the end of the world. Then we shot past the stripped and burnt bones of what was once a car on the right-hand shoulder. There was no telling its make or model. Billy had lived in New York for several years. Your car breaks down here, he told me, you walk away. It'll be stripped within the hour, and you don't want to be there when it happens.

I remembered watching game two of the 1977 World Series, between the Yankees and the Dodgers, at a friend's house when the sky shot from the Met Life blimp showed a school as big as a city block burning near Yankee Stadium in the Bronx. Howard Cosell, America's top sportscaster, stated grandly, "Ladies and gentlemen, the Bronx is burning!" Like it was a joke. Like New York City was a lost cause, the drunk, jobless relation who throws up on the bride at a wedding.

My friend's father had had a few beers, and he started ranting at the TV about what a cesspool it was up there, how we ought to just bomb it all, getting angrier the longer he went on until finally his wife brought him a sandwich. I can't even remember who won the game, but I remember thinking you could get on a subway in the Bronx, where the fire was, and be at Tiffany's in less than an hour. Conversely, you could be at Tiffany's and be only an hour away from the wasteland. The irony, the dichotomy, thrummed in my chest, a subtle vibration, like a calling.

Now from that wasteland, rap, break dancing, and graffiti art had erupted like bright, crazed flowers from cracks in the sidewalk. The graffiti artists were kids from the projects with names like Blade, Duster Lizzie, MIDG, and Slave Fabulous 5, toting illegal cans of Krylon spray paint. They climbed over or cut their way through chain-link fences into train yards in the middle of the night, poor kids risking arrest and physical assault from gangs so the art inside them could get out, so they could watch their letters, their abstracted names, shoot by on a subway platform. On weekends I rode the subway to Queens, to Brooklyn, to the elevated trains, and took the stairs down to the street where I watched them pass above me. I sketched what I saw. The trains roared and rattled, their brakes squealed, they snaked in and snaked away. The graffiti looked to be influenced by everything from Russian Constructivism to comic books. Letters bounced on legs and leapt and jousted. Over-endowed cartoon females reclined over subway doors, split and came together with the thin sliding metal. The drawn figures could be unexpectedly cute, childlike and happy, something you'd put on a baby's bedroom wall, while the words disrupted and electrified. I considered that I'd been disrupted. I'd been electrified. By this city. By Alena. Wasn't that the idea all along? Isn't that why people came here and gave themselves over so that they might change, so that something might change them?

This particular car, the one I'd put my hand on, was covered in a form called Wildstyle. The letters overlapped and interweaved in layers. Arrows and spikes jutted in angles. There was a word there somewhere but I could only make out a glimpse of it before it sank back into the morass. It was so complex and beautiful and familiar I suspected it had been painted by the legendary Dondi. Jennifer took me to an East Village art opening last year and there his art hung on the wall, some scrawny brown-skinned kid with a sweet smile from East New York who'd be going back to the projects after the show.

Jennifer wouldn't let me live it down if I didn't ride his car at least one stop, so I got on. Inside it was almost empty, a few people headed somewhere half asleep. Someone had splattered the inside of the car with black Krylon. As the subway pulled away and rumbled downtown I decided to get off at 34th so I could walk back up to Times Square. I stepped out, touched my fingers to the car's exterior again, and watched the train roll toward Brooklyn.

Above ground I started toward Times Square in the dim light, passing peep shows and XXX video stores, shuttered Chinese take-out shops, and the northern remnants of the garment district. I was still so excited from riding in the Dondi car I almost stepped in the small puddle in front of me gone thick and clay-red. Blood, a pool about nine inches in diameter. I stepped over it, glancing side-to-side, and picked up my tempo, aware of how isolated I was along this dark stretch of 7th Avenue. Stupid, I told myself. Keep your head out of your ass. Ahead Times Square floated in a mist of light like an enchanted kingdom.

When I crossed 42nd Street, Times Square was popping, but since Monday's a slow night for tourists, the performers were out more for themselves. A white preacher yelled into a microphone about sinners and the coming end of the world. A Black Muslim preached, with his muscle-bound, cross-armed entourage behind him, about the superiority of the black race and the evilness of the white. A group of kids of every shade break-danced on sheets of cardboard, spinning and rising and twisting in impossible angles while one of the crew carried a tip jar around the semicircle of people watching them. At two different street corners pairs of black kids rapped, their words buzzing through small amplifiers as they battled.

All the while against the sky, goddess-sized models reclined semi-nude across billboards. Lights and signs strobed and ran and swirled overhead, dripped and sprayed colors, drenched the street. Prostitutes and pimps lay back in the shadows along with drug dealers who whispered "smoke smoke, coke coke." Street people stumbled past, and the meager theater crowd hitting the few shows that didn't go dark on Mondays mixed with the rest of us to find the bars. Cops strolled by, stood on street corners, watched it all. I was sweating. I was dirty. I was looking forward to a shower but couldn't imagine going home.

I turned left at 45th Street and headed toward Charlie's, an old ground-floor theater bar near Port Authority. Inside, the ceiling was low enough to touch, and strung with Christmas lights. A tiny ancient woman in a big blond wig who was there every time I stepped in sat in the back at her table, smoking and sipping whiskey, leaving bright red lipstick prints on her glass. I took a seat at the bar. The bartender took my order, then moved away from me with the clear grace of a dancer. When he brought back my beer I looked into his face. It was unnaturally thin, and his hair was obviously dyed brown. Another AIDS victim. I pictured him younger, beautiful, a chorus boy for Fosse, for Bennett, while he worked here between gigs. I took a drink from my bottle and looked out the window at 45th Street. I didn't know what to make of this, of anything. It was all beyond me. I only knew I loved it. Even what was horrible.

~

The next day I found a pink tulip in my desk drawer at work. I was transfixed at how perfectly its shade complemented its green stem. I wanted to lift it out and smell it. It was always a challenge at the end of my shift to remove the flowers she left me with no one seeing. In her apartment lobby that night I noticed the flowers on the front desk were pink tulips. At her suggestion, she told me, the superintendent changed the flowers weekly.

I rode the elevator up. I opened the unlocked door to her apartment and stepped inside. I followed her to her sheets on the floor of the living room. After we were done, she lay on her side looking out her window. I curved into her from behind. "We're going to have to talk about it sometime," I told her.

"Why?"

"Because time is going to run out."

"We've still got more than a month."

"Then what?"

79

"You know," she said. "You know, and I know."

Yes, I knew what I'd signed up for. But I couldn't help but wonder what would happen if she left him for me. What would it do to us? Would we survive it? Could I be there for her and her daughter? I would try. I would do all I could. But Alena was used to stability and money and I had neither. Would her daughter hate me? No doubt. But there was also this, what I felt in my bones, and it was definitely *not* the deal I had signed up for—a need to separate her from that man. Because she deserved better. Whether it was me or someone else. But what would such a breakup do to the child? Alena told me that Carina loved her father madly, that he was actually a very good daddy for a daughter, that he truly adored her. "Just not me so much," she said, "or at least in the way I need it."

In her office a few months before we began our affair, she showed me a photograph of a beautiful little girl at a beach. "Carina," I said.

"No," she told me smiling. "Me."

Now I buried my face in Alena's hair. Her daughter was asleep in her room, no idea her foundations were quaking.

"Sometimes I wish . . ." Alena said quietly, "sometimes I wish something would happen to him."

"While he's in Italy?"

"Yes. And that would solve everything."

So now, I realized, we were speaking of his death. "Why is he in Italy?"

"Business," she said. "He left me alone for two months so he could do business. Would you leave me alone for two months?"

"No."

"Ever?"

"I'd know better."

"You'd know *me* better. And even forgive me for it. And maybe even love me more for it. And that's the way it is. That's the way things are."

It was true. I would forgive her so long as I could have her. I loved that aspect, her needs, as much as anything else. More. I pulled her closer. Our bodies matched, fit, linked.

She sighed. "Am I being fair to you?"

"Don't."

"What?"

"The only thing that's not fair is . . ."

"What?"

"I'm scared of what someone might lose."

"Besides my husband?"

"Yes. But even him." She didn't answer, and my fear seemed to spread over the carpet like mist. "I dunno," I said. "I don't know what I'm thinking. I'm . . . I should . . ."

She turned and put her mouth to mine to make me shut up. I was grateful. I could feel my blood rushing toward her body. She looked into my eyes. "Don't be getting too serious, okay, baby?" she said. Then she smiled. I loved her smile, its shape, its arc, the texture and warmth and hunger of her mouth. And her dark eyes, playful now, grounding me, turning our sudden gloom on a dime. And everything was okay again. There was nothing I'd ever wanted more than this. And here I was. Here we were.

"We'll be careful," she said.

"Yes."

15

New Braunfels, Texas, 1971

I am eleven. Kari is seventeen. She sits perfectly still with her eyes shut, her hair tied back, in front of the vanity. Her skin is almost white. Kari wants me to cover up the tiny freckles around her nose with makeup but I talk her out of it again. They make her look more delicate, I tell her. What I don't tell her is they help keep her face from looking too flat. They set off her features. I lean into her side, swirl the tiny brush in the eyeshadow as I study her, and begin again, painting her eyelid powder-blue, stroke by stroke. I learned how to draw makeup on Kari in no time. It was as if I already knew how. Now I make the color deeper, stronger on the inside, then spread it outward so it almost blends in with her skin on the far side. I step back to see her whole face better. "What do you think?" I say. She turns to the mirror. She nods, and I keep going. I apply the lipstick to her bottom lip, then stop, getting an idea. I pick up a little sponge brush from her makeup kit, rub it against the lipstick, and paint her bottom lip in a downward motion.

"What are you doing?"

"I think this might make the color smoother. It might make your lips less sticky."

"But what if I need to put more on later?"

"It's okay. We're just trying this." I stop to look at it. It looks better this way.

"Should I press my lips together?"

"No," I say, and begin painting her upper lip.

Afterward I take the eyeliner brush and draw a thin black line across the arc of her eyelid. I make it thicker as I follow its shape outward. Then I angle it up just past her eye, matching perfectly her other eye that I've finished. Kari calls the mark a "lilt." It's something I saw to do, and it got Kari noticed at school. One of the popular girls came up to her at lunch and asked about her eyes. Her name was Jackie, and she called Kari later, invited her to a party. That's why I'm drawing her makeup on her. I have to get her eyes perfect for the party.

"What if Jackie asks me to show her how?"

"Then show her."

"I'm not as good as you."

"You don't have to be as good as me. Besides, maybe you don't want her to know. She'll steal your look." I lean back and look at her mouth. It's a little wider than you'd expect for her face. I get an idea to bring that out to separate her from the other girls. I pick up the darker red lipstick, put a little on the brush, and very carefully outline her lips. The curves are delicate but were hard to notice until now. I feel my heart speed up, excited at what I've done. I want to trace my finger along the line, but instead start blending it into the middle, into the pinker lipstick there. And they fill, like magic. Boys will want to kiss her. Everybody will want to kiss her, to touch her mouth. "Kari," I say, "you're going to look so good."

When I finish she stands. She turns to the right, the left. She's wearing a T-shirt and jeans. The shape of her body has changed. Her curves bend gently, like an eyelash. Like a sliver moon. Her breasts aren't big. They'll never be big but they don't need to be. They need to match her body, and they do. She's grown taller. My sister is beautiful, but she doesn't look like herself anymore. She looks more like Amanda and Catherine. How could this happen so quickly? I'm still small, the smallest in my class. Will this happen to me? Will I change so quickly too? Sometimes she and I make each other nervous and we don't know what to say. She's stopped reading to me.

Kari turns to look at herself over her shoulder in the mirror and strikes an expression I've never seen before that makes my heart ache, that takes my breath, that makes me want. How did she do that? Then she smiles, just slightly, seeing in the mirror what she's done, seeing what she can do, that hurts me in a whole new way. And I helped her. I helped draw her face so she could do this. But it doesn't come from what I drew. It comes from inside her *through* what I drew. There's something in her look I will never understand, and will always want to know, but never will. And it will always hurt. I will always want it. She is so beautiful that I am afraid.

She catches my eye in the mirror and sees me watching her. "Thank you, John," she tells me.

I want to brush her hair.

~

I sit on the edge of my bed, look out my window, and wait. There's almost no wind tonight. The trees and limbs barely move. Kari was supposed to be home by midnight, but Mother is already asleep so it doesn't matter. Did she have fun? Did Jackie like her? Did the boys?

My radio is set to a station in Austin, and the DJ says, "Tommy from San Marcos wants to dedicate this to Mary Beth. Here you go, Tommy. And Mary Beth, it seems . . . you've got a friend." Then James Taylor starts singing "You've Got a Friend."

And I wonder why Tommy picked that song. I wonder if he and Mary Beth had a big fight and now he's trying to apologize. Or he's trying to tell a girl he's her friend so she won't be afraid of him, and then he can get to be her boyfriend. Or maybe something bad happened to Mary Beth. Maybe her father died.

A car turns at the corner and drives down our street, and it's Kari's white Ford Torino that used to be Mother's. After my sisters pass their drivers' license test, Mother gives them her car. Then she gets a new one. It'll be my turn next. Kari's car bumps up on the curb, then she turns off the engine and sits for a minute with the headlights on. Finally her door opens, and Kari walks a little funny, angles off to the left on her way up the hillside. I stand in my doorway and wait for her. Her keys scratch at the front door and then it opens. Grandma's snoring rattles from her room. When Kari sees me from the top of the stairs she looks startled.

"What are you doing?" she says.

"Making sure you're alright. Are you alright?"

She nods. But I can tell there's something she doesn't want me to know. She teeters a little on her feet. Some of her makeup is gone, or has faded. But she looks like Kari again, my sister, not the girl who was in the mirror. I smile so she's not nervous. "Did you have fun?" I ask.

"Yeah," she says. She touches her fingers to the handrail. "Yeah," she says again.

"I *told* you that you were pretty."

She nods, then goes in her room and closes the door. Soon I hear her fan. I watch her door for a minute, then I go in my room and lie down on my bed but know I won't be able to sleep. So I wait and give Kari enough time to get in bed, then I get my flashlight and walk past Kari's dark door and down the stairs, keeping my feet on the edges so the steps hardly creak.

Kari forgot to lock the front door. I open it, step out, and close it without making a sound, then walk down the grass toward Kari's car. A car's coming down a side street so I run and crouch beside her white Torino. When the car turns my way, my heart starts to thump. What if it's a police car? What if it's Mike driving by? But when the car moves past, it's just another car going down the street. It turns at the next corner and disappears.

I shine my flashlight in Kari's car, and the light hits two cans on the floorboard. They're beer cans. They're Budweiser. I open the door and grab them, then close it quick, but it's too loud. I'm scared the noise is going to make the neighbors come out on their porch or the lights go on in a house. But it doesn't happen. I hurry up the grass, around the side of our house, and push the beer cans deep into our trash.

16

"He's downstairs," Mother says at Kari's doorway.

"Just a minute," Kari says, waving her hands.

"Be still," I tell Kari. She made me smear her eyeliner.

"Don't let this one get away," Mother tells her.

"Please. Please let me finish," Kari says.

"Thank god *John* knows what he's doing."

I feel my throat closing. It's hard to take a breath. Finally Mother shuts the door and goes downstairs. Kari's breathing fast. She waves her hands like she wants to shake them off. "God," she says.

I put my hands on her shoulders and rub the muscles. I know just where to press. "It'll be okay," I tell her.

"I can't *believe* her!"

"She doesn't understand."

"Why can't she understand?"

Kari's too loud. The boy will hear. I haven't met the boy. I want to meet him but I have to work with Kari. It's October. Kari's a senior. The boy's a captain on the football team. She's never gone out with anyone on the football team and she's too nervous. I don't even know his name.

"What's his name?" I ask. She starts breathing too fast again. Her head tips toward the vanity. "Are you dizzy?"

"Yes."

"Take a deep breath."

"I can't."

I hold her hand. I squeeze it. "Try, Kari. Just try." I put my other hand to her belly like Amanda showed us to do. "Breathe against my hand," I tell her.

"What?"

"Push my hand out with your belly." She does, and I feel it go out, then in. I guide her breathing. We work together to slow it down. "You're going to be fine," I tell her. "You're so pretty. You've got nothing to worry about. What are you worrying about?"

I take my hand away. She looks at me in the mirror and whispers, "I never thought he'd ask me out."

"And now it's happened."

"Yes."

"And why is that bad?" She stares at me. "And why is that a bad thing?" I say.

Her breathing has slowed to normal. "It's not bad," she says. She looks surprised that's her answer.

"Why are you acting like it's bad?"

"I don't know."

"So it's good?"

She nods. "Yes."

"It's very good, right? It's great." She keeps nodding. "So think about that. How it's great. You're going to have fun tonight, Kari. I know you will."

She watches me for a second. Then she falls against me, wraps her arms around my waist, tucks her head against my chest. "John," she says.

～

Kari goes down the stairs ahead of me and turns back. With a look she tells me to stay, so I stop halfway down the stairs. She runs to him, and I hear them talking but can't see. Then they go to the door and I see him from behind. He's big. He's even bigger than Charlie. When Mother calls out from the kitchen, "You two have fun," he looks back toward her. His hair is dark and short. His face is big and square.

"Hey," I say, but Kari pulls him out the door and they're gone. She didn't tell me his name.

～

Mother says his name is Gary Phillips and colleges are trying to recruit him to play football. She says he plays defensive tackle and is very handsome.

"He's big," I tell her.

"Isn't he, though?" She opens and pours a Coke over ice and adds to it from her bottle in the cupboard. She stirs it with her finger, licks it, then looks at me and smiles. Her eyes are wet. She lifts her glass. "Anything you can do to help," she says.

"I'm trying," I tell her.

~

Finally his car pulls up and parks behind Kari's car. He drives a brand-new Mustang and it's silver and Kari says his daddy bought it for him. But it is very late. It is past one o'clock. Mother is asleep. After she fell asleep in her chair I woke her and helped her to bed. What if Kari and the boy came back and found her there like that? What would he think? I watch their car from my window for a long time, but they don't get out. I want to see him walk her up the hill. The night is cool and cloudy. It's supposed to rain. I can't see any stars.

Then her door opens and the interior light flashes on. Kari gets out and closes her door and the light goes out. She takes a step up the grass, then turns to look back. Isn't he coming? Finally his door opens and he steps out. Kari begins walking slowly up the hill by herself. She doesn't look back at him anymore. He doesn't hurry to catch up, doesn't stand close to her, doesn't take her hand. She looks at the ground. He says something and laughs. Before he reaches the porch he turns and waves goodnight, then goes down the hill to his car, leaving Kari alone on the porch.

I hear the front door open and close quietly. I hear her come up the steps. At the top she sees me standing in my doorway. I smile so she's not nervous. "Did you have fun?" I say.

She nods. "Yes."

"Is he nice?" I ask her.

Her mouth twists a little. "Yes," she tells me. She goes in her room and closes her door. I hear the fan come on. I go back in my room and shut my door. I crawl in my bed under the covers but can't sleep, so I sit up, watch the street from my window, the leaves that are drying in the trees, that are changing color, that have already started to fall.

~

"I don't want him to know you do my makeup," Kari tells me.

"Why?" I say.

"I just don't."

"Hold still." I brush her eyelashes with the mascara brush, I try to separate each lash just like on TV. I lean back and look at her. Then I look at her face in the mirror. "He should like you anyway," I say.

"He does."

I start on the lashes of the other eye. It's the next Saturday, the second Saturday in a row they've gone out. I didn't think he'd ask her out again. A part of me doesn't want to finish, to let her go out the door.

When I'm done she looks at herself and says, "Thank you, John." She takes her turquoise blouse from the closet. "Wait here," she says.

"That blouse will be too cold," I tell her.

"I'll wear a jacket."

She leaves to go change in the bathroom. I sit on my stool and see myself in the long mirror. I look like I did last year and the year before, but Kari does not. I imagine Amanda sitting at her stool, then Catherine, then Kari, except Kari's smaller, more like me. I'm behind them holding the hairbrush.

I walk out Kari's door and stand at the top of the stairs. Kari's running water in the bathroom sink. I walk down the stairs, each step creaking. Does the boy hear me coming? He's talking to someone. Then I see him sitting on the couch holding our phone to his ear. He's smiling and laughing and talking. His face is big and square.

When he sees me watching him he gets a funny look on his face. He doesn't stop talking, but keeps looking at me, then away. He's not laughing anymore. Then he says, "Great. Seeya later," and hangs up.

"Who were you talking to?" I ask.

He narrows his eyes, then one side of his mouth lifts in a kind of grin.

"John," Kari says behind me. She's at the top of the stairs. She's so pretty it takes my breath. It scares me. The turquoise blouse and her blue eyes, her blond hair, her curves like a sliver moon. Her makeup. It's all come together. I brought out what she could be, and now it's who she is. "I told you to wait," she says coming down.

"I wanted to meet him."

"Yeah, Kari," he says. "We needed to meet."

When I turn back to him he's standing. He's so big it seems he takes up the whole room. Part of me wants to run from him, but I don't. I hold out my hand. He takes it, smiles, and squeezes it to let me know he could crush it.

I say it anyway. I look into his face. "What's your name?" I ask him.

17

When I walk into the living room they are on the couch lit by the TV, and he's got her, twisting around her and pressing her into the back of it. He's kissing her but I can hardly see her, can only see her hair behind his head, her arm around his shoulder, his hand on her leg at the edge of her white skirt. He's touching her thigh. His fingers are sliding under her skirt.

"Kari!" I say. Her name leaps out of my mouth without my realizing, then hangs in the air. I see my sister's thin arms, her small hands pushing at him. They come apart and his face is red.

"What?" she says to me.

I don't know what to say. I don't know if I meant to say anything at all.

"John," she says. "What do you want?" She stares at me. "John," she says again.

"Mother," I say.

He laughs. "Mother," he says.

"What about Mother?" Kari asks me.

"Where is she?"

"John," Kari says. She is angry. She is embarrassed. "She went to bed," she tells me. "You know she went to bed. Why are you asking me this?"

"Isn't it time for you to go to bed," he says to me.

I look at Gary Phillips. I look in his face. "What is your name?" I ask him.

He starts to move and Kari puts her hand on his leg to stop him. "John!" she tells me.

"What?" I say. She stares at me. I know what she wants me to do. So I finally do it. I leave. I go up the stairs toward my room. They're arguing below, then the TV is turned up loud. I go in my room, close the door, and sit on my bed. I stare out the window at the limbs that aren't moving. My legs shake. My hands are fists.

I get the flashlight out from under my bed and click it on and off. I walk to the door and back, then in front of my window and back. I don't know what to do. I head for the door again, opening it and stepping past Kari's room, which was Catherine's room, Amanda's room, the room with the vanity, with the long mirror where we all used to be. I walk down the stairs quickly, as quietly as I can. Grandma's snore is rattling. Johnny Carson is talking. The audience is laughing. Ed McMahon is going "Hi-yo . . ." I don't want to look into the living room, but I do anyway. And in the TV light I see them on the couch. I see Gary Phillips on top of my sister. I turn and run. I run down the hall to Mother's door and open it and she's lying on her side on her bed. I shine my light on her but she doesn't wake. I push her shoulder but she doesn't wake. "Mother," I say. "Mother!" She mutters, "John," and covers her face.

I walk back and forth. I walk back and forth in front of her, then I stop. I leave. I go out. I walk down the hall into the living room. He is on top of her and I stand in front of them. I see my thumb pressing the switch on the flashlight and it flashes on. When I point it at his face he looks like a monster.

"Son of a bitch," he yells, coming for me. Before I can get away he's got me around my waist and I'm up in the air, I'm way up, I'm over his head, and the flashlight falls and I hear it shatter, I hear it break and the batteries fly away. He's laughing. He's tossing me up and catching me, and if I fall I can feel the hit. I can feel how my head will hit and my neck will crack. And the lights go on in the room and Kari's crying. She's saying "Stop, please stop," but he's laughing, and I am in the air over his head. "Relax," he tells me. "Relax." He holds me up facing the ceiling, and if I move I will fall. His hands tell me that. So I stop fighting. I stop moving. "That's better," he says. "That's right." And Kari's crying, "Stop please stop please." And people are laughing on the TV. "He's so light," he says. "He's so small. Like a little kitten. Or maybe a mouse, how he scurries around."

"Don't call him that," Kari says.

"Don't call him what?"

"Just don't."

And I am up near the lights. I am near the ceiling. I hold my arms out to my side. I hold my legs out straight. My back is bent. My balance is perfect. I'm floating on his horrible thick hands, one on my back, the other against my bottom, where his fingers press. The flashlight is broken. Kari is crying and hitting him, and he's laughing.

"What?" he says. Then he brings me down, tucks me under his arm like a football and I can smell him. "He's just so little," he says. "We were just having fun." And she's crying. "It was a joke," he says. "We were just playing, having a good time. Right, John?" He bounces me under his arm. My arms and legs hang over the ground. "Right, John?" he says. And he's bouncing me. His hand is holding my side. I can feel his thumb on my side, his fingers pressing into me. And I just want it to stop. I want it all to stop. So I say yes. And he says it again, we're just having a good time. And I say yes. And he says no hard feelings, we're just kidding around, and I say yes. In front of my sister. Who's crying. Then I'm on the ground. And I'm trying to run but my legs don't work right, and I trip on the edge of doorway and fall to the wood floor and land hard on my elbow. I scramble up. I run away from them, I run up the stairs and to my room and close my door. But there's no lock. There's no lock on it to stop him from coming in. And are the stairs creaking? Is he walking up the stairs? I crawl under the bed where he's too big to fit. My chest is heaving and I can't make it stop. So I put my hand to my belly and try to breathe. I press down and let the air go out, and I push up with my belly and take the air in. And soon I'm breathing okay. I'm breathing. The stairs aren't creaking. He isn't coming. But I can't go downstairs again. I can't come out from under the bed. And I've left her alone with him.

~

My elbow aches. It's starting to stiffen so I stretch it. I hear the front door close and his car drive away. I tell myself I have to get out from under the bed, and so I do. I look out the window to make sure his car is really gone, then step into the hallway. Kari's light in her bedroom is out, and I can hear her fan humming. I go down the steps as quietly as I can in the dark house. I stand at the edge of the living room, and for a moment I think I see him sitting on the couch, his big body waiting for me. I want to run even though I know he's not really there. I see the flashlight on the coffee table where Kari must've set it. The back end is gone and the batteries are missing. I touch its glass and my finger is burned. No, it's cut. The glass is cracked. The flashlight is broken. The one my daddy gave me. I put my finger to my mouth and taste blood. I think, *this is how blood tastes*. I go to the front door to make sure it's locked and see Kari forgot to lock it. He could come back, walk in, do whatever he wants. Quick, I push the button. I slide the chain. I turn the deadbolt. His smell is everywhere. On the couch where he was on top of her. I look at the TV. I'm scared it could come on, could start talking to me. And what would I do? The house is silent. The limbs outside are not moving. The leaves have fallen. I left her alone with him. I helped make her beautiful for him. I can't hear the wind blow or the house creak. I can't hear anything at all.

18

New York City

The car shook and jolted beneath the river toward Brooklyn. I imagined the Brooklyn Bridge above us and the thousands of people pouring across it the day it opened. The largest and fourth largest cities in the country joined in May 1883, connected by an architectural marvel, a triumph of engineering and imagination. At least twenty-seven workers died while building it. Thirteen years before it was finished, the man who designed and engineered it tried to help put out a fire deep below the water in one of the chambers of its massive supports and suffered the bends, wrecking his health for the rest of his life. He was too ill to visit the site, so his wife replaced him, kept pushing the project forward as he watched from a window in the distance. She was the first to ride across the completed structure, carrying with her a live rooster as a sign of victory. It was like no other bridge in the world. Like so much of New York City, it seemed to me haunted and beautiful. It seemed to belong to other times even as it belonged to mine. My first year in the city I walked across the upper deck at sunset, and I remember how the light fell on the water and the boats and the buildings. I thought of Walt Whitman and his "Crossing Brooklyn Ferry."

> Just as you feel when you look on the river and sky, so I felt,
> Just as any of you is one of a living crowd, I was one of a crowd,
> Just as you are refreshed by the gladness of the river and the bright flow,
>   I was refreshed.

What would he have thought about me, about what Alena and I were doing? I knew full well I'd stacked the deck using him as a voice of conscience.

If I were being honest with myself I'd have picked someone less renowned for sleeping, or wanting to sleep, with everyone, if not everything. Someone with a less desperate need to merge. Even in this poem he overtly forms a union with his reader. It dawned on me that his lines, since I'd memorized them, were inside me, had taken up residence. I'm sure he would have liked such a thought. I think back to when I first read the poem. I was a junior in high school and in love with a girl for the first time. She was older than me. She wanted to move to New York.

The car lurched and a beer bottle rolled out from under a seat and hit the far side with a glassy ding, then crossed back toward me. I stopped it with my foot, then after a moment released it to let it roll down the runway again where it clattered and chimed and threatened to break, but didn't, at each contact. It was Thursday. The night was hot and thick and the subway's air conditioning couldn't cut through it. I was sweating. I felt like I needed a shower, though I had had one only a few hours earlier. Down the subway car I spotted a thin black woman in a green dress staring at me disapprovingly. What did she see? What was she thinking? She had the look of a regular churchgoer. Well, I decided, there she was—the moral alternative to Whitman. When I nodded to her she turned away.

As I stepped off the train at Grand Army Plaza I considered maybe it wasn't me, but only my letting the beer bottle loose to romp freely down the subway car that bothered the woman. The station felt like a steam cooker. I hurried above ground, anxious to get off the oppressively humid street. I dashed against the light across Flatbush to the phone booth. Even the phone felt greasy when I lifted it.

"The door's unlocked," she told me. Her voice sounded slightly reserved. Insecurities pattered about me, but I ignored them. They were par for the course.

I slipped into her air-conditioned apartment as if it were a pool. The unit churned in her window. I told her of my miserable ride over and asked for a glass of ice water. For the first time since our first night we took a moment to sit on her couch quietly, not talking, not touching. She sat a few feet from me in her bathrobe, her legs crossed precisely, ladylike. I sipped at the water. She started to say something, but stopped herself.

"What?" I said.

She shrugged and turned away. Whatever was on her mind didn't look like good news. I gave her a moment to gather her words, then the little figure toddled into the room from the hall. Ran, actually, past the white sheets on the floor toward her mother, her feet sounding against the carpet in child steps. Then stopped, then froze as she looked at me.

I remained motionless, fully lit by the overhead light. I didn't make eye contact, didn't look at her. I didn't look at anything. I did my best to disappear, as I knew how, as I learned somewhere, to cease behaving like a living animal and so to stop looking like one. I breathed in and out imperceptibly. I kept my gaze soft, unfocused and downward, my face expressionless. I could've been a chair, a vase, a bird in a tree you thought you saw for a moment before it blended into the leaves around it. In my peripheral vision the child was scooped up by her mother and carried away.

Afterward I sat alone for many minutes. I kept glancing at the front door. I considered standing and walking out into the night, ending it there and then. As I should have. As I would have if I were a good person. I looked down the hallway toward Carina's room. My legs began to jitter. I looked out the window. The clouds were so low I could only make out the bottom half of the clocktower. I picked up my glass of water. Everything seemed misplaced. I put the glass back down. It seemed partially culpable—if I hadn't asked for it, then this wouldn't have happened. Then I realized if we hadn't taken a moment, a normal moment to just sit beside one another on the couch to allow me a sip from a glass of water, we would've been farther along in what we did, and her little girl would have walked in on that. I stood. I walked toward the kitchen, then back. I sat on the couch again, then stood. I heard a door softly closing down the hallway, and Alena walked into the room.

"I'm sorry," she whispered. She turned off the overhead light, then came for me, guided me back onto the couch. "I'm so sorry. I thought I closed her door securely."

"It's secure now?"

"Yes. She can't open it. She can't reach the doorknob." She sighed. "It could've been worse."

"No kidding."

"This is the first time she's ever gotten out of her crib. Soon she'll be everywhere, into everything."

"Speaking in complete sentences. Understanding what she sees."

She took my hand. "Not yet. Not yet." She pressed my hand to her chest, then lowered herself to the floor, pulling me down after her, giving me no choice but to follow her from the couch onto the carpet. She flurried over me, removed my shoes, unbuttoned my shirt. She twisted out of her bathrobe and kicked it away before curling into me, her thigh over my waist, her arm and shoulder weighted across my chest. I had no leverage, couldn't rise if I tried. "John," she said. "You're still with me. Say it."

There was an anguish in her voice I'd never heard before. "Sure," I said. The word tumbled out of my mouth of its own accord. I watched it fall. "Of course."

She looked down at me, the warmth of her body seeping through my clothes. "Listen to me," she said. "Take a deep breath, John." I tried. I shook my head. "Relax," she told me. "It's okay now. Carina's asleep. I attached a screen that came with the crib to its top. I'll do that every night from now on. She's safe and can't get out. It won't happen again. I promise. She has an air conditioner running in her room, a window unit. She can't hear a thing. Four more weeks. Just four more weeks."

I pulled her to me so she'd stop talking and found her shaking. When she pushed away I knew what was next, though I didn't know if I was capable. I was wondering how to end this, thinking of the neighbors who might see me the next time I stepped out her door. In my mind the sound of her daughter's footsteps cycled, and more than anything I remembered the little girl's presence, her focus as she stared at me, the machinations in her head turning, pointing her toward an answer she couldn't quite reach before being swept away.

As if reading my thoughts, Alena moved faster, almost frantic to get me inside her before I bolted, and had me unzipped and out. On cue my body ignored my concerns, my second thoughts, my considerations of what would be right or good or prudent or necessary, and offered her this one sure thing. I was ashamed at my weakness.

"In case you don't come back," she said as she took me.

"How could I not come back?"

She fixed her hands on my shoulders, placed her weight perfectly so I couldn't rise. Her eyes shut, her face angled away in concentration, as if trying to block everything out but where she'd claimed me. The shame I felt bonded me closer to her, the erotic charge of regret, the awareness of my needs and how I didn't want what I wanted, how wrong we were to do what we were doing, and were doing it anyway, on the floor of her home, her daughter in her bedroom nearby, the clocktower shrouded in the distance. She bit her lip. "You'd better come back," she told me.

"I have to come back," I said, and tears spilled down my face.

"John," she said. She brushed a finger across them and looked touched, as if I'd brought her the most perfect gift. Then her expression shifted, and she bore down on me, staring at me with determination more than anything else, pushing me across the line mechanically now, grimly, crudely, watching me, insisting I go.

As I left her building and climbed into a cab, I saw the haze rested higher around the clocktower than earlier and I couldn't make out the time. I leaned against the window and stared out at the old decrepit brick buildings down Flatbush Avenue, the dim streetlights, the homeless bodies on cardboard rolled against a fenceline, and realized I was memorizing it all because soon I would not be seeing it. This street, these buildings, she and I, who we were together, it would all be in the past. It would be in past tense, in how I spoke of it, in how I remembered her.

~

The next day in the office I was exhausted. I'd hardly slept all night, seeing a small figure dart at the edges of my vision whenever I began to doze. I looked up from my computer to watch Alena through the glass wall of her office. She and Jeremy were talking again. They'd been talking all week. Yesterday they even went out for lunch together. People might be starting to wonder if *they* were the ones having the affair. It was an odd position to be in, fighting off feelings of jealousy triggered by a gay man, who also happened to be Alena's trusted confidante, who could blow the whole deal if he got one too many drinks in him. Jeremy, who I felt was involved with us on some personal level, who would know things about me no one but she would know. Neither of them smiled as they spoke. It was unlike them. What could they be talking about? The corner she and I were painting ourselves into? The fact that her child, who he adored, nearly walked in on us at the worst possible moment?

Finally he got up and walked toward his desk. As he passed by he put his hand on my left shoulder. Briefly his fingers pressed into the muscles and that whole side of my body released.

"No need to be so tense, John," he said, taking his seat behind me.

"If you say so."

I looked back toward Alena's office. She turned from my gaze but was clearly watching us. At five o'clock she gathered her things and made her way to the door. "Have a good weekend," she said to everyone. She stopped on the other side of the door, partially in shadow, and looked back at Jeremy and me. Her eyes shifted slightly from one of us to the other, her expression filled with what I could only describe as love, or longing, or sorrow. Then she was gone.

"That was some look," Jeremy whispered. "You could live your whole life and never have anyone look at you like that."

I nodded. I couldn't know if Alena was thinking what I was, that we'd been foolish and lucky. But something was up with her. I had till Sunday to make a decision, but in truth I knew I'd already made it.

19

"It's for the best," Jennifer told me. It was Saturday evening at Noho Star, a brightly lit bistro in the Lower East Side. I'd just told her of my decision. "Honestly, I was getting worried," she said. "I hadn't heard from you in awhile."

"I've been preoccupied."

"Just a little. So you have a plan?"

"The plan is I tell her."

"Tomorrow night?" I nodded. She stabbed her fork into her pasta and twirled it. "Well, I'd rehearse, if I were you."

"What I'm going to say?"

"Yes."

"I can be direct with her."

"If you say so."

"She's the one who's got everything to lose."

"She'll see the logic of that."

"She already does. We've talked about it."

"Sounds like you're set then."

"Something was definitely on her mind yesterday. Like she was thinking along the same lines." I watched Jennifer lift the pasta to her mouth. She followed it with a sip of wine, avoiding my eyes. "You're not buying it," I said.

"Not at all."

"Then what should I do?"

"Rehearse. Get your list of reasons down pat. Be firm and don't waver. Don't expect her to make it easy."

"Jennifer, if you'd seen that little girl walk into the room . . ."

She shook her head as she ate mechanically. She didn't want to hear it. "You got lucky. In what you were, or should I say, weren't doing at that moment."

"I keep thinking about Carina. Do you think I imprinted her? Will I be some shadowy figure that appears in a dream when she's in therapy twenty years from now?"

Jennifer shrugged and looked up. "We all get imprinted, darlin'," she said, letting her accent roll across her tongue. "The question is, what do you do with it?"

~

I stood before the mirror in my apartment and hung my cross on its chain around my neck. I wasn't specifically religious, but I felt objects carried meaning, and that there was much more going on around us than we could ever know. But there are rare moments we get a hint, something out of the corner of our eye that disappears as soon as we look at it. So why not a cross? Why not incense and candles and prayer and red wine? I touched my finger to the cross beneath my T-shirt, felt its shape against my chest. A girl once gave it to me. It steadied me.

My ride to Brooklyn was long and hot and strained. I saw no beauty in the stained mosaics in the stations or the graffiti-laced subway car. In my head I ran through my list of reasons for ending the affair. They were practical, irrefutable. As I stepped off at Grand Army Plaza I found myself reacting sentimentally to everything I saw, every grease stain and overflowing trash can. I saw a rat scurrying along the track. Was I going to miss the rat too? I told myself to snap out of it. Then it hit me how much she'd put on the line for me—her home, her family. It was hard to comprehend it. Whether she cared that much, or wanted me that badly, it didn't matter. Whether punishing her husband was a part of the deal, and that was always part of the deal, I didn't care. I stood at the dark street corner waiting for the light to change, realizing I'd never do anything like this, never know anyone like her, again. It didn't matter, I told myself. If it had to end, it was time to end it. If I cared about her. However she might respond. Unless . . . unless she would be willing to leave him for me. I could ask, even though she had made me promise not to, and though I felt in my gut she wouldn't. But if she did, then what? How could we manage? Would Carina ever accept me? And if she couldn't, how could her mother? The thought was exhausting, seemed so much weight to bear. Were Alena and I even capable of an ordinary day-to-day relationship?

The sky was cloudless but hazed, no more than a few stars showing through. I looked down Flatbush Avenue to see the string of green traffic lights change to yellow, then red. I crossed and phoned her from the corner. Walking down her street I picked up my pace, built momentum. I turned down her sidewalk before I saw someone standing in the lobby, an old skinny man in a jacket talking to a young woman. I spun away before they spotted me and scurried to the sidewalk, then continued up the street before glancing back. They still hadn't come out. To avoid appearing even more suspicious, I turned left at the end of the block toward Flatbush, then walked back up the long slope to Sterling. When I passed in front of her building again, the lobby was empty. I hurried to the door and pushed the button that said "Marino," her husband's name. The buzzer sounded and I entered. When I pushed the elevator button the door didn't open. I looked up to see it was parked on the sixth floor. Finally it began its descent. Fifth. Fourth. Taking forever. Anyone passing outside would've seen me. Anyone could've stepped into the lobby, gotten on the elevator with me, and followed me to her floor. Her husband even. What if he surprised her, came back early? Finally the door opened. I ducked in, pushed 7, and the doors closed, thankfully. See, I told myself. We'd been crazy. Foolish. Stupid. I walked down her hall. I opened her door and stepped inside.

"Finally," she said. "I thought eleven would never get here."

"But . . ."

"Don't talk. I don't need you to talk. We can talk after."

"Wait," I told her, trying to pull back, but she pushed me against the door.

"What is it?"

I blurted it out. "Don't you know how risky this is? We're putting so much at risk. We need to stop now before . . ."

"Before what?" she said, and I was sinking. She was guiding me down to the floor.

"Before something goes wrong."

"Something's already gone wrong."

The voices inside me were thrilled and horrified, ashamed and proud at how helpless I was at her body, at how little effect my words were having.

"But . . ."

"Keep talking," she said as she unbuttoned my shirt. "I'm pretending I'm listening to you." But she hesitated when she exposed my cross. "John," she said, then bent down to kiss it.

I thought of my sweat coating the cross, the salt now on her lips, and that sacramental gesture finished me, wiped out what resistance was left. She pulled me on top of her. We did it there on the carpet by the door. I put my hand over her mouth to muffle her cries so they didn't reach the hallway.

~

Afterward we lay on the sheet in the living room looking up at the ceiling. And I knew what she knew before I even arrived—I was hers. I always would be.

She released a long, deeply drawn sigh. "So," she said.

"What?"

She paused. "There's something you don't know. About Jeremy."

Because of her hesitancy and the tone of her voice, because of that sigh that rolled out of her before she spoke and the weight it carried, there was little point in her even saying the words. But she continued. "He's sick."

I closed my eyes. His beauty would be stripped away in front of us, and he would die.

"I'm going to lose him," she said. "I'm going to lose you."

"You've been talking to him at work. This is what it was about?"

"Yes."

"I thought you were talking about us. I thought he might be counseling you to break it off. You were trying to tell me something when Carina walked in on us. Was this it?"

"Yes. He's known he was HIV positive for some months. But his lymph nodes were swollen so he went in for a checkup. It's begun."

"How's he handling it?"

"He's very brave. Braver than me. I didn't realize how irreplaceable he is, of course, until now."

I felt a twinge of jealousy, which made me ashamed. "I've seen it. Your connection when you're together."

"I'm going to need you, John. I can't be alone with this."

I hesitated. "I came over tonight to try and end it."

"You didn't try very hard."

"Actually, I was determined. I just failed."

"Why would you want to end it?"

"Because of Carina. After what happened I thought . . . I wanted to do the right thing."

"John, please don't do the right thing. She's my responsibility. She's *my* daughter. Your responsibility is to me, and if you want to leave because you're tired of me, then tell me that and I'll accept it. But I won't accept this other reason." She turned her head toward the window. "I want you. Make me feel alive while Jeremy dies, while my husband does his business deals in a country he doesn't understand. Soon Carina will be too old and what you and I are doing will be impossible. I need . . ." She turned back to me. "I need to be who I am with you and to feel the way you make me feel. Please. Stay with me a little longer."

20

Jeremy and I didn't have to say anything. Our eyes caught. Looks passed between us. We took the elevator down together after work and made small talk, ignoring the larger subjects that accompanied us. We separated at the street and didn't linger in each other's presence. I wondered how, when, the conversation would start. We could go to a bar and get away from the office. Not mention anything until after the first drink, then be there all night. But I wasn't ready to open the door to it and all its weight. I couldn't speak about it yet, though I was thinking about it all the time. Him, Alena, me. Carina, Alena, me. Alena and me. Alena.

But the week hadn't ended before, sitting at my desk, I heard a dense, heavy weight, the sound of a downed animal, hit the floor behind me. I turned to see Jeremy in seizure—on his back, his arms extended, his legs straight out, flailing at the thin cubicle walls, shaking as if he were being electrocuted. I froze, couldn't take my eyes off him even as Marjorie ran past to grab his arms and Carla from proofreading picked up a phone to call security.

"Grab his legs," Marjorie yelled. I continued to stare. "John!" she screamed, and I snapped out of it. I scrambled to the floor and tried to hold him, but he was so strong I was almost useless. I bore down with all my weight.

Within minutes a young man and a woman from EMS arrived carrying a first-aid kit. Marjorie gave way to them and the woman grabbed Jeremy's head as the man took his shoulders.

"He's HIV positive," I blurted out. All three stopped to stare at me as the huge body shook in our hands, as his eyes rolled back horribly white into his head, as his jaws clenched and his heels pounded the floor. I was ashamed I said it. I wished I'd never said it. But how could I not say it? And why didn't I tell them the whole truth, that he had AIDS? "Do something," I said.

They turned back to Jeremy and carefully guided him onto his side. Marjorie stared at me. Something in her mind clicked into place, her hands that had gripped Jeremy moments before held from her sides as if toxic.

~

When I stepped into the workroom the next day no one looked up. I walked down my aisle to see Jeremy's empty desk behind mine, then took a seat and started up my computer. As it ground to life, I pulled open the drawer where Alena has left a flower for me each week. Of course it was empty. It was Thursday. Tuesday she'd left a daffodil. I slipped it into my bag after work and placed it on my seat on my subway car, as I'd taken to doing, sending it to Brooklyn.

An interoffice memo appeared on my computer. When I opened it, it read, "Our friend and colleague, Jeremy Crawford, suffered a seizure last night in the office and is under observation at St. Vincent's Hospital. This is all we know, but I'll keep you posted as we get more information. For now he is not receiving any visitors. We are buying him a gift, so please come by the office if you'd like to contribute. Thank you, Alena."

I shook the tension out of my hands before I began working on the stack of charts that had been left on my tray. There was little conversation in the room, but Lizbeth, a young Dominican proofreader, came by to quietly ask if I knew anything more about him. I could feel others listening.

"Why would I?" I heard the touch of defensiveness in my voice.

"Well, I just thought you two were . . . friends." She looked at me, caught awkwardly.

"Right. Of course," I said. I attempted a smile. "But I really don't know anything."

"I'm just worried," she said.

"Me too."

Alena and I avoided interacting. At five o'clock she left, and Marjorie and I were alone in the room. In my peripheral vision I kept seeing her look my way. Finally she came over. "So," she began. "Is it alright if I ask you something personal?" I looked up at her without answering. "How well do you know Jeremy?"

"Why?"

"I want to know how long he's had AIDS."

Now I saw what he would face. "I don't know that he has AIDS," I said, I lied. "I just know he's HIV-positive. It's different."

"How long has he been HIV-positive?"

"Why?"

"He held my baby last Christmas."

I wanted to grab her by her collar and shake her. I wanted to shake her until she was crying. "It's not the same," I told her.

"I still want to know."

"You'll have to ask him, Marjorie. I just found out last week."

"You people think you're protecting each other, but you're putting everyone else in danger."

"What do you mean, 'you people'?"

"How long has he had it?"

I fought back the urge to spill everything to Marjorie, to wave my affair with Alena before her like a flag. But I didn't. And I realized the value in the cover she'd given me, the rumors she'd no doubt spread through the office. I only had to swallow my pride and let it stand. "You know everything I know," I told her. "And if you could catch AIDS by being held, this whole city would have it."

~

We lay on the sheet, her head on my chest, the air conditioner whirring in the window. In the dark room the reflected streetlights illuminated our bodies in black and white, in grays and purples. We never did it with the lights on. I once asked her why and she responded that it made her shy. This from the least physically reserved woman I'd ever known. But there was often an element of shyness about her, as if she was shocked by her own wantonness, carried a touch of shame at her needs. "I feel like myself in the dark," she said. It allowed her imagination to open, I thought, as it did mine. It gave us a place to be, and to hide.

"How long will Jeremy be in the hospital?" I asked.

"They're holding him for observation for a few more days."

"Do they know what happened?"

"It could be a lot of things. Regardless, there'll be something to follow."

I remember the two of them stepping into the office last Christmas after shopping for clothes together. They'd played dress-up in a nearby upscale clothing store like a pair of children at their parents' closet, and their faces beamed from the holiday season, from the cold and the snow outside, from being in one another's presence. I could imagine them modeling for each other in front of the dressing rooms and the full-length mirrors. I felt a twinge of pain at the sight of them. They looked like they belonged together.

"What kind of flowers did you send?" I asked her.

"Red and white roses."

"Red for love. White for innocence and purity."

"I just liked the way they looked."

"Everything means something."

"How do you know what flowers mean?"

"My sister."

"Which one?"

"Kari. She always had them around. She put them on the . . . on the . . ."

It hit me then, for the first time. She stopped at some point.

"The what?"

"The white vanity in their room. In a thin vase."

"Why did you hesitate?"

"I just realized. She stopped bringing flowers into the house."

"When?"

I thought back, trying to remember. "About the same time she stopped reading to me."

"She read to you?"

"They all did, but she did it the most. She was six years older than me. Our other sisters had left. Kari was trying to manage puberty, high school, a small Texas town. Our mother. God knows what. I was just a little kid."

"It's a difficult age."

"I wonder . . ."

"Yes?"

"I wonder if she still brought flowers into her room secretly. After I was banned from it." I saw the room. There was Amanda, and Catherine, and Kari. White lilies in a vase beside her.

Alena rose up on an elbow to see me better. "Why were you banned?"

I hesitated to talk about it, though there was nothing so horrible to tell. Still, it was hard to find a place to begin. Maybe I just didn't want the distraction. But Alena wanted it. So why not? Why would I hold anything back from her?

"I didn't approve of her boyfriend," I said.

21

New Braunfels, Texas

"John," she says. "Please. You have to."

Kari stands in my room. She is so thin, so pretty. But her hair is messed up. Her face is worried.

"I don't approve of him," I say. Amanda would not still be with him. Catherine would not still be with him. After what he did to me.

"John," she says. And she's desperate.

"What?"

"But John." She takes a step toward me. "He told me he loves me. He really said he loves me." She says it quietly, hopefully. She smiles and can't see me. She is looking past me to another place, where she thinks he is. But he has tricked her. He is somewhere else.

"John."

And she is so unhappy. And she can't help who she is. And I can't either. I can't help that I am small. Or that my daddy died. Or that my sisters have gone away. Or that this one doesn't read anymore and has picked a bad man. I can't fix any of it. So I say it. "Okay. Okay." And I follow her into her room. We start again. I paint blue eyeshadow across her eyelids and follow the shape of her eyes in black eyeliner. I draw the lilt at the edge of her eyes and outline her lips in a darker red than the center. I make her beautiful for him. But my heart starts beating wrong; it skips, it hops, and I am almost sick. I step back.

"What?" she says.

"It's okay," I tell her, but it's not okay. Then I see the one thing I can do. And I'll have to do it slowly so she doesn't notice. But I can change the way she looks. I study the bones on her face and see exactly how to do it. I can put shadow between her eyes so they seem too close to her nose. I can add darkness to her cheekbones so it looks like she doesn't have them. I can cover her freckles with base so her face appears flat. And I will never use the brush on her, even if I have to tell her I lost it. Yes, I will tell her I lost it.

~

"Hey little guy. We're still pals, right? Didn't mean to scare you the other night."

It's Saturday afternoon. She's called me into the living room where Gary Phillips stands. He looks pleased with himself. His face is square and big. "Go on," she tells him.

"I brought you a present," he says, and holds out a flashlight. It's silver like mine was, but it's shorter and has a black rubber head. I turn to Kari. I see that what I'm doing with her makeup is working, but I need to take it further. Her nose comes to a little point. I could highlight that to bring it out, then darken the bridge.

"John, why are you looking at me like that?"

"Like what?"

"Gary brought you a flashlight. And he's sorry he broke yours."

I reach out for the flashlight, but as I grab it he holds onto it for just a second, to let me know that he could take it from me. That he can do whatever he wants. Then he lets go and it's in my hand. I want to click it on and shine it in his face.

"What do you say, John?"

I try to look into his eyes, but can't.

"John," she says.

"Thank you," I say, and my voice is too small. I turn and leave to get away from it. Upstairs I set the flashlight on the floor outside my room, then sit on my bed and watch the street until they drive away. Afterward I carry it down into the kitchen. Mother is heating something on the stove, stirring it with a big wooden spoon. I smell it's spaghetti sauce. I step on the metal button to the trashcan, and the lid pops up. I drop the flashlight inside.

"Hi, John," she says at the sound.

I sit at the table. "Mother?"

"Yes."

I'm scared to say the words aloud, but I do. "The other night. Gary Phillips."

She turns to me. "Yes?"

"He was on top of Kari."

She turns to the stove again. I watch her stir the sauce. "Thank god."

I stare at her back. "I don't approve of him," I tell her.

"That's sweet," she says.

~

"Wait," Kari tells me. She catches my hand. It holds the mascara brush. "Something's wrong."

"What?"

She stares into the mirror, turns her face side-to-side. "Did you do both sides the same?"

"Yes," I say, I lie.

"It doesn't look right."

I added darkness to the right side of her face and light to the left. To make the right side sink in. To make her face lopsided. To mess up how everything naturally works so well. But I went too far.

"I'll fix it," I say. But she doesn't let go of my hand. She looks into my eyes and knows. But he's a bad man, I want to say. Don't you understand? Can't you see? Amanda and Catherine could see. But Kari can't. She doesn't trust me now. And she shouldn't, because I lied to her. She'll never forgive me. She lets go of my hand, then asks me to leave. And thank you, she tells me, but she can handle her own makeup now. I know she can't, but it doesn't matter. Because she'll do better than what I was trying to do. Which was to make her ugly and drive him away. I don't know what to do, but she has asked me to go, and so I go. I stand outside her door as she slowly closes it.

~

Kari sees him every weekend. Every Friday and Saturday night. And her lips are too red and her eyeshadow is too blue and she makes circles of rouge on her cheeks like a doll. Instead of making her more pretty, her makeup now hides how pretty she is. Amanda would say it makes her look cheap. Gary Phillips approves, Kari tells me. Thanks for the help, Kari tells me, but he likes her better this way, she must've learned something from

Amanda and Catherine after all. In the afternoons I sit in the swing in the backyard and I read. I read *The Hobbit*. I read *Lord of the Rings*. The wind blows the swings. The birds fly from the tree. Kari won't let me into her room anymore.

I call Amanda, but I don't know what to say. So she tells me about college, how it's a lot of fun but she has to study all the time. She tells me to study and make good grades so I can go to college and *get out of that house*. She says she has a boyfriend.

"Is he nice?" I say.

"Of course," she tells me. I can imagine her face from the sound of her words, surprised I would even ask that. "Is everything okay?"

"Yes."

"Really?"

"Kari has a boyfriend."

"I heard."

"I don't like him."

"Well . . ." she says. "What does Mother say?"

"She says he's handsome."

Amanda sighs. "Joujou, even if he's not the *right* guy, it's good Kari has *a* guy. It'll give her confidence. The next guy'll be better. That's how it works."

"Amanda?"

"Yes?"

"I miss you."

She doesn't respond for a moment. "I miss you too, baby," she says. "Listen. It'll get better. Have you got a girlfriend yet?"

"No."

"Get a girlfriend."

"I'm too young."

"No you're not." I hear noise in the background. Voices are talking to Amanda. "Yeah yeah," she says to them. "Just a minute, alright?" Then she talks quieter. "Joujou. I've got to go."

Then she says some more, but I can't hear it over the noise. I can only hear my name. "Okay," I say. "Okay."

22

I scurry through the house without making a sound, through the shadows, down the halls. I freeze and disappear against the drapes and the walls. He doesn't even see me anymore, but I see him. I see him grip her wrists and how small her hands are against his. I hear her say "Ow," and "Stop it," and "It's not funny." And she hits him, slaps at him, and he laughs and grabs her again. I watch his car from my window when they park out front and stay inside too long. I could sneak up on them, find out what they're doing, but I don't want to know. In the morning I see beer cans in the backseat of her car and her doors are locked. Kari looks like a different girl now, not my sister, or the girl in the mirror, but just another high school girl with too much makeup done poorly. She doesn't look for me in the house, doesn't often see me, but when she does her eyes go down to the floor, and so do mine as she passes.

During the week she sees him on Tuesdays and Thursdays. She helps him with his homework in the living room. On Friday nights I hear her footsteps tumbling down the stairs, then she runs out the door in her white skirt and socks, in his blue letter jacket that swallows her. She looks happy then, she looks to the distance like she can see him. At the football game she sits in the stands with the other girls who have boyfriends on the team, and they cheer for their boys in the cool air, under the huge lights on silver poles that click and hum and shine on the bright green grass with perfect white lines. The football players throw themselves against each other, and the cheerleaders jump and yell, and everyone in the seats rises to their feet, everyone claps and hollers.

On Saturday nights she and Gary Phillips go somewhere else. They go out to eat. They go to the drive-in movie. Someone has a party, and they go to it. They go places I don't know about.

Then football season is over. But the team didn't do as well as expected. They lost three of their last five games. And they lose their last game and now won't get to go to the playoffs. Late after the game from my window I hear Gary Phillips yelling inside his car, and Kari's inside with him. I see our neighbor's porch light come on across the street, and Mr. Sobek stepping out onto the porch in his housecoat and slippers. He walks across his yard toward the car and stops halfway into the street. Gary Phillips is still yelling inside the car.

"Who is that?" Mr. Sobek says. "Do you have any idea what time it is?"

Then Gary Phillips stops yelling, and his door opens with a loud pop and he steps out. Mr. Sobek takes a step back. Gary is so much bigger than him. "Time for you to mind your own fucking business," Gary Phillips tells him.

"Gary," Kari says.

Mr. Sobek tries to look around him into the car. "Kari Martin. Is that you in there?"

"Hey, old man," Gary Phillips yells. "Did you hear what I said?"

"Are you okay, Kari?" Mr. Sobek says louder, but he sounds scared.

"Yes," she tells him. "I'm really fine, Mr. Sobek. Go back inside your house, it's okay. Gary! Gary, please get in the car."

"That's right, Mr. Sobek, go back inside your house where it's safe," Gary Phillips tells him.

"I'll call the police," Mr. Sobek says.

"Call them."

"I'll do it," he says, backing away.

"Call them. Run into your house like an old woman, lock the door, and call them."

"It's okay, Mr. Sobek," Kari says, climbing out of the driver's side of the car. She grabs Gary Phillips' elbow. "We're leaving. I'm so sorry." She pulls him back inside. Mr. Sobek jumps onto his lawn as the Mustang peels away and fishtails, leaving a black rubber streak across the pavement.

The next day Gary Phillips comes to our house and he and Kari and Mother talk quietly at the kitchen table. When they're finished, Mother puts a bottle into a bag and hands it to him. He and Kari go out the door and across the street. I watch Kari knock on the door. When Mr. Sobek opens it, Gary Philips hands him the bottle. They talk at the door for awhile before Mr Sobek lets them inside.

Later Kari tells Mother that Mr. Sobek forgave him. Mr. Sobek's boys used to play football for New Braunfels High too, and he understood how disappointed Gary must feel. But he should look forward, not back, Mr. Sobek said. After all, he's getting scholarship offers. He could be big man on campus somewhere that mattered, maybe even go pro. From my window I saw them shaking hands on his front porch, Mr. Sobek smiling, clapping Gary Phillips on his back.

But as the weeks go by I see worry in Kari's eyes. "He doesn't know what to do with himself without football," she tells Mother.

~

The weather's getting colder. Some of the houses have already started putting up Christmas lights. Amanda says she's coming to visit for a couple of days at Christmas. Catherine has a job and can't get away. Kari stays behind her makeup. I can see her eyes, but not her face.

One night when I think she's in her room I push open the door to the upstairs bathroom, and there's Kari standing at the mirror, fresh out of the shower, her face clean, a bath towel wrapped around her body. I see marks on her arms, on her wrists. Fingerprint bruises from where he has gripped her. We stare at each other, frozen. In one hand she's holding a small pink sponge with flesh-toned makeup on its bottom. She's been covering the marks with makeup. How long has she been doing this? And I see the right side of her face is redder than the left up by the cheekbone. Then she steps back, and her hands and arms start moving over the bruises trying to cover them, but how do you cover your arms with your arms, your hands with your hands, and keep from showing what's on them?

"John!" she yells at me.

"The door wasn't locked," I say.

"You're a liar!"

I twist the silver doorknob in my hand and it hardly moves. She's right; it was locked. "The door wasn't shut right," I say. "I'm sorry."

She runs at the door and slams it so hard it hurts my ears, it knocks me back. "I hate you," she yells. And I back away till I'm at the stairs, then I'm going down them. She's still yelling, and I'm out the front door and down the grass, running down the street until I can hardly breathe, till I have to stop, bending over, my hands on my knees. And I can't hear her anymore, only my panting and my heart in my chest.

~

Kari won't look at me anymore. Gary Phillips comes into the house and sits on the couch. Kari is afraid. I see it in her eyes when she doesn't know I'm watching. I see it when she comes in one night and she's not walking right. I know what he's done. I know what he's doing.

Gary Phillips and Mother talk about him and Kari going to the same college. Wherever he's offered a scholarship. Texas A&M wants him. So does Texas Tech, Oklahoma, Purdue. Kari says she doesn't care where they go. Gary Phillips thinks he's going to be a professional football player. He thinks he's going to be rich and famous. What I think is this: He is big and strong, but he is also stupid. He makes mistakes. Those other football players, the smart ones, will run him down, will break him. What would he be like without football?

23

From the corners and the shadows of the house I study him. I watch where his eyes fall and where they don't. I walk where they don't. It's that easy to become invisible. Especially when you're small like I am, when your footsteps make little sound.

I know he's drinking and has Kari drinking. From my bedroom window I see them stagger up the grass to the house. Kari's key scratches into the lock to open the door. They get on the couch. I don't have to watch to know. But I keep my door cracked open so I can hear if something goes wrong. And I know I didn't do what I should have the time before. I know what to do next time.

Amanda called on Sunday. She has to spend Christmas with her boyfriend's family in Oregon. She told Mother first, then she talked to Kari and me. I told her it was okay, that I understood. She would visit soon, she promised. It's okay, I told her, what matters is she likes where she is now and is having fun. And didn't I help her? Didn't I help her to leave? And didn't I help Catherine? Yes, she told me. And Catherine's doing good, she said, and I am the best brother. But sometimes I don't think I am because of what went wrong with Kari, and I don't tell Amanda about that because I don't know what to say. Or maybe I don't want her to know.

What good will it do Kari to leave this house, this town, if she goes away with Gary Phillips? She would be better off staying here with Mother forever. Even if she can't stand up to her, even if she folds into herself when she's around her. Even if she would never blossom, never become the beautiful girl I know she could be. Sometimes I pretend my daddy left me a rifle. I crawl up on the roof with it and wait for Gary Phillips to come for

Kari on a Saturday night. When his silver Mustang turns the corner too fast, I fire a single shot. It hits the front tire, and his car crashes into a neighbor's car and blows up. The cars burn and it looks like an accident. The flames are red and yellow and white. They go higher than the houses.

But there is no gun, and I don't know how to shoot a gun. If Daddy was here he would put a stop to this. He would not allow it.

~

All the houses on our block are strung with Christmas lights. They're outlined in reds and blues, in greens and whites. I walk down the street after dark and look in the front windows of other families' houses to see their Christmas trees. They're covered with ornaments and lights and tinsel. One night Mother has Kari and me bring in the big box from the garage that holds the same plastic Christmas tree we use every year. We dump everything onto the living room rug—the base, the trunk, the green plastic limbs Catherine called pipe cleaners. Mother is excited, running around the tree sticking in the limbs and singing to the Christmas carols playing through the radio. But the tree isn't looking right. She isn't following the colored markings on the limbs that tell where they go. The longest aren't always going on the bottom. It's going to be shaped funny.

I try to tell her the ones marked black go on bottom, the purple go next, then the maroon. She starts laughing. Holding a limb in her hand, she sits down laughing on the rug and says, "Good lord, what difference does it make?"

I hurry to stick in as many limbs into the right places as I can before she starts again. "It won't be balanced," I say.

She falls back onto the floor laughing at me. "I'm sorry, John," she says. "I'm sorry. You're just so . . . my god . . . fastidious." She turns her head toward Kari trying to get her to laugh at me too, but Kari looks down.

"Mother, the neighbors will all see it. They'll see it in our window," I tell her, but it's coming out too loud. "I don't want to be embarrassed."

She stops laughing in an instant, like a faucet turned off. She sets the tree limb down beside her on the rug and lies still for a long moment. Then her hands press to the floor and she pushes herself up like she's real heavy. "Embarrassed," she says. "Don't you mean ashamed? Are you ashamed of us? Of me?"

I've said too much, I've gone too far. I'm holding a limb in my hand marked purple. "No," I say. Kari takes a step back. "White Christmas" is being sung through the radio by the man who sings "White Christmas."

"I just want it to look okay," I say.

Mother looks at the tree. "You're right," she says. "Of course you're right. You're always right. It is embarrassing. It's awful." She starts crying. "I wish . . ." she says.

And I know where it's going now, what I have to do. I have to help, and the thought just makes me tired. "It's going to look fine," I tell her. "Isn't it, Kari?"

"It's going to be beautiful," she says.

Mother shakes her head slowly. "I've failed. Across the board. I'm such a failure."

And there's nothing to do now but go to her. So Kari and I help her up, and hug her, tell her how much we love her, then lead her to her bedroom where she falls on her bed crying. We leave her there, curled up on her side, to fall asleep.

Kari and I bring in the ladder from the garage and go back to finish the tree. I do most of the work, but Kari helps. We pull out the limbs stuck in the wrong places and put them in the right places. We string the lights on the tree. We take the ornaments out of their boxes and hang them on the limbs. When she looks in my eyes for the first time in so long, she looks like my sister again. The radio plays Christmas carols. And I'm sorry for what I said to Mother, but I'm glad she got upset and left me and Kari to finish the tree together. I know what I feel doesn't make me good, but I feel it anyway.

While Kari's holding the ladder and I'm putting an ornament high up, she wobbles the ladder just a little. "Hey!" I say. And she wobbles it again. "You better watch it," I say, and she's laughing. I can't remember the last time I heard her laugh.

I have to help her.

~

It's late on the Saturday night before Christmas, and I've gone outside to turn off the Christmas lights that Mother paid a man to string up on our house. I pull the plug out of the outdoor socket and our lights go out. The sky is dark and there are stars everywhere. Far away I hear a train. Then I hear a different sound, a car coming, Gary Phillips' Mustang. I run into the house, then up the stairs to my room, and just as I get to my window I see it skid into our curb. I hear yelling inside the car even though the engine's still running. Kari's door opens, and the light flashes on for a moment so I see Kari inside, then Gary Phillips grabs her and closes the door and the light goes off. Then it goes on and I can see her again, then it goes off. Then on, and she tumbles from the car, tries to run up our grass and away from him, and he's crawling out her door after her.

I am running. I run through my doorway. I see my feet going down the stairs. I see my hand opening the front door and I'm running toward them, where they're standing, where he's got hold of her arms and is shaking her like a rag doll, like she's got no bones. And I am on him. I'm grabbing his jeans and his jacket. I'm climbing up his back onto his shoulders. He's yelling and his hands are flying, trying to grab me, but they can't find me, I'm too quick, I'm too small, I'm too high. My arms are hooked around his neck and my feet are digging at his back and my hands are grabbing at his face, and we spin and spin as he yells. The lights are whirling past and his horrible thick hands are on me trying to push me off, but I am not falling. I am not falling yet, and I bite down hard on something to hang on better, and because I want to. I taste blood and don't let go.

Then I see the stars and I am falling. My arms are out, my feet are pointed, my back is arched. I am falling with the stars above me. It is such a long way down it seems I will never hit.

24

New York City

"You did *what?*"

Alena, propped up on her elbow, looked down at me. Only then did I realize I'd never told this story to anyone. "I bit off his ear." The fact filled the room like helium and we started laughing.

"His whole ear?"

"Well, most of it. They said they found it in my mouth. They had trouble prying my mouth open."

"Lucky you didn't choke on it. How far did you fall?"

"He was at least six-four, and I was higher than his head."

"That's a long way for a little boy."

"They said I landed flat on my back. It knocked me out. I open my eyes, and my sister and the neighbors and my mother are there looking down at me. And the cops. I remember the red and white lights from the cop car spinning round and round. I thought they were Christmas lights at first."

"What happened to this guy? Now that you'd defeated him."

I liked the way she said "defeated." "They took him away," I told her. "Locked him up. We struck a deal with his family. He doesn't get within a hundred feet of Kari, and we don't file assault charges. Assault charges could've cost him his scholarship."

"Did it work?"

"Yes. Football was more important to him than my sister."

She paused. "And you all lived happily ever after?"

"No."

"No?"

"I mean, who does?"

I'd said too much. It felt like my stitching was unraveling, like I wouldn't hold entirely together should I try to move.

"But we have our moments," she said. "Don't we?"

~

I carried a document into the duplicating department, which was, as usual, clattering, banging, thumping. Manny and Jackson were feeding the machines. These guys would probably suffer hearing loss from working back here. Louis looked up from his desk at the back of the room.

"How many copies?" he yelled out.

"Twenty by end of day," I yelled back.

He nodded, then turned back to his paperwork. He was an old-school Bronx Italian with an accent straight out of *The Godfather*. Though short, he was built like a tree trunk, and he was the last guy I'd want mad at me. Still, you got to know him, you realized he was a good guy, loved his family, was fair to his underlings. I began filling out a form for my document with the name of the analyst, pick-up time, etc. Since the event with Marjorie it seemed these guys had been keeping a distance, if not flat-out avoiding me. Maybe they didn't know what to say. Maybe I was paranoid. But whether they thought I was gay or bisexual or straight, if I was close enough to Jeremy to know his HIV status, I was suspect.

Some of the younger women in the department tried to befriend me, teasing me in the halls and opening up about their personal life, their boyfriends and what shitheads they could be. Alena found it all amusing. Marjorie stopped speaking to me entirely. I was okay with that. It made everything easier.

~

I watched Alena beneath me on the sheet. I rolled into her then out, like a wave onto a beach, in a rhythm that sought no resolution, that went on and on. She opened her eyes, closed them. For the most part she kept her eyes shut when we did it. I kept mine open so I could read her, watch her face, see her breath catch, a lip quiver. But her eyes opened again and stayed open. They were so dark I had no boundaries, and I was falling. And it was a hundred years ago in Italy, five thousand years ago in Crete. Did I know her there? Did I know her then? She blinked, and I was back, above her on the floor of her living room in Brooklyn. A trace of sorrow passed across her face like the shadow of a bird. For a moment I thought she might cry.

"Please," she said.

"What?"

"Please. Don't stop. Why did you stop?"

I hadn't even realized it. She closed her eyes, turned her head away from me, and I began again. I placed my hand to the side of her face and held her to the soft floor. I ran my fingers down her cheekbone, inched along the bridge of her nose. My other hand found her face. My fingers entered her mouth.

Afterward I stared down at her panting, the rhythms of our breathing locked into each other, her eyes still closed. A droplet of sweat fell from my face to her cheek. As I brushed it away she began rocking her head slowly side to side. "We could off him," she whispered quietly, as if accidentally speaking a half-formed thought. She wasn't talking about Jeremy. She opened her eyes. "I just said something awful," she admitted. She hesitated, then, grabbing my hair, she pulled my ear to her mouth. "I said, *we could off him.*"

She released my head, then watched my reaction as her words rang through me. I was a little surprised I found nothing foreign in them. I shrugged. "Well, we *could.*"

She stared at me, then after a moment turned to look out the window toward the clocktower. "I can say anything to you, be anything. Even myself." She looked back at me. "Why haven't you asked me to leave him?"

"Because you asked me not to. And because you wouldn't."

"But how do you know?"

"I know you."

"How can you be sure unless you ask."

I hesitated. "Do you really mean that?"

"I was just wondering."

The thought filled me with an undefined distress. But even so, there was only one answer for such a question. I took a deep breath. "Leave him for me."

She hesitated. "You don't mean it."

"But Alena, I do." I wasn't optimistic about the prospect, but the truth was I would never be able to say no to her. "If you think I'm bluffing," I said, "call it."

She hesitated. "Listen," she whispered. "If it wasn't for my daughter, I would leave him for you. I want you to know that. I'd shame my family and my church, which means more than you could understand. You're an American. You have no idea. But I'd walk away from the money, from the security and everything else. And it'd probably be a disaster. We probably wouldn't last a year. But I'd try, I really would. But with my daughter it's just too much."

Something in me sank at her words, while something else lifted. "Okay."

"That's all you have to say? Okay?"

"Yes."

"I've never said anything like that to anyone."

"I'd do the same for you."

"If you had a wife, you'd leave her for me?"

"Of course."

"But you don't."

"And you have a husband, and you won't."

"I told you why. And when I say there's nothing else that would stop me, I would hope you'd believe me. Have I ever been anything other than honest with you? Have I ever spared your feelings?"

"No."

"And I never will. That's how you know you can trust what I say."

I hesitated. "Then what would you have me do?"

"See me through this. Get me to the other side. Protect my family."

That included her husband, the man we were just talking about "offing." A man toward whom I felt nothing but disdain. A man who was entirely overmatched by his woman and covered it with bravado and money. A man who didn't deserve her. But protecting Alena meant protecting Carina. So protecting Carina meant protecting them all.

25

New Braunfels, Texas

"John," she says.

We sit on the swings in the backyard. Kari's seat is too low for her now. Her legs stretch out and her heels push at the grass that's grown back over where her feet used to scrape. My heels still don't reach the ground. I have to push off with my toes. I take hold of her chain and rock myself side to side. It's cold out so we've got our coats on. She's wearing a pink knit cap and scarf, and her cute face peeks out. When I shake her chain she smiles a little but doesn't turn her head to look at me.

"You were right about him," she tells me. "Of course. As if I didn't really know, but . . ." She's not wearing any makeup. She looks so much better now, like Kari, but also older. She looks like two girls at once—my sister, and a stranger. "I'm sorry," she says.

"Don't be sorry," I tell her.

"It's like I've been dreaming."

"It's okay."

She suddenly sits up straight. "John, I've got to start applying to colleges. I was waiting for Gary to decide where he was going."

"How much time do you have?"

"Not much. Will you help me?"

"Yes," I say, and my voice is so loud and high that we both laugh. She reaches over and takes my hand. "Where do you want to go?" I ask her.

"Someplace he's not going. Someplace far from here."

During the week between Christmas and New Year's we work together every day, and even Mother helps. Kari's grades are good and her SAT scores are high, and we fill out applications to a bunch of universities in the north-east and a couple in Florida.

Her college materials are spread over the coffee table and I help her look through them. "Why do you want to go so far?" Mother asks as she flips through the brochures.

"To get away from him," Kari tells her.

New Year's Eve passes with the three of us watching the ball drop on TV in Times Square, except Mother's fallen asleep in her chair. When the crowd counts down the last seconds, Kari and I count with them: "Ten, nine, eight, seven, six, five, four, three, two, one!" Then the ball slides down the pole, and the New Year's song plays, and everybody in Times Square is kissing and happy and dancing and blowing horns, and fireworks are exploding in the sky. It seems like the New Year always begins in New York City. That is where it happens, where it breaks like a thunderstorm, and the rest of us wait for the water to run down to us.

"Happy New Year!" Kari and I say, and she leans over and hugs me. Her body still doesn't feel right. Will I not feel right to her after I change? Will she notice I don't feel like her brother anymore?

～

The first week after the weather turns warm, Kari gets accepted to Florida State. They are the Seminoles. Their colors are garnet and gold. Their student body is 24,500. Scholars and athletes of every race and nation go there. Each day Kari and I look at her Florida State brochure, then we look at all the other ones. The 4th of July passes. We find out what dorm Kari will be staying in. Then one day Mother tells me that Aunt Phyllis needs a place to live and how would I feel about her moving in with us. I know Mother's already decided. "We've got a lot of room," she says. "We'll have even more after Kari's gone."

I tell her it's okay. It doesn't matter. Because everything has turned around. Kari's going to get away. Her story can begin. She can go to college and find the right boyfriend and get a good job. She can be happy. And I helped her. I want to tell Amanda, though of course she already knows most of it. We talked on the phone on Christmas Day.

"Joujou," she said, "you could've really been hurt." But I heard something in the sound of her voice I liked.

"I didn't care," I told her.

"Don't ever do anything like that again."

"He was hurting my sister."

"Promise me you'll be more careful. Still, it was very brave."

"I know."

She laughed. "Did you *have* to bite off his ear?"

"Yes."

She laughed louder. And I started telling her more things about Gary Phillips, how he wasn't anything like Mike or Charlie, how he was a drinker, how he scared Mr. Sobek, but then I stopped talking. I remembered Gary Phillips holding me over his head in the living room, and his hands on me, his fingers on my bottom, and how I couldn't move. I didn't want to tell her about that. I didn't want to tell her how he was on top of Kari on the couch.

"Joujou. Are you there?"

She didn't need to know. She's so far away, what good would it do? And now it's all okay. Gary Phillips is gone. Kari's going to leave. It would just upset Amanda.

~

It's August, and Aunt Phyllis moves in before Kari moves out. She takes the room between Grandma and Kari, which is Catherine's old room. She's big and when she hugs me she pulls me into her. It's hard to breathe, but I let her do it. Like Grandma, it takes her a long time to go down the stairs.

Her being in the house makes me worry that Kari won't leave for Florida State. I don't know why. Kari says that would never happen. But Aunt Phyllis is always in Kari's room, always talking to her. It is 916 miles from New Braunfels to Tallahassee. Kari is going to drive the whole way by herself. It will be an adventure, she says. I want to go with her but Mother asks how would I get back? I could fly back on a plane, I tell her. She says that's foolish, I'm too little, and if Kari insists on going so far away she can drive there by herself.

I help Kari pack. I help her pick out which clothes to take. Mother gives us some money and Kari drives us to Bachmeier's department store downtown to buy her new clothes. Afterward we sit at a window booth at Cowboy's Diner, and she buys me a hamburger and fries. She looks out the window and I see how the light falls on her face. She's still so pretty, but it's harder to notice. She's stopped wearing makeup and wants to be invisible again, like I am.

The day before she leaves I get a bucket and sponge and drag the green hose to the driveway and wash her white car. When I climb up on the trunk to scrub down the top I look to see her watching me out the window like Catherine used to. She waves at me. I scrub the car. It seems like the car will go faster if it's clean and pretty. It won't break down along the road.

I wake up the next morning before anyone else. I check the oil in the car, the water, the brake fluid, just like Charlie showed me. When Kari comes downstairs I've already made coffee and have her cereal poured. We're sitting down to eat when Aunt Phyllis walks in. "Cold cereal," she says. "We can't send her across the country on cold cereal."

She starts pulling pans out of the cupboard and banging them, and frying eggs and bacon, and the smell is thick and Aunt Phyllis won't stop talking and now I'm scared. I had Kari almost ready to go. She was almost gone, but now there's Aunt Phyllis and toast and jelly, and now she's decided to cook sausage and make gravy, and when she pours the milk into the hot skillet it hisses and pops and splatters.

Now Mother's downstairs, and even Grandma, and we're sitting around the table and Mother and Aunt Phyllis are talking so much they don't notice Kari's stopped eating. She's hardly eaten a thing. Soon she gets up and leaves the table. I slip away and find her in her room sitting on her stool in front of the vanity.

"I can't do it," she says.

"What?"

"Leave."

My heart beats so fast I can hardly breathe. I turn her away from the mirror. I take her hands in mine. Her fingers are long, her hands are elegant. Mine still look like a little boy's. "Kari," I tell her, "you have to."

"I can't."

"It's what we worked so hard for." And I'm thinking what if she doesn't go, what if she never leaves, but stays in her room or dates boys like Gary Phillips? What would become of her? What would Amanda and Catherine think of me? What would Daddy think? How can I leave if Kari doesn't leave first?

"Do you want to stay here forever with Mother? With Grandma?" She doesn't answer. "Kari!"

"No."

"Then you have to go. You have to make yourself do it. Once you go, you'll be glad. Like Amanda and Catherine."

"I'm so scared."

"Everybody's scared. Weren't you scared when you first went to grade school? And then when you went to junior high?"

"Yes."

"And then high school. Weren't you scared?"

"Yes."

"But you did it anyway. And see? You were popular. You made good grades and got to go to football games and parties and even dated a football captain."

"But that went wrong."

"There'll be better boys at college. Amanda says they're better there."

"She does?"

"Yes. They're different." If Kari doesn't go now I feel like she never will. She'll stay here and become an old woman. I yell, "Kari, don't you want to get out of this house?"

The words hang for a moment, echo around us in the room, and I worry Mother heard it, but I also don't care. Kari finally nods her head.

"Okay," I say. "Okay." Her breathing is shallow and fast, but she nods again. "Take a deep breath," I tell her. I put my hand on her belly and she breathes into it. "It's just like standing at the edge of a swimming pool," I say. "All you have to do is take a step, just make yourself take a step, then everything will change. Everything will be different."

She looks into my eyes. "I'll be different?"

There's something that scares me in the way she said it, in the way she looks at me. I try not to show it. "Yes," I say.

She looks away. Her breathing slows. She nods again. "Okay."

"We will all drive away. . . . Say it. Amanda, Catherine, you, me."

"We will all drive away."

"Yes?"

"One after another."

～

I try to lift Kari's suitcase up and into the trunk but it is heavy. Aunt Phyllis, who has followed us down to the street, takes it from me and drops it in, then slams the trunk shut. Mother has come down from the porch and stands at the edge of the yard. She looks lost there. She doesn't know what to do. Kari stands back from her car and stares at it. Her backseat is piled high with her stuff. The sky is blue. There aren't any clouds. I'm starting to sweat from the sun. I move toward Kari, but Aunt Phyllis beats me to her, hugs her, pulls her into her. "Bon voyage!" Aunt Phyllis shouts.

I take Kari's hand and pull her away to the driver's side where I open her door. I'm afraid something's about to go wrong. Quick, I hug her goodbye. "Go, Kari," I whisper.

But she hesitates. She takes my shoulders in her hands and guides me a step back, then holds me still as she looks down at me. I'd forgotten how tall she's grown. She's looking at me different, like she's just realized something. She looks toward Mother and Aunt Phyllis, then back.

"John," she says. I see she's worried. Worried about *me*.

"Kari, go!" I yell and push her so hard she falls back against her car. She stands there a second, then gets in, and I slam her door shut. She starts the engine and grabs my hand through the window. "Now," I whisper. I pull my hand away and her car lurches off. Then I'm running after it. I put my hands on its trunk and push, and the metal's so hot it burns. "Go!" I yell. "Go, Kari! Go go go go go!" Her car pulls away from me and I'm still reaching for it. She hits the gas and her car goes so fast she's speeding, she's tearing away. And I'm yelling. And I can still feel my hands burning. I can hear my shoes hitting the pavement. She turns the corner at the end of the street and is gone. Like that. Like magic. Like an accident. And I stop running and stare after her. I look back at the house, the empty windows along the top floor, mine in the corner by itself. There's Aunt Phyllis on the sidewalk. There's Mother in the yard. There's the house. My sisters are gone. I look back down the street. I begin running. Running toward where they disappeared.

~

A car slows, crunching the rocks as it rolls up to where I sit on the curb. Aunt Phyllis behind the wheel of her Oldsmobile and Mother beside her. Aunt Phyllis leans across Mother and says, "John?" I don't answer. "Did you run all this way? What on earth?"

I ran until my legs quivered and I fell, scraped the palms of my hands where I caught myself on the pavement, and the world stopped. My hands are bleeding and dirty from the street.

"John," Mother says.

Driving back toward the house the light looks different. The street looks different. Mother turns over her shoulder to look at me. Her makeup cracks around her mouth and eyes.

They follow me up the slope to the house. Even Aunt Phyllis is quiet. Mother opens the door, and I step inside. Everything looks wrong. The couch, the TV, the window, like it's all been replaced.

The stairs creak in a weird way. My room looks wrong too, like someone else messed it up. I stare out the window at the street, where no sisters will walk up the grassy slope, where no boys will come to take them away.

After everyone's gone to sleep I walk into Kari's room, Catherine's room, Amanda's room, our room that will never be my room. I sit on the stool and look at my face over the white vanity. Now I am the only one left in the mirror. If there was makeup I could make myself look like I am dead. A dead little boy. But there is no makeup. It's gone, and there is no girl to put it on, and brush her hair, and smell the way her hair smells, and draw a perfect line along her eyelid, and lean into her body. They're all gone. Kari has escaped, and Daddy would be proud. But I will not use makeup again. I won't draw with it. I won't draw anymore or paint. I am a boy. I won't tell my friends.

I see how long my hair has grown, almost to my shoulders. When I close my eyes and run my hand over it, it makes me think of Kari. It makes me think of Amanda and Catherine. I see them in the mirror, all of them, my sisters, but when I open my eyes it is only me. A boy who is too small for his age, whose hair has grown too long. I pick up the scissors and cut off a strand. Snip, it goes. I hold the strand up. It is dark and curls like Amanda's. I let it fall, then cut off another strand, then another, until I don't know who it is in the mirror anymore, until my hair is so short my scalp is bleeding.

26

New Braunfels, Texas, 1976

I am a junior in high school and I've broken my nose. I sit at the kitchen table of my best friend and doubles partner, Paul Malik, my head tilted back, my nose spread across my face and, I fear, my looks ruined for life. We're waiting for Paul's dad, Dr. Malik, who is on his way home from his office to assess the damage.

My tennis coach decided we'd use a piece of football equipment for our workouts today, specifically an "agility trainer," which is a long, flat, horizontal frame supporting criss-crossing wires that form two-by-two-feet squares nine inches off the ground. You start on one end and high-step through it. I was wearing a gray sweatshirt with a hood and a pouch up front where you tuck in your hands to keep them warm. When my turn came to run through the contraption, my mind and focus were elsewhere and my hands were buried in the pouch, so they could not break my fall when my left foot caught in a wire and my momentum hurled me face-first to the ground. The next thing I remember was hearing laughter. I opened my eyes and saw a steel pipe, maybe three-quarters of an inch high directly in front of my face, then the dirt behind it. As I rose I heard a girl shout, "He's bleeding," followed by a voice in my head that asked the question, "I'm bleeding?" Then I felt the roaring and rumbling, the geyser the steel pipe had tapped. Blood surged in a stream out of my nose with more velocity than I thought possible.

Marty, Paul's nineteen-year-old sister, hovers around us in the kitchen. Her best friend, Laura Teagan, is in another part of the house where she and Marty have been watching afternoon TV. They often meet for TV reruns after their classes at Texas State, and sometimes Paul and I join them. Laura has long dark hair and blue eyes, a combination I've never seen anywhere except TV. She's so gorgeous it's hard not to stare. I have a terrible crush on her, but I'm not stupid enough to try anything, especially since she's a freshman in college and I'm just a junior at New Braunfels High School. Even there I can't manage to stand out from the bigger, louder, more brightly colored boys. Or, I sometimes think, I just don't want to.

But now I've broken my nose due to my own awkwardness, never mind that agility and balance are what I pride myself on as a tennis player. I tell Marty, "I don't want Laura to see me like this." I speak through my hands. I can't remove them from my face. Marty disappears. A few minutes later she and Laura walk by, both careful to avert their eyes, and drive away in Laura's blue Camaro. Only then can I pull my hands away.

~

On a Saturday night four weeks later, Paul and I, along with a friend named Howard Michaels, who scored two sixpacks of beer, hop in Paul's Trans Am and head to the Century Drive-In.

The long-term damage to my face turned out to be minimal, leaving just a subtle rise along the bridge of my nose. I'm a little embarrassed at how strongly I reacted to my injury. I catch myself tracing its shape with my forefinger and pull my hand away, then pop open a beer and take a sip. The drive-in is showing a movie called *Rollerball* set in the future where corporations own countries, and apparently the only sport that exists anymore is roller derby. James Caan is the nation's most admired athlete, so the corporation is anxious to get him in the fold, but Caan, of course, is a rugged individualist inclined to buck the system. You can pretty much figure out what's coming from there, but it's still a fun movie. Paul leaves for the bathroom and Howard tells him to bring back some popcorn. Fifteen minutes later when I hear footsteps crunching on the gravel behind us, I look in the side mirror and see it's Paul, except two girls are with him— Marty and Laura Teagan.

They're laughing, and when the car doors open we're all lit inside, spotlighted for the other cars in the lot to see. Marty climbs in the backseat next to Howard, and Laura crawls over me to straddle the bucket seats between Paul and me, explaining to Marty that she wants to "see better." They're buzzing. They've been drinking. Laura hasn't even looked at me, said a word to me. As the doors close and the lights go out, my heart seems to stop because of the sudden darkness, because of her being beside me in the dark, because our shoulders touch, because of the scent of her perfume. She shifts, and as her right thigh settles against the length of my left I feel her warmth through our blue jeans. My brain races at the sensation, then clouds over as my blood surges southward. She leans into my side and twists around to tell Marty a joke. She laughs, then tells another before reclining across my body and locking her blue eyes into mine, somehow managing to make such a move seem natural. Her arms around my neck hold her there, smiling slightly, inquisitive. She tilts her head, my fingers touch her hair, and before I can stop or think, I'm kissing her. It is my first kiss. It is such a long, deep falling.

When I finally manage to pull away I'm amazed to see her still in my arms looking up at me. What has happened? She smiles a little quizzically, then lifts herself toward me.

Soon we are walking beside one another across the white gravel, under the stars and night, then in the cramped backseat of her blue Camaro grappling to fill any gaps between us. *Rollerball* playing on the movie screen, James Caan fighting the good fight.

I have no sense of how much time passes, but at some point we stop at the same instant and sit up, staring at each other before turning away. After a moment she rests her head on my shoulder, and I look out the windshield at the cars and screen and white gravel, the images flickering on the huge screen.

"It's getting late," she says.

"Yes," I manage. She lifts her head. I watch her breath rise and fall beneath her blouse and at her throat.

"We should see each other again," she says a little unsteadily. She looks relieved when I nod. I consider her boyfriend. I've heard her complain about him to Marty, how he doesn't "get it." "Alright then," she tells me. "Goodnight, John." I nod again, then push open the door and walk alone across the white gravel slopes to Paul's car.

On the way home, my friends try to get me to talk about her. They've always teased me over my reticence with girls, at the fact I've hardly dated. Now they're almost as shocked as I am at what they've seen. I deflect their questions and eventually they begin to chatter about other things. It is a relief when they drop me off at my car. Soon I pull over to the curb in front of my house. The windows inside are dark, including my room at the right upstairs corner. But I see a dim glow coming from the kitchen—Aunt Phyllis waiting up for me again at the kitchen table after putting Mother to bed. I decide to open the front door quickly and dash up before she has enough time to get to her feet. "Did you have a nice time?" she'll yell. "Yes," I'll holler back as I hurry to my room.

But something's up. Something's different. As I run up the stairs she's telling me to wait, though I'm hoping if I keep going she won't bother to come up. I hurry into my room, close the door, and lock it. Then I hear her heavy footsteps, and the stairs' slow creaking under them, and her voice, "John, John." I want to run, but there's nowhere to run unless I leap out the window. I imagine myself hitting the ground, sprinting down the street. But I know I won't, and there'll be no getting rid of her. I don't want to see her face, for her to see mine, as if she'll know what happened tonight and that will take it from me. I wipe my mouth to remove any trace of lipstick. She knocks at the door. "John," she says. "John. Open up, John." Finally I turn the lock, hear the tumbler tumble, and pull the door open, having left the light to my room off so it would be harder for her to see me.

I look into her round face. "Yes?" I say.

She hesitates. "Kari turned up," she tells me, trying to smile.

Something locks in my chest. "Where?"

"Fresno."

"Is she okay?"

"Yes. She called Amanda from a Motel 6. She'd run away from that awful boy she was with."

"What do we do?"

"Nothing. Amanda's going to drive down to get her. She says she'll handle it. Anyway, it's good news." She tries to smile again. "Right?"

"Yes."

"So you can stop worrying."

"Thanks."

"Because I know you were worrying. We all were."

"Thanks, Aunt Phyllis," I say. "Goodnight."

"Because how could you not worry?"

I nod. "I have to go to bed now."

I close the door as she's standing there, then lock it, which I know is rude. Still, I've found rudeness to have little impact on her. I sit on my bed and look out the window. Now I can't shake thoughts of Kari, how she didn't even make it through her first semester. I feel guilty because I only want to be thinking about Laura, not worrying over when my sister will vanish again, or call for money, or whatever it is she's going to do. My mind wears itself out trying find an answer for her. She was so smart; why didn't things work? There's nothing I can do to help, except talk to her if she calls, and she rarely calls. I'm only a high school kid. That's what I tell myself. It's not my fault. It was never my fault. A trace of Laura Teagan's perfume sweeps past, and I see her over me, her hair falling in a curtain around our faces. She smiles, and I can breathe again. I close my eyes and feel her kissing me as surely as if she were in my room. I smell her skin beneath the perfume. I feel her hair brushing my neck and shoulders. I can't break the kiss until she does.

I can't imagine how this happened. Her, of all the girls in the world. Outside the window the limbs in the trees are shifting slowly. Their leaves are drying, changing color, already are starting to fall.

27

Since Laura lives at home, I never call her. We have a standing date on Wednesday nights. If anything changes she calls me, though it's only happened once so far, and I ran to pick up the phone before Aunt Phyllis reached it. Otherwise Laura passes a message to me through Marty, then Paul. Marty is her alibi since Wednesday is their official "girls night out." Laura sees her boyfriend on the weekend.

She waits for me in her car, hidden from the street behind Crocket Junior High, where we both went to school. I park behind her in my blue Ford Capri that used to be Mother's and watch her get out of her car. When she sits beside me there's a touch of mischief in her smile. She seems younger when she's with me, as if we're the same age. We head away from New Braunfels to one of the nearby small towns where we explore their town squares and get something to eat. Once we caught a movie in San Antonio, thirty miles south.

During the drive back I try to behave nonchalant, I make small talk, but it's hard to hear me or her, the way my blood rushes in my ears as we make our way to Hill Street Park and a particular mesquite tree under which we park. I turn off the engine, the lights. We hesitate, then my mouth is against hers, her chest is rising and falling against mine. My hands have needs of their own, my fingers their own wants. They're ravenous at the slightest contact, and I am crazy drunk with it all. She rolls, turns, and leads me like a dancer, like a matador, never pushing me away but controlling the landscape I travel: her arms, her hands; her mouth, her throat; the long arc of her spine, her thick mane of black hair. I never push for more as every inch I already have overwhelms. I lose myself, am electricity.

I don't expect her to break up with her boyfriend. How could she and I ever manage the normal boyfriend-girlfriend things? The family dinners and the Valentine's Day cards, the casual phone calls, the double-dates? What would her parents think? And her friends would judge me. I would look like a high school kid in their eyes, and then, in Laura's. Only a boy. Which I could never bear. Which is a position I will not put myself in. I know it's one she will not put herself either. Even so, she continues to wait for me on Wednesday nights behind Crockett Junior High.

~

Tonight she has surprised me. She has done something wicked, taken me to see her boyfriend play football for Texas State with Marty and Paul along for cover. To an outsider it would look like a "little brother" outing. The sky above us is black and cold, and there are few stars to be made out through the stadium lights. The cheerleaders tumble and jump, the boys on the field hurtle into one another, and everyone in the bleachers stands and cheers. A few of the players on the field are sleek and beautiful in their movement, but I'm glad to see her boyfriend isn't one of them. He mostly wallows on the front line as the second-string right tackle. His name is Roger.

Paul is seated beside me, I sit beside Laura, Laura sits beside Marty. Five minutes into the second quarter Texas State scores a touchdown, and my hand slides under our blanket and rests on Laura's thigh. Her hand immediately grabs it to pull it away, then hesitates. At her hesitation I press it back on her thigh. She allows it, covers it with her hand. Her chest rises and falls.

After the game I meet Roger. He's thick-bodied, six inches taller than me, and at least seventy pounds heavier. Handsome in that large-jawed, football player sort of way, I will admit. I offer my hand, feeling some hesitation over the lie of this act. When he shakes it his hand swallows mine. He hardly looks at me when I congratulate him on his team's victory. I know I'm being two-faced, but I'm starting to enjoy it. Besides, to whom do I owe my allegiance? Him or Laura?

As he talks to Laura and Marty he's already forgotten about Paul and me. We are, after all, high school juniors and inconsequential to someone with no imagination. Then Laura, to my horror, asks him if he wants to join us for ice cream. He shuffles his feet, mutters something about "the guys" and "the team" needing to get together at some local bar. Laura tells him she understands but will miss him. He returns the sentiment, then, magnanimously it seems, he pulls her to him and kisses her forcefully. I find it a very hard thing to watch, but can't look away. It goes on longer than it should. It's meant for show, a bad stage kiss, hardly nuanced. In fact, it is brutish. It seems an affront to kiss such a girl in such a manner. I sense Paul glancing toward me and am careful not to meet his eyes. Finally Laura puts her hands to Roger's chest and pushes back, managing to break the kiss. She looks down, her hands still placed against him. "Okay, then," she says, in a tone that is neutral, that is a lie, that gives away nothing of her embarrassment. For the first time I feel sorry for her. What is a girl like her doing with this guy?

~

We're in my backseat parked under the mesquite tree in Hill Street Park. Her head rests in my lap as she looks up at me. I run a fingertip along her cheekbones, then across her eyebrows. I trace the shape of her lips with a fingernail. I memorize every curve and angle, every rise and fall of the shape of her face. I stroke her hair. I could do it all night. I could do it forever. And she tells me. Her parents are pushing her to marry Roger. She says she doesn't think he's "the one." She asks me if I think there really is "the one." Is she stupid to wait for him to show up? What if he doesn't?

"Yes," I say. "I think there is 'the one.'"

"What about people who get married more than once?"

"Maybe there's several people we're supposed to be with. Maybe somebody is 'the one' for awhile, then over time they become somebody different. They change. People change. And then you find the next one you're supposed to be with."

"That sounds sad."

"I think what's sad is being with the wrong person from the get-go."

"Roger will stay in New Braunfels. That's one reason my parents love him. But I want to live in other places."

"Where?"

"New York City," she says quietly.

"Really?"

"Just once. You know, before I'm old." My mind swirls with images of the city. "But Roger . . ." She shrugs, shakes her head. "He does treat me well."

"Want to know what I think?"

"Yes."

"If he was enough you wouldn't be here with me."

She hesitates. "Unless there's something wrong with me."

"Or something right with you, not wanting to commit your life to the wrong guy, get stuck in the wrong town."

"Then why don't I break up with him?"

"Yes. Why don't you?"

She shrugs. "I've tried. I get lost." She looks away. "John?"

"Yes?"

"Is it okay . . . if we never . . . you know."

"It's okay whatever we do."

"Have you yet? Done it?"

"No. Have you?"

"Yes. Not with Roger though. My boyfriend back in high school. The summer before he went away to college. He was a year older than me."

"What about Roger?"

"He's saving himself."

"For marriage?" She nods, and we both start laughing. "I mean . . . for religious reasons?"

"Yes. No. I don't know. We shouldn't laugh."

"Want to know a secret?" I say.

"Please."

"You're the first girl I ever kissed."

She stares at me. "You're kidding." I wonder if I've said too much, made a mistake. "No one's ever kissed me like that," she tells me. "That kiss is why we're here."

"I've never felt like this about anyone."

"John . . ." and now I see she's worried, "you know we're limited . . . with . . ." She sighs.

"I know I can't be your boyfriend."

"Really?"

"It wouldn't work."

"That's okay?"

"Yes. But I want to I ask you. . . . Why me?"

"There was that thing you said. After you broke your nose. You told Marty you didn't want me to see you like that. I felt so sorry for you. I'd never thought that way about you before. I had noticed how cute you were, but . . . still, you said that, and then I knew you had feelings for me. It was so sweet and sad. And then Marty and I were at the drive-in, and we knew you were going to be there, and we'd had a little too much to drink. And then, well, that kiss."

I start tracing the shape of her face again with my fingers. She takes my hand and holds it to her chest.

"You should get a girlfriend," she says.

"Why would I want to go out with someone else when I can see you?"

"I mean after."

"After we're done?"

"Yeah," she says. "Sure."

"Okay." Instead of smiling at my matter-of-fact response, she studies me, then pulls herself up and starts digging through her purse. I worry I sounded too flippant. "It's going to be a tough comparison, though," I say.

"Then don't compare."

I try again with a line from a movie. "How do you keep them down on the farm, after they've seen Par-ee?"

"Hush," she tells me so sharply it stings. She shakes her head, whether in frustration or in anger, I'm not certain. "Here," she finally says, and pulls out a tiny gray cotton bag. She straddles me so quickly I'm caught off guard. I feel her sudden weight, the heat of her legs beneath her skirt. Immediately I start to respond. I'm still not over my shyness at that, at how little control I have, as if there's another part of me that has its own designs, that pushes me this way and that. I tell myself this is a sophisticated girl. She'd be disappointed if I didn't respond. Besides, I couldn't move if I wanted, couldn't shift so she didn't feel me there specifically. My heart beats faster. She opens the gray bag and pulls out a silver chain. At its end a thin, silver-white cross with a silver-white circle at its center hangs in the air. Its form is so simple it's perfect.

"What does the circle mean?" I ask.

"It's a Celtic cross." She fastens it around my neck. "My grandmother gave it to me." She presses it to my chest with a finger, then drops it inside my shirt.

"It's too much. Your grandmother . . ."

"Hush," she says again and leans closer. I feel the warmth of her breath against my mouth. "I want to give you something to remember me by," she whispers. "Something that matters."

She kisses me. I feel her lips, her tongue in my mouth. My hand settles on her bare thigh at the edge of her skirt, and the image of the cross plays through my mind. The two lines float apart in space, then drift back together. They symbolize where Christ died and bled, but could also represent a human being standing feet together, arms extended. In math, straight lines extend infinitely, which would make the cross a never-ending horizontal line bisected by a never-ending vertical. On earth that would be the mortal plane bisected by the line connecting heaven and hell. It's north-south, east-west, finite-infinite. It is all there in the form.

She breaks the kiss and looks down at me. I take a sudden breath, then let it out in a shudder. "Thank you," I say. I don't know what else to say. My hand is still on her thigh. It slides up farther, now under her skirt.

She shakes her head, and I stop my hand but don't remove it. She touches her forehead to mine. "I hate you sometimes. A little bit."

"Don't hate me," I tell her.

"You're so sweet I hate you." She lifts herself up and starts tugging at my jeans. "Help me," she says.

"What?"

"Help me break up with him. Give me a reason."

"What?"

"I've already applied to Kansas State. I'll be leaving in January." She pauses. "I mean, if they let me . . . let me in. Shit, it doesn't matter. I don't care. I want this, John. I know you want it too."

"But why the circle?" I ask.

"The what?"

"On the cross."

She smiles slightly. "A circle never ends," she says. And I'm out, shocked at my exposure. She lowers herself, and I'm in her. Her eyes shut. Her mouth opens. I can't believe I'm in her. She puts her lips to my ear and whispers, "John, it's the moon."

28

New York City

As I walked across Grand Army Plaza toward the stairs leading to the street, I could still hear the clanging, feel the jostling of the subway car. Tonight I watched the riders alongside me going home. I caught their eyes. Though I've always found pride in my ability to disappear, to blend, I did not disappear this night, with my long dark hair and jeans and T-shirt, my sweat shining on my face and neck, my dark eyes that couldn't help but look at each of those riding with me. I wanted to reach out, to know them, to tell them about the woman waiting for me. Even the drunk sprawled out at the other end of the car who I could faintly smell, even the obese, likely diabetic woman across the aisle with her feet swelling out of her shoes, even the bone-thin white girl with dyed black hair and scars on her arms, even the plain mixed-race girl with a freckled face and a thin gold wedding band on her ring finger, even the three tightly wound Latino boys making too much noise who clearly could be dangerous if someone looked at them the wrong way, but I couldn't help but look at them. And what's true is I didn't look at them the wrong way because I was in love with them, all of them, riding the downtown 4 train, ferried beneath the river toward my stop at Grand Army Plaza with its *P* emblazoned on its walls, in love with every inch of this fragile city, every stain and loose screw, every pimp and whore and cop and cliché, and yes, though it hurt to admit it, even every guy in a suit.

I cast my eyes toward my fellow riders as I stepped off the car to make my way to the love of my life, and felt they sensed something of the kind by the way they looked at me, particularly the women. I nodded slightly before the doors closed. And how could I ever hold myself above them or anyone else, whatever they did, however they lived? Was I anything more than an adulterer, putting a child and a family and the woman I loved at risk?

In this city where Washington fought and Isadora danced and the punks punked and the junkies junked, I found her. I found myself, how I best walked and sang and breathed and prayed. And how I loved. Now I knew.

So what to do with this knowledge she gave me, that this city gave me? Honor her request to do everything I could to protect her, except stop, until he returned. I'd been careful, but not careful enough. I could take nothing for granted any longer. As I walked toward her building I noted every barrier I crossed and considered how to minimize the risk at each step.

I called from her corner. She told me, "The door's unlocked," and I stepped onto her street. I glanced around to see if anyone was within sight and if I was in their sightline. If so, I would keep moving past her building. If they were behind me, I would circle the block. If they were in front of me and headed my way, I'd let them pass and keep moving to the end of the street, then double back. I would repeat these steps as many times as necessary, till there was no one around, till the street was empty, from now on.

Next I hesitated, but didn't stop (as stopping draws attention) on the sidewalk in front of her building in order to give anyone stepping off her elevator a moment to clear the corner. But the lobby was empty so I turned up her stone pathway. I opened the first set of doors, pushed the black button, and waited in that lit glass box between the doors. On display, I thought, like a goldfish in a bowl.

I jumped at the sound of the buzzer even though I was expecting it, then quickly pushed open the inner door so it didn't relock. I heard it buzzing behind me as I continued, noting the flowers on the desk had been changed to white roses. I told myself to focus, keep moving.

I walked around the corner to the elevators and looked up at the numbers. I pressed Up and watched them light one after the other as the elevator descended, hoping it didn't stop, which would mean it was picking up a passenger. I glanced to my right toward the front door, then warned myself against glancing at the front door because if someone was walking in through it they would see my eyes and more likely remember me. I moved to the far side of the elevator so any passengers getting off wouldn't cross my body to exit. If any stepped off I'd nod passively, my eyes vaguely focused in the general area of their torsos, giving them nothing to fix on, nothing to remember, and disappear. I'd use my skills, these particular talents, like I'd been training for this my whole life.

The doors opened to an empty elevator, and I stepped in and considered what to do if any tenants entered the lobby behind me and followed me on. I'd move to the back, making room for them to press their button first. If their floor was below Alena's, then I'd push a number above hers, and after they exited press the correct number. If the passengers pressed a number above hers, I'd press a number below, get off on that floor, and take the stairwell up. If the passengers picked *her* floor, 7, I'd push a button at least two floors above it, then take the stairwell down, giving enough time for those preceding me to get inside their apartment, and peer through the small window on the stairwell door to make sure the hallway was clear before stepping out.

If while rising to her floor the elevator stopped and picked up a passenger who was also headed to 7, I would consider myself fucked and accept it. I'd be forced to get off on 7. I would not make eye contact. I'd head straight to the stairwell and disappear down it. Which would be suspicious but matter little since I wouldn't be coming back.

I told myself this last scenario wouldn't happen. I banked on it. I focused my attention back where it belonged, on the woman waiting for me in the darkened living room in her bathrobe, her door unlocked. I stepped off the elevator onto her floor. This was where I would most likely be seen, caught, remembered. I walked down her hallway listening for locks turning, doorknobs twisting, doors opening. My heart rate increased. I began to sweat, ready to jump at any sound. If anyone stepped out of an apartment on her floor before I reached her door, I'd disappear down the stairwell. Which would be suspicious but matter little since I wouldn't be coming back. Otherwise I walked quietly in a straight line, not looking at her door, and only at the last second, when I was sure I was alone in this hallway with its thin brown carpet and harsh fluorescent lights, did I reach for the silver doorknob and pray the door opened. It opened. I stepped through, closed it, and locked it behind me. I breathed. I was safe for awhile; she was safe. I turned to see her moving toward me down her dark hallway in her white bathrobe, her feet bare. I took her in my arms, felt how perfectly her body fit mine, listened to the air conditioner rumbling in her window, felt the cool air against my skin overheated from the summer night and the long journey from Manhattan.

This is how it would be for each night we had left. We would make love while people across the city were dying from making love. While Jeremy was dying from it. Specifically, in his case, from toxoplasmosis, also called "the cat disease." It's the reason pregnant women are warned against changing their cat litter boxes, but of course it's simply the form AIDS took in his body. Alena told me he'd asked me to visit him in the hospital, in the AIDS ward at St. Vincent's. No one else from the office had been invited.

29

Austin, Texas, 1980

I sit on one of the couches scattered along the hallways of the Texas Union and look out its windows onto the UT campus and its enormous live oak trees, green-leaved year-round, even in early December. Christmas break is a week away. I'll have to drive down to New Braunfels for a few days, though I doubt any of my sisters will make it. But since I'm only an hour up the road I don't have an excuse. I work part-time at a health foods store so I can afford a small apartment and not live in a dorm where I'd have to clear out entirely every Christmas or leave Austin during the summer. Outside the window, students wander along the sidewalks in light jackets. A few squirrels dance around on the yellowing grass. I pick up my backpack and pull out the poem I wrote for the poetry class I took as a lark to fill an upper division credit. A girl I know is pregnant. I wrote about the moon and the swell of her belly. I wrote about water. I said her baby's a swimmer about to break free, like a seal, hairless and shiny into her arms. But what I didn't expect, what was pointed out to me in class today, is that the line-breaks on the page, the ends of the lines when taken together, form a shape. You see it when you just look at the page instead of trying to read the words. There's a curve, a moon, a pregnant woman's belly. It's so obvious I feel dense for not noticing it. No one in class believed I didn't consciously design it so, even the teacher.

I'm a junior. I've majored in English only because nothing else interests me. It doesn't interest me that much, but I like to read. I look out the window, then back down at the page. I feel a little ridiculous about what happened with the poem, but something deep inside me is trembling with it, thrilled. I shift my focus from the shape of the poem to the individual sentences, then the words, and then their letters, the combinations and groups of four, seven, eleven, two. And the lines and curves that make each letter what it is, that define it. The tiny marks meeting the bottom of the straight lines, the curves on the bottom where the round ones rest, like a wheel, something that could roll or bounce away, but won't, because they belong with these other letters, these groups. These groups are now their identity, their family, their tribe. The *r* in "curves" knows it's found home beside the vowel sound of the *u* and the soft consonant of the *v*. It bridges the sound from one to the other. It has a purpose, like all letters in all words. If they weren't necessary they wouldn't be there, even the silent ones. They would have left long ago.

For my class we have to turn in a poem every week and, excited by how the day went, I start to scribble out some words, hoping to find my next poem. Kari's name appears, then the words "sister," and "blond, and "loser." And I feel guilty at what I've written and scratch through it. I write out the word "lost" and scratch through it. I write the word "trouble" and scratch through Kari's name.

"John," someone says. Startled, I look up to see Larry Silberman. "What are you doing?" he asks.

"Nothing." I shrug. "Writing for a class." I focus on his horned-rimmed glasses, his slightly greasy black hair and the acne he battles, his thin frame and bad posture. Larry is a Radio-Television-Film major and a photographer and chronicler of the local punk scene.

"You'll be ready at seven?"

"Sure," I say. He nods and walks away. The Armadillo World Headquarters is closing and Larry wants to go out and take some photos. The Armadillo is—soon to be *was*—Austin's version of the Fillmore East or West, an old airplane hangar that in 1970 a hippie named Eddie Wilson renovated and turned into one of the top places in the country to hear Texas, American, and world music. I've gone there to hear Frank Zappa, Koko Taylor, Bonnie Raitt, Bob Marley, and Bruce Springsteen, among others. The Armadillo was where the right wing and the left in Texas, the rednecks and Texas hippies, made peace with one another, as much because they all loved Willie Nelson as anything else, and he'd claimed the Armadillo as his home. The last time we heard the place was closing, the employees volunteered to work for free to keep the doors open. There were stories of how Eddie cooked huge pots of beans and rice so no one would go hungry. But there'll be no more volunteers or beans and rice. Austin is suffering a boomtown moment. Office buildings are going up everywhere, and the land was bought out from underneath the Armadillo where it had blossomed, reeking of cannabis, like some undeniable and gorgeous native plant. Larry wants to document what he can before they bulldoze it.

~

I stand in the men's bathroom at the Armadillo, peeing in front of the mural of the green army man, a larger-than-life painting on the white concrete wall behind the urinals of a soldier, complete with helmet, rifle, and a lot of attitude all but leaping from the wall. The voice balloon painted by his mouth says, "If I catch any of you pussies whacking off in here I'm gonna turn you over to the Guacamole Queen." I'm reading these words for at least the fiftieth time, but now noticing the lettering and how it seems to rise off the two-dimensional plane. Suddenly it and the army man flashes white to the sound of a pop behind me. Someone has taken my picture from behind.

"No pictures," I shout. It's an absurd thing to say and I recognize Larry's laughter. He's sneaked in to snap a shot of me pissing in front of the army man.

"For my scrapbook," he says. "You know?" I zip up and turn around but Larry's already halfway out the door. "You're a part of history now," he yells. "Your backside, anyway."

I head to the sink and wash my hands, then look up. It dawns on me this will be the last night I'll see myself in these mirrors. I stare into them until a skinny guy in a cowboy hat bangs the door open. When I walk out to track down Larry, Ray Wylie Hubbard, one of the Texas "cosmic cowboys," is performing onstage and people are dancing below him. Above the band hangs the enormous banner that has been draped over the stage as long as I've been coming here showing blues legend Freddie King playing what appears to be, by his expression, a particularly painful and exquisite note while a full-fledged armadillo bursts from his chest. At the edges of the stage, folks mill around smoking, talking. The smell of marijuana is thick and growing. I see a flash of light in the darkness. Larry, I figure.

I wander toward the entrance to the women's bathroom for a last look at another favorite mural—The Guacamole Queen. Painted glaring at you out an open window, she looks like the love child of Janis Joplin and Ma

Barker. Her arms are thick as ham hocks, and boxed over her image in a voice balloon it says: "Rikki, The Guacamole Queen Has a Message for All Men. 'If I catch any of you guys in the girls' john I'm gonna mash you up and spread you on a salad!'"

The lettering jumps out 3-D, as thick and muscular as her image, a take-no-shit goddess and guardian. As I stare at her I figure she's probably based on a woman working in the kitchen. I could walk back there and find the flesh-and-blood Rikki whose goddess-image and source of celebrity will come tumbling down with the walls of this place.

The letters around Rikki look to be subtly shifting. I wonder if I might've gotten a contact high because the armadillo bursting out of Freddie King's chest appears to be eyeing me. The dancers in front of the stage call to mind hieroglyphics. I see one flash of light. A second goes off at the side of the stage. Then another, and another. A war of tiny white explosions—people committing to Kodak the images of this place where they'd fallen in love, for the first time in their life heard music from Senegal or Jamaica or Tibet, or found home.

I'm suddenly so heartsick I turn and walk toward the exit so I can step outside and clear my head, but by the doorway I'm arrested by a black-and-white poster of Townes Van Zandt, the troubled and brilliant singer-songwriter from Fort Worth.

"Hey," a female voice says softly from behind me.

I turn to find a woman older than me, maybe in her early thirties. Good looking. A brunette almost as tall as I am and a little on the fleshy side. "Hi," I reply.

"C'mere," she says as she takes my left hand in her right. Her hand feels warm and comforting. In her other hand a joint burns between her fingers. She pulls me a step into the shadows and puts the burning end of the joint carefully between her lips, brings her face to mine, and blows a cool white stream of smoke into my mouth. I take it deep into my lungs and hold it in like oxygen. The smoke presses against my chest but I fight its release. "Thanks," I mutter, white smoke curling from my lips.

"A farewell gift," she says and kisses me, lingers a moment longer on my mouth than I expect, then pulls away. Finally I let the breath go. She tilts her head as she watches me. "It's gonna be okay, baby," she tells me. "You say goodbye, you say hello." She smiles and puts her hand to my cheek, then turns and walks away.

I turn to the poster of Townes on the wall. I see his face drawn gaunt as a coyote's, his facial bones exaggerated, rendered even more prominent than they are in life, and the scar beneath his right eye deepened. I see the lines on paper that make it all so and the geometry that rises from them, how the letters around him sink into the paper as if in counter-relief, then seem to rise again. Each word has a life of its own, as does each letter. The lines and the shapes and the type work together like gears. I see it all, the pieces and the whole. I reach up and carefully peel back the poster from the staples holding it to the wall.

~

As Larry drives me back toward my apartment I can't stop staring out the window at the billboards we pass and their designs of women and lettering, the neon signs in bar windows spelling out beer brands in red, white, or blue, Mexican restaurants with enormous monikers carved out in audacious script under spotlights. I look down at the poster in my lap.

"Are you alright?" Larry asks.

"I guess. I'm pretty high, really. A woman gave me a hit."

"You told me. Anyway, there was enough smoke in that place to get everybody off."

Larry didn't drink or smoke. "You get some good pictures?" I ask him.

"Yeah. Cheer up. We've still got Raul's."

He's talking about a punk rock club near campus, but I'm not really listening to him. I'm staring at the poster. As soon as I get home I thumbtack it to a wall, then sit and stare at it for an absurdly long time, taking it apart in my mind, reconstructing it, following how the lines of the text and the image work with one another. Suddenly I've looked at it too long. I need to see other images, other designs. I pull books off my shelves and examine the jacket covers. I scrutinize the Shiner Bock beer label in my hand, the soda labels in my refrigerator. I dig cereal boxes out of the cupboard, laundry detergent out from under the sink, and in general trash the place. I finally force myself to stop. I sit and turn on the TV only to be swarmed by logos and all the elements of their designs—the odd fact that there is no period after the *Dr* in the script that says "Dr Pepper," the utterly specific curved yellow arches of the *M* that's immediately identified as McDonalds, the crudely stenciled letters around the asterisks that spell out M*A*S*H. These gestures of line and space that burrow into your mind and set up shop.

I'm seeing, I mean *seeing* letters everywhere, their shapes on billboards, logos, television. I see how they and the colors and shadings and shapes around them are working. And the tumblers click and say, "Here you are, aren't you?" I've stepped through a door and stumbled into an ocean. My ocean.

30

Austin, Texas, 1982

I've been summoned by Zoe. I follow her with my produce cart loaded with empty boxes down the narrow aisles of Whole Foods, then through the swinging aluminum doors to the backroom. Zoe continues toward the back door, and when she opens it the summer sun is blinding. After I unload my boxes I step out to see her smoking as she waits for me, seated on a concrete retaining wall that keeps a small house, its yard, and a scrawny mesquite tree from spilling over into our lot. Zoe's a whippet of a girl with a bob cut, an "It Girl" in the Austin music scene. Her boyfriend, Kyro, is the leader of an art-punk band called Face, one of Austin's most popular bands. Everyone expects them to break through nationally like REM, 10,000 Maniacs, The Dead Milkmen. Zoe is Kyro's public face, his go-between. Notoriously introverted, he needs one. The heel of her right foot beats against the wall in a steady rhythm as I approach her.

"I hate to smoke alone," she tells me when I walk up. She offers me a cigarette. I shake my head no, then sit beside her. She blows out a quick puff of smoke. "So," she begins. "Where'd you learn to draw?"

I'm caught off guard by this, but I remember last week seeing her staring at one of the posters I sketched for a display of Shiner Bock in the store, and a few days later I spotted her examining a small sign I made for the high-end juicers. She's always been friendly—she's friendly to everyone—but she's never taken a specific interest in me before.

"I'm self-taught," I tell her. "So far."

"You're a natural." She looks into my eyes. Her gaze is intense. This isn't small talk. "When did you start?"

"It was odd. I only . . . discovered it a year ago Christmas. Before my last year at UT. It came out of the blue."

"How?"

"Well . . ." I hesitate. She leans toward me, then I find myself spilling everything. "I was at the Armadillo a couple of weeks before they tore it down. You know, saying goodbye. And there was so much weed in the air I'm sure I was getting high from it. Anyway, I was staring at this poster of Townes Van Zandt when some woman . . . I didn't see her coming . . . she takes my hand, leans up to my face, and gives me this tremendous power hit."

"Really."

"Enough to make me cross-eyed. And then . . . she kissed me."

Zoe's head tilts. "She kissed you?"

"Yeah." I feel a bead of sweat run down my neck and into my T-shirt. "Then she walked away. And I turned back to this poster. It might have been a Jim Franklin poster. I dunno. I'm not sure who drew it. But . . . this probably sounds crazy." And I start to doubt myself even as I'm speaking, like I know I should stop. "Something shifted. I could see *into* it," I try and explain. "It was like I woke up . . . to a way of seeing."

She takes a puff off her cigarette and looks away. I've said too much. I wish I could take it back. The way she was looking at me caught me off guard. She's never looked at me like that.

"You didn't draw before?" she finally says.

"No."

"Not when you were a kid or anything?"

"No, I never drew or painted. In high school or junior high or studied it or anything. I never thought about it. That night it just popped into place. Like it'd been there waiting." The heat from the retaining wall seeps through my jeans into my thighs. A beam from the sun slipping through the leaves presses against my right shoulder. A droplet of sweat runs down from my temple and I turn to wipe it off. When I look back she's smiling faintly as she studies me. She looks away again, off at Lamar Boulevard in front of the store, the cars rolling past.

"That's a great story," she says. "Maybe that woman was a hallucination. Or an angel. There to wake you . . . with a kiss." She giggles. "Like Snow White."

"Don't tell anyone."

"No, no." She pats my knee. "I promise. Don't be embarrassed. It's just too perfect. It's got fate written all over it. So what are you going to do with this message from a strange woman out of the shadows of the Armadillo World Headquarters? Which is gone. Which doesn't even exist anymore."

"Don't make too big a deal out of it. My drawings are just little things I knock out. You know, geometric shapes and a dancing pair of olives, or whatever. And 'Buy Me!' It's the text I'm into as much as anything."

"The what?"

"The text. The letters. How they look. I can spend an hour making an *h* look right." She stares at me. "I know that sounds crazy."

"Maybe it's obsessive or whatever," she says. "But all artists are obsessive or whatever. You should see Kyro once he gets an idea in his head."

"Really?"

"His latest thing is this second-hand synthesizer he bought. He's up all night trying to figure out how he might use it. Frankly, I don't think it'll pan out." She puffs on her cigarette. "Don't tell him I said that."

"Sure," I say. Why would I? I don't even know him.

"I don't want to wreck his creative process so I'm not saying anything, but it's hard to imagine how a beat gets under the sounds he's coming up with. But what do I know?" She stubs out her cigarette on the wall as she gets to her feet. "He starts here next week, by the way. I got him a job."

~

When I first meet Kyro I'm sitting beside her on the wall again. He's tall, lean, dark-haired, and intense. Soon both of us are joining Zoe during her cigarette breaks. The standard line he feeds me as he walks up is asking what I'm doing with his girl. "Nothing," Zoe answers, then he jumps subject and launches into a treatise on Arthur Rimbaud one day, Max Fleischer the next. He appreciates I can keep up with him more or less, and Zoe appreciates he has someone besides herself to babble to.

"We like your signs," Zoe says one afternoon, prodding Kyro. He has to shield his eyes from the August sun glaring off a parked white delivery van as he looks at us.

"You have a good eye," Kyro mutters. "Want to design a poster for my band?"

"Sure," I tell him.

"Okay," he says, and turns and walks stiffly back to the building, then inside the store. What just happened?

Zoe turns to me smiling. "How exciting," she says.

"What if my poster sucks?"

"Then he'll let you know." Yes, he would. And bluntly, as was his nature. She laughs, seeing my anxiety. "It'll be terrific, John," she tells me. "Just don't think about it too much."

After work I park my car on Guadalupe Street in front of the UT campus and start walking, examining the posters stapled to the wooden telephone poles, taped to the metal light poles, one band after another and another. I notice the better posters can be made out from a distance. The least successful are gibberish until you're on top of them and by then, of course, it would be too late—you would've lost interest and walked right by.

I buy a handful of standard colored paper—pink, sky blue, mustard, pale green—and lay them out on my dining table. On impulse I draw a rectangle within one of the pages, then begin scribbling marks around it. The scribbles turn into letters, and the letters turn into the name of the band, "Face."

I sit back in my chair thinking I might have a thread to follow. I grab a razor blade and a ruler, then cut out a medium-sized rectangle from a piece of white paper, lightly make a pass at its backside with a glue stick, then place it perfectly centered on a clean, mustard-colored piece. I begin sketching the word "Face" at a thirty-degree angle across the page, serif and sans serif, large and small, thick and thin, upper case and lower, crossing and bleeding over the blank rectangle. Then when I can't squeeze in another word I peel off the white piece from its background, leaving its shape—an empty perfect rectangle on the mustard page outlined and defined by the text. There I draw two dots for eyes and a horizontal line for a mouth, simple as you can get: a face. The space around it is frenzied with letters, while the face itself is almost empty. On impulse I draw a second version and knock a chip off the upper left-hand corner, turning the rectangle into an irregular pentangle, which complicates the simple design just enough. I draw a thin line a half inch from the bottom of this empty space and print beneath it: "Saturday 7/10. Black Cat Lounge. 9:00 pm."

I lean back and look at it. Then I get an idea to duplicate the face with a second white piece of paper. I cut it out, glue-stick a strip along its top, and stick it precisely over the original. I add the eyes and the mouth, then I lift the top page up then down, up then down. I'm getting more ideas—flip books, note pads, business cards—but I decide to stop and get Kyro and Zoe's reaction before going further. He answers the phone when I call and tells me to come over.

Kyro and Zoe rent a small three-room house off Congress Avenue in South Austin not far from the Continental Club, something cute and shabby and brightly colored that the wind whistles through. They keep a green plastic Christmas tree up with twinkle lights year-round. Zoe makes a pitcher of iced tea while Kyro and I alternately stare at, then avoid the folder I set on their coffee table containing the poster. As soon as she sets our glasses down in front of us, I lurch forward and open it. "Ta da!" I say too quickly, trying to cover my fear.

Kyro stands and bends over the poster like a praying mantis. He leans back, then looks at Zoe. "Did you see this?" he says.

"I'm right here," she answers.

"This figure . . . face," he says tapping the sketch. "I really like its reductive aspect."

"It's just a first draft," I tell him. "The final version would be bigger. I figure 17 by 11. I really want to go to town with these letters. Vary the font style, the depth and thickness, hand drawn and stenciled in actual type to create a tapestry effect that'll frame the spareness of the image."

"Yeah yeah."

"He's cute, too," Zoe says.

"In a blank sort of way," Kyro responds.

"He's the answer to the smiley face," she tells him.

"God," I say. "I can't believe I didn't see the connection."

"No no," Kyro tells me. "If anything it's a reference, part of an argument."

"He could be your logo," Zoe says.

Kyro freezes and stares into space, then leans forward and picks at the bottom edge of the head. "Is this part of the design?"

"Peel it off," I tell him.

He lifts it to find the mustard-colored replica underneath. He laughs out loud, a short crisp, "Ha!" "Ha!" he says again and heads toward the kitchen with the top page.

"We can stack them as high as we want," I call out, "I figure people might peel them off and collect them, or stick them onto other things. We could find glue that would work for this. It's all more trouble and expense but those little faces could be everywhere. To save money we could do a simple black and white version. What I've got here would be the formal, color poster." He doesn't answer. I look at Zoe. "What's he doing?"

She shrugs as she examines the figure, then puts her hand on my knee and pats it absently. At her touch adrenaline shoots through my system. Kyro rattles around in the kitchen.

"We could make a bunch of little faces," she calls out to him and finally, to my relief, removes her hand. "Stick them everywhere. Draw the figure on sides of buildings. No words, just that face. People will wonder what it means."

"We hold off on the full poster until we've established the icon," Kyro announces as he walks back from the kitchen. He carries three juice glasses and an open bottle of red wine I recognize from work. $5.99, from Spain, on sale.

"I see you're breaking out the good stuff," Zoe tells him. She pats my knee again.

"I ask for a poster and I get a poster, a logo, and a marketing device," he says filling our glasses. "Muchas gracias, John."

"De nada," I tell him, as casually as I can manage.

～

On the drive home I'm so excited I have to concentrate to keep from speeding. I keep dreaming up variations on the poster all the way back. As I open my door I see my answering machine showing a flashing numeral 1 in the dark room. I hesitate, then hit play and hear my mother's thin, reedy voice. She can't reach Kari. Her phone's been disconnected, and Mother's worried she's taken off again. She wants to know if I've heard anything from her, if I know how to find her, then starts to cry before she apologizes and hangs up. This is par for Kari. She's probably just neglected to pay her phone bill and they've shut it down. But still, she's pulled me into her orbit once again on what had otherwise been an amazing night. I resent her for it. I resent her and feel guilty for it in the same instant.

31

New York City

On Thursday, with Alena's permission, I took off the first part of my shift and made my way to St. Vincent's Hospital on 12th Street in the Village. I stopped at a nearby florist shop, picked out a dozen daisies, and placed them in a clear glass vase. I liked the flowers' simplicity, their yellow centers, their white petals.

As I approached the hospital I thought of our company's last Christmas party, how Jeremy quickly claimed the seat beside Alena at dinner. I ended up at a table nearby next to David Rohmer, our boss. He'd had a few drinks and was in good spirits. He told me he'd been an actor in the late sixties with an experimental theater company. He'd known people at The Open Theatre, at La Mama.

"It was a lot of fun," he said, "except for the part about starving. You should've seen me." He touched his shoulder. "I had hair down to here. Sometimes I'd do women's parts for a gag. We all did that back then."

"Do you miss it?"

"Sure. Sure. But I got married. The world changed. You know. Suit and tie. And I wasn't that great an actor, truth be told. But John, here's the deal, and if you tell anyone I told you this I'll say you're lying and it will not reflect well in your annual review. But with your particular talent . . . you see, the great thing about your art form is that you could actually make a living doing what you love. Maybe a *good* living. Of course, that means you'd have to pursue it. And by that I mean at some point you might have to align your art . . . with your *job*. With *where* you work. If you catch my drift."

He raised an eyebrow, as if daring me to ask whether he was advising me to leave the company. Suddenly Alena stood between us. "What are you two talking about?" she said. "You look so serious." She wore a plum-colored, knee-length dress that made her appear almost modest. She took David's hand and pulled him up. "C'mon, David," she said. "We're dancing."

"Think about it," David called back. I followed them to the crowd on the dance floor where most of our department had thronged. There was Berne Mason doing an overly enthusiastic dance with a proofreader. There was Kristy, the young, adorable new hire from Kansas, dancing with Maya from East Harlem. At some point Jeremy took me by the shoulders and guided me in front of Alena who was doing a controlled little shuffle on her high heels. She caught my eye once, smiled, then focused somewhere behind me. I tried not to think about the fact that I'd found myself dancing with her, tried not to react overtly to the gestures we sent back and forth. Then the hand of Jeremy, our maestro, conducted me away to a middle-aged secretary who looked thrilled at joining our group.

The party ended close to midnight, and Jeremy and I were standing outside considering sharing a cab when Alena stepped between us and hooked us both by our elbows. "C'mon," she said, quickly pulling us down the steps to a black sedan. "I called a car service."

Jeremy had the back door open for her, and I ran around to the far side and hopped in beside her. "Boy-girl-boy," Jeremy said as our car pulled away, as Alena's hip and the length of her thigh rested lightly against mine on one side and Jeremy's on the other. There she sat, her hands folded demurely in her lap, between her gay boy and her straight boy. She looked happy. We all did. We might've been three sixteen-year-olds escaping a party together, piled into the back seat of a car, subtly, physically connecting.

The affair was well in motion then, even if none of us were aware of it. Because Alena's husband had, a year earlier, blanched at her surgery, her scar, her inability to have any more children, and maybe more than anything else, her specific needs, like them or not. All he would've had to do was give her proof she was still a woman in his eyes, convince her he preferred her this way. And really, how hard could that have been, to say yes to his imagination and hers? They could've redefined themselves to one another, become hard-core lovers, and given everything else to their only child. But because he came up short, Alena and I had come together. And

I stood outside the massive structure of St. Vincent's Hospital holding a thin vase of daisies for her confidant, and now mine.

I looked down at the flowers. They looked too simple and cheerful to be exposed to such a place. It seemed they would wither under its weight. Jennifer told me AIDS had turned into a cash cow for the hospital, that in the wake of the CDC and the government's slow response, a gifted team of St. Vincent's doctors, led by the now-legendary Dr. Ramon Torres, had gone cowboy in their approach, throwing medicines together like Pollack did paint, and opening up the game. The first AIDS survivor, if there ever was one, was predicted to come from St. Vincent's. Jeremy's family, with their money and political pull, had secured him a tiny private room.

When I stepped through the doors into the hospital, the odor of disinfectant repelled me physically. I had to push through it to the desk where I asked for directions to the AIDS ward. The attendant gave me a look I was unsure how to interpret, though it was hardly welcoming.

I found the ward teeming with patients, families, caregivers. The dying were everywhere, almost all male, slumped in soft chairs, propped up in wheelchairs, one body strapped to a cot by a wall. I felt a need to move faster through it, then felt an urge to run down the halls to escape the smells and white surfaces, the mourning and the despair and the matter-of-factness about it all from the staff.

I turned down one corridor, then another. I held up my scrap of paper with Jeremy's room number to the light, then looked down to see four patients, all male, rowed up in wheelchairs along the wall, IVs dripping into their arms. I hesitated, but when the first man looked up I continued walking. His face was mottled with purplish lesions. Like leeches, I thought. Doctors used to use leeches to treat patients. The second man, his face drawn to bone, cut his eyes toward me, then away. The third was sleeping fitfully. I was overcome by a sense I would never find my way out. I was terrified, then horrified by my reaction, but that didn't stop it. All these men, dying now because of following their hearts and desires. Like me. Like Alena. Like Jeremy.

The last man, his face barely more than a skull inset with eyes, watched me closely. "Hello," he said.

The fact of his voice stopped me. I swallowed. "Hello," I said. I looked down at my flowers. I was embarrassed by them. They were too carefree.

"There. That wasn't so hard, was it?"

He smiled and his eyes opened to a shade of green so intense they were startling. He must've stopped people in their tracks with them each day of his life. His smile made me able to see beyond the disease, to *him*. I was ashamed at my initial response. "You have amazing eyes," I said.

"Aren't you the flatterer."

"What are you doing out here?"

"Waiting for a bed to open."

"Sorry."

"It's just the velvet rope, darling," he told me with a wave of his hand. "St. Vincent's is the *only* place to be. Trust me, I'll get in soon enough. You look lost. Are you lost?"

"Yes."

I showed him Jeremy's room number and he told me where to go. I extracted one of Jeremy's daisies from its vase.

"Why, thank you," he said. As he reached out to take it, he was careful not to touch my hand. He smelled the daisy, then looked up, his eyes bright. "You made my day."

"I'm glad. Be well."

"It's too late," he told me. "Be careful."

When I finally located Jeremy's room I saw him through the open door lying on his bed. I was so relieved I almost forgot why I'd come. An IV dripped into his arm as he watched a small TV attached high on the wall. I rapped on the doorframe, and he turned his head. "John," he said. "So happy you could make it."

I stepped inside, feeling instantly located by his presence. "Wouldn't miss it for the world."

"A little scary out there?" He noticed the flowers I'd brought and smiled. "Is it the daisy week?"

"Yes." I made room on his undersized dresser and set them among the others, the roses and the lilacs, the mixed arrangements.

"It's so romantic. So sweet. Daisies."

I felt a bit exposed by them. "How are you?"

"I have an awful headache. I guess you heard."

"Yes."

"Toxoplasmosis. The cat disease." He started laughing. "It's so pathetic. I don't even have a cat. And now they say I've developed the brain fever."

He repeated the phrase in the style of a horror film. "*The Brain Fever*. I'm going to start saying crazy shit any minute now."

"Knock yourself out," I told him and pulled up a chair. "You look good, Jeremy. It's so good to see you." I meant it. I was relieved he still looked like himself.

"Thanks. It's catching up with me quickly though. I'm suddenly rather batty. My looks are holding, but my mind is not. The cat disease gave me encephalitis. One thing leads to another. God knows what else is coming. I don't like the idea of losing my mind and rotting away for eighteen months, only to die. What's the point? That's the average, you know. Actually, I think I'm further into the cycle."

"Eighteen months is a long time. Any day they could come up with a cure."

He waved me off. "That's what everybody says, and nobody believes it. Forget all that. Listen, do you know why I didn't want anyone from the office besides you or Alena to come?"

"Why?"

"Because I don't like anyone else." He laughed, a little too loud and long. "But also . . . also I'm afraid I might squeal. Get excited and spill the beans. Tell everyone about two of my favorite people and what they're doing with each other deep into the night. I can just see the words coming out of my mouth as I scramble to catch them. Truth is, I'm not stable. It's so odd. It happened so quickly. Maybe it's the drugs, too. Maybe that's most of it."

I considered how someone from the office might show up invited or not. "I appreciate your looking out for us," I told him, trying to mask my fears.

He shook his head. "Not to worry. My family has come to get me. I'm being transferred to Minneapolis next week. That's my plan. Get out of town before I blab."

"Jeremy, that . . ." I was so relieved I didn't know what to say. "That's beyond generous."

"Not at all. I should be with them now anyway." His eyes fell on my face. "You really look good. You look . . . sure of yourself."

"Thanks."

He leaned toward me. "I'm very jealous of you. But honestly, I don't envy you a month from now. Are you paying attention, John?"

"Of course."

"You're going to have to keep your wits. Love is a tyrant. It thinks it is justified any behavior, including setting fire to it all. Then you wake up in ashes."

There was more to what he was saying, some story behind his words. Where did he pick up the bullet? Was it worth it? Did he love that person? Did he still?

"Jeremy . . ."

"Yes?"

"What happened?"

"Oh . . . life. Life happened. Love happened." He smiled. "You look after Alena and that little girl, okay? You do what's right."

"I will."

"Otherwise I'll come back and haunt you."

Tears began running down his face. They made his beauty, which would soon be leaving him, even more potent. I felt an urge to place my hand on his neck, to stroke the long, drawn muscles. Instead I reached over and brushed away his tears with the back of my fingers. It felt odd. I'd never touched a man's face like that. "It's gonna be okay," I told him.

"I know it is. That's what I wanted to tell *you*. But now you're telling me. I messed it up. Ask Alena. She knows. I can't manage anything anymore." He jerked his head. "Oh god," he said, pushing my hand away. "The virus is in the tears."

"You can't catch it that way," I told him. "If you caught it that way we'd all have it by now."

"Go wash your hands anyway."

"Okay, okay." I washed them in the small sink, then returned to his bedside. "I don't even know where you're from," I said.

"Saginaw, Michigan. But home is Minneapolis. That's where I'm headed. Home, and then *home*." He looked upward.

"Hang in there. Things can change."

"Don't worry. I wouldn't *do* anything. I honestly don't think I'll have to." He looked up at the TV. "Hmm . . . alright then. Alright. I see by our programming it's getting late. I cleared this slot for you so we could talk. But other guests will be arriving soon."

I stood. "Will I see you again?"

"Unlikely. Better this way. I'd rather you remembered me being pretty."

"I will." He smiled. "I've valued our friendship, Jeremy. I didn't think I would at first. In fact, I didn't like you."

"It was mutual. We were both in love with the same woman. In our different ways, of course. She played us against each other."

I was surprised at the thought even as I realized on some level I'd known it. "I got the impression you helped my cause."

He laughed. "You needed help. You were in such pain."

"Thank you. More than I can say."

"Can I tell you something naughty?"

"Sure."

"Do you know why I want to come back as you in my next life?"

"Why?"

"So I can fuck Alena." His eyes glistened at the transgression. "And the life after that . . . I want to come back as her. Can you possibly imagine why?" He watched my face intently.

"I think I get the idea."

"So I can fuck you." He smiled, pleased with himself. "Is it okay I told you that, John?"

"You can tell me whatever you want."

"Because I'm going to die?"

"We're all going to die."

"Keep your head on straight. Don't do anything rash."

"Same for you, Jeremy. Nothing rash."

"I'm in my element," he told me, waving me off. He pointed to his dresser. "That large manila envelope. It's yours."

I walked over and picked it up.

"A memento," he said.

32

Austin, Texas

Is it always a parent's fault if a child fails? Kari turned up at a Motel 6 outside of Needles, California, after being evicted from her apartment and disappearing for three weeks. She'd given the manager Amanda's number, and Amanda had agreed to cover her bill. That was a mistake, they tell us at the Windom Recovery Center, a high-priced addiction treatment center north of Tucson. Take some heart that she agreed to come to the clinic, they said, but know odds are she'll backslide. If she does, you'll have to let her find her own bottom. Don't try to stop her fall. Her bottom will be far beyond yours. You can't protect her, so protect yourself. She'll pull you down after her if she can.

At Amanda's insistence we'd all flown out to support her when she checked in. Stupidly, I got to the airport late and just missed my flight. I arrived four hours later than planned and didn't get to see Kari before she was admitted. "Consider yourself lucky," Catherine told me. We'd taken three rooms at the nearby Holiday Inn, which no doubt was filled with relatives of "guests" of the clinic. This morning we met at the center and were led to a small conference room where we now sit, my mother on one side and my two beautiful, dark-haired sisters on my other, while the counselors advise us. We're shocked at their words. We expected they'd tell us it was somehow our fault, that we'd have to pull together to support her. But instead they insist we let her hang herself out to dry. To not do so would only enable her and cripple what chance she had of recovery. It could, in fact, kill her.

Afterward we join together for lunch at a nearby cafeteria, filled again, no doubt, with people associated with the clinic. We're all finding it hard to talk. Any subject but Kari would be superficial, and we're all sick of talking about Kari, about how to deal with her. We meet again for dinner and separate shortly afterward to get an early night's sleep. I figure Amanda and Catherine regret choosing to share a room, but who knows? Regardless, I'm glad I don't have to talk to anyone.

The next morning we meet in Mother's room to say goodbye. She says she wishes we'd scheduled later flights so we could have breakfast together, but it's obvious none of us can wait to get out of this place. Amanda rushes away in a flurry—she has to make a business meeting that afternoon in Atlanta. Soon after, Catherine and I share a cab to the airport. I haven't really seen her in years. We don't talk much along the way, but when we hug goodbye it seems she's never going to let go. "I can't believe how you've grown up," she whispers. "I wouldn't have recognized you." When she finally releases me she can hardly look at me. Her eyes dodge about. "God, life can be hard," she says.

On my flight back to Austin I stare out my window at the darkening sky over the curve of the horizon, then down at the patterns of lights below. Did Catherine hold me so long because she didn't want to look in my eyes? It's probably common for families at the center to feel uncomfortable, even ashamed to be around each other. Then again, we see each other so rarely these days. Thank god Amanda is handling most of this business with Kari. I reach for my notebook to begin sketching, but my hand is jittery, jumpy. I shake it out, then try to breathe down the length of my arm to my fingers. I first relax my little finger, then my ring finger, then my next, and the next till my entire hand tingles. I begin working on logos for imaginary companies, a game I play to loosen up when I need to draw but am short on ideas. "Crown of Thorns Christian Bookstore." "La Turista Mexican Restaurant." "R. Munchies Edible Underwear." Feeling better, I start working up a sketch for a poster for Kyro. I riff on the old Indian head sign-off image from TV and have him shout "Face!" in a word bubble. Then I draw a huge-headed baby with worried eyes and the word "Face" spelled out on his building blocks. Next I draw a magician with a dubious grin lifting his black top hat and, along with it, the top of his skull as the word "Face" floats out from the dark space underneath. I draw the square-faced logo beside the club date. I'm on a roll. I feel good. I sketch until the plane lands.

I decide to treat myself to dinner since I've done several weeks' work in only a few hours and feel certain Zoe and Kyro will love it. I drive to one of my favorite Mexican restaurants where I order a margarita and a plate of enchiladas while I continue scratching at my notebook. I draw a delicate arc on a page, a sliver moon, and stop at its familiarity. It's Kari's body, the subtle curve of her torso, the bend in the hourglass. I mark through it, then tear it out. After our family dinner Amanda told me Kari didn't care that I missed her at the Windom Center check-in. She said Kari didn't care about anything. It'd been hell getting her out of the Motel 6 and into the car, but once they made it to the center she went in quietly. You have to let her fall, the counselors told us. You have to protect yourself. Sure, I think, I tell myself. Life has to go on. What else is there for it to do?

I still feel the urge to sketch but am wary of it now. I've sketched so much already I know I should disengage or risk burning out. So I put the notebook away and order a second margarita. My mind continues to spin. I need to wind down, give it a few hours off, have a little fun. I finish my meal and head to the Continental Club.

The Continental Club is on Congress Avenue just south of the river from the capitol building. It's probably my favorite club in town, though punk and new wave bands like Kyro's rarely play here. Everybody else does though, from hard-core country, to country punk, to blues, to rockabilly. It's an old roadhouse bar that's been here since the fifties. Even Elvis played it. Inside the lighting is red, the walls are painted bordello red, and the ceiling is a sooty, thick black. Huge, dusty, somewhat tacky paintings of Europeans sipping demitasses in cafes and bars and promenades, circa WWII, hang on the walls. In the backroom a worn, red coin-slot pool table sits squarely in the center, and at the rear corner of the ceiling an actual and rather large motorcycle appears to be crashing through the roof as a type of sculpture/art piece.

Tonight the music is rockabilly, and Johnny Nitely and his three-piece band is kicking up a swarm of dancers on the floor, a bunch of mid-twenty- to late-thirty-year-olds who've learned swing dancing and the jitterbug. The dancers obviously practice, whipping each other in tight spins and circles. Some of them even dress the part—girls in poodle skirts and guys in jackets and skinny ties. The darkness and neon of the bar and the familiar bartend- ers and waitresses, who if they're not gorgeous are more than cool enough to make up for it, provide relief for me, as does the energetic racket from the band.

I sit on one of the ragged, red-upholstered stools at the bar and order a Jameson and a beer. Which is something I don't usually do, a voice inside me notes. So what, I think. It's been a long couple of days. I order another shot. I hesitate, then lift it, toasting Kari. Poor Kari. I take a sip and set it back on the counter. When I turn to look at the band, Johnny Nitely, with his blond pompadour, leopard-skin vest, and skin-tight silver pants, lowers his upright bass toward the stage at a forty-five-degree angle and hops onto its side as if mounting a small whale. He thumps maniacally, his eyes rolling back in his skull like a deranged preacher. The dancers spin faster and faster, approaching a frenzy. A girl at the edge of the dance floor glances at me, catching my eye, then turns back to the dancers. She's a strawberry blond, more preppy than I usually see in here. She looks back at me again, bouncing on her feet. So I do it. I move to her.

"I can't jitterbug," I yell over the music.

"I can't either."

"Perfect."

As we hit the edge of the dance floor I manage to steer us clear of dancers who know what they're doing, who would likely wipe us out on contact, and fake my way through a basic swing step as well as I can. Which is, frankly, quite a bit better than she can. Not that I'm complaining. She's cute and quite happy, I'm noticing. My guess is she's in a sorority and slumming tonight. Soon we're at the bar and she's ordering us shots of tequila, slamming her shot glass down on the wooden counter, drawing irritated glances from the bartenders, which bothers neither her nor me. She's funny, this girl. She's full of sass and tequila, and so am I.

～

I wake to the smell of bacon, coffee, and eggs. My sheets are pink. The walls are pink. The room smells faintly of lavender. Three sizable turquoise triangles are fixed to the wall over the bed, the sign of the Tri-Delts. A few stuffed animals are strewn over the floor—a brown teddy bear, a white pony, a gray Eeyore donkey. I sit up. I am naked beneath the sheets. I swing my legs over the side of the bed, pick up my underwear and slide them up over my legs, then follow with my jeans and black T-shirt. The smell of breakfast is calling, but before I leave I walk to her white vanity where I spot a picture of a group of girls posing in front of a sorority house. Beside it is a photo of a clean-cut, thick-necked young man posed holding a football like he's about to pass it. The shot looks to be from fraternity flag football.

I look past the photo to see myself standing in the mirror behind her vanity. My white Face logo on the upper left-hand corner of my black T-shirt is a bit smaller than one would expect, which appeals to me. I smile into the girl's mirror. I look happy. I am, in fact. I look nothing like the boy in the photo. I try to remember the girl's name. Marsha. Yes, it's Marsha.

"Good morning!" she says when I step into her kitchen. "I was hoping this would wake you up. You were out. Like, in a coma."

"It smells great."

"Thanks."

She stabs a strip of bacon from the pan and lays it on a paper towel alongside half a dozen other strips.

"I'm really hungry," I say.

"I'll bet!" She doesn't look at me but she's smiling. She's wearing an oversized burnt-orange UT T-shirt that covers her to mid-thigh. Nothing else as far as I can tell. "How do you like your eggs?" she asks. She turns to me and grins. I see a half-dozen eggs, over-easy, resting on a plate.

"Over easy."

"Great!" she says and returns to her cooking. I walk past her to her refrigerator where there are three photos of the boy featured on her dresser attached with magnets. In one she's wearing a formal beside him in a suit. In another he's throwing another football. In a third they're going down a waterslide together. She's between his legs, and the water's spraying around them as they laugh and scream.

"Who's this guy?" I ask.

"My shithead boyfriend." She looks over at me and smiles in a matter-of-fact way, then turns back to her cooking. "Coffee?" she asks without looking up.

33

Austin, Texas, 1983

At work Kyro pulls me aside. He tells me Zoe had found out her final grade in her summer-school trig course at UT was 79, and she was unable talk her way up to an 80. The prof apparently wasn't only immune to her charms but made a point of being so. Took pride in it. "She holds herself to a high bar," Kyro says. "A B is a failure for her." I know that being unable to talk her way from a 79 to an 80 would be even worse. She called him at work crying.

Since they only have one car I often drive her to shows when she can't or doesn't want to go in early with him. I'm on their permanent guest list, and I love the shows, especially when I get to hang out with Zoe. Her attention is so focused and generous that when she turns it your way you feel like you could do anything. As a bonus, her attention makes me look good to other girls. So when Kyro asks if I can drive her in so she won't have to endure the pre-show, I tell him I'd be happy to.

"And keep an eye on her."

"Of course."

She greets me at her front door wearing a purposefully ragged "Never Mind the Bollocks, Here's the Sex Pistols" T-shirt, cut-off shorts, and holding a bottle of red wine. She grabs my hand and pulls me inside where she immediately pours me a glass.

"I mean, fuck the motherfucker," she says, only a little drunk at this point. I sit beside her and sink into their slightly broken-down, second-hand sofa. "Who does he think he is?"

"Who made him God?"

"Exactly! These people. I mean, it's all bullshit."

"You'll still graduate."

"Sure. I just. I just . . . sometimes I think about grad school."

"A C won't kill that. What's your GPA?"

"3.57."

"With the C?"

"Yeah. I did the math. Upper division is 3.64."

"You kidding me? No problemo," I tell her. "Unless you're going to Harvard. You're not going to Harvard, are you?"

"Hell no!"

"Listen, you're an undergrad. Schools don't expect perfection. I only wish my GPA was as high as yours. You're in great shape."

"Really?"

"Yeah. When do you graduate?"

"Next May."

"Screw this guy. Life's too short to be sweating a meaningless GPA shift."

"I second that emotion," she says, refilling my glass.

Soon we're heading out. Zoe grabs my *Remain in Light* tape and shoves it into the tape player, and we yell out the lyrics all the way to the club. We pull into the parking lot, but before my car has stopped she's out the door marching across the gravel toward Club Foot. Inside she heads straight to the bar where she buys us each a margarita and a shot of tequila. She downs the shot, grins at me, then begins working on her margarita. I can hear Face starting up a song, their trademark layered melodies floating over a driving bass line. Before I finish my drink she's ordered us a second. After draining it she takes my hand and guides us toward the music, firing her spent plastic cup into the trash as we cross onto the dance floor. Soon we're dodging around the white pillars spaced throughout the floor. We run, hop, chase each other like a couple of kids while Face performs on the stage above us. Until she stumbles over another dancer's feet. I just manage to catch her before she hits the concrete floor. She hangs limp in my arms, laughing. I look up at Kyro at the keyboards. He raises a single eyebrow.

I hoist her up. Still laughing, she dances away to join a trio of women with whom she starts doing some sort of sixties go-go boogaloo. She's pretty good at it. I see Kyro watching her intently from the stage. I point to her and mouth the word to him, "Home." He nods and focuses back on his keyboard.

The only way I can talk her off the dance floor is to suggest we take a cigarette break outside. She staggers out the door, then leans against the wall where she can't quite manage to connect the tip of the flame from her lighter to her cigarette. Sweat shines on her face, spots her T-shirt.

"Maybe I drank too much," she says once she finally manages to light it.

"You had a hard day."

"No shit." She grimaces. The alcohol's really starting to kick in now, as I figured it would once I got her off the dance floor and gave her a moment to slow down. She's getting heavier, sinking against the wall. She blinks a few times.

"Sleepy?" I ask.

"No."

"Listen. It might be time to get you home."

"But *why*? We're having *fun*."

I back ten feet away from her. "Walk toward me in a straight line."

"Sure thing, officer." She throws down her cigarette, then takes about three steps before veering off the curb where I catch her. She starts laughing in my arms. "Sweet Jesus, I'm shitfaced."

Driving her home down South Congress, she starts patting my leg. "You are so great," she says. "I think you are just the best!"

"You're great too," I tell her.

She puts her hand on my thigh and leans toward me. I wish she hadn't. And I wish she would go farther. And now I don't know what to do. I don't want to openly reject her in her condition by pushing her away. I don't want to reject her at all. "Wanna know a secret?" she says.

I look over to see her grinning at me, inches from my face. I turn back to the road. "It might not be a good night to tell secrets."

She leans close to my ear and says softly, "I love you. I really do."

She hesitates, then falls back to her seat. I turn to see her smiling at me almost shyly. "I love you too, Zoe," I tell her. "I love you guys."

"The three of us should all get married," she says. "You, me, and Kyro."

"It wouldn't be legal."

"Don't be a sticky wicket. Our vows would be sanctioned by a higher law."

"Okay. We'll all get married."

"Yay!" she says. She sticks her head out the window and starts singing "Going to the Chapel."

When we reach her house she's so wasted I have to hook an arm around her waist to walk her to the door. I hold the screen door open for her as she fumbles to put her key in the lock. It finally turns, and the door opens into the dark living room. She glances back at me. "Wanna come in for . . . coffee?" she asks, then grins a little oddly, as if puzzled at herself.

I hesitate. "Might not be the best night for coffee."

"I know." She lets out a breath I didn't realize she was holding. "You're right," she says and begins patting my cheeks with both hands like she might a baby's. "You are . . . the best boy. You are . . . a good friend."

Her gesture seems so innocent and playful that I don't react in time when she pulls my face to hers and kisses me. And then I can't stop it. Or I won't. It is the sweetest kiss. It is gentle and clever and clear, like Zoe. Finally she breaks it. She looks down at the ground, then back up into my eyes.

"That's the only kiss like that you'll ever get from me."

"Okay."

"Because I'm drunk."

"I'm drunk too."

"But I won't regret it."

"Me either. Now go to bed."

"I've been a good girl, and you've been a good boy."

"Yes, we have."

"No. I mean, we've *really* been good."

"Yeah. And Kyro's been good too. He really loves you."

"More than anyone ever has. He's number 1!"

"And we have nothing to be embarrassed about. Because we were good."

"That's right."

"And I do love you, Zoe. Like a sister. Or something . . . or something else."

She hesitates. "But it's a good thing, right? Something else? A good thing."

"Yes. It's the best."

34

New York City

I stepped out the doors of the hospital carrying the envelope Jeremy gave me. I didn't want to risk bending it in my backpack. The early afternoon sun seemed too bright, the sky too blue, the people around me moving too quickly. I wasn't due back at the office for two hours, so I crossed the street and headed up Greenwich Avenue toward a tiny dive bar.

Inside the walls were dark wood, and the air almost too cool. I took a seat on one of the stools and ordered a shot of Jameson. There were a few men at the bar and a lone woman. A young couple was seated at a small table in back. The jukebox played, of all things, "Amarillo by Morning" by George Strait. Out the window pretty people walked by. I didn't want to go to work. I didn't want to go anywhere. The ground felt to be shifting beneath my feet and I needed to be still for awhile in the hope that it stopped. I took a sip of the whiskey, then walked to a payphone in back to call Alena.

"It's me," I said.

"Do I hear country music?"

"I'm in a bar."

"Work's light tonight. Take the rest of the evening off if you want."

"I'd like that."

"But please don't get drunk. See you at eleven."

I walked back to my seat where I knocked the shot back, then ordered a beer. I glanced around and wondered if any of the men or the woman at the bar, like me, had come from the hospital. I wondered how much business had picked up since the AIDS crisis really kicked in, and how the owners felt about such fortune.

The manila envelope rested on the wooden bar in front of me. I finally picked it up, peeled off the tape along its edge, and looked inside. As I suspected, it contained a photograph. I turned to look out the window again, watched the pedestrians step through the shadows of the buildings and the narrow creases of light. Then I pulled out the photograph, a ten-by-twelve-inch black-and-white shot of Alena. Bare from the shoulders up, she looks out a window covered in dots of rain, the fingertips of her right hand touching the glass. She might be wearing a towel below the frame, or her bathrobe with the shoulders pulled down, or nothing. The location was not her apartment. I wondered what she was looking at in the distance through the rain, or looking for.

One of the lesser parts of myself began careening around inside me in rage and fear, shouting that she and Jeremy had slept together. But it was such a small, weak part, I wasn't really listening. I was convinced that was not a possibility in their relationship. Jeremy had told me as much, which didn't mean he hadn't touched her in ways I never could.

~

"I need you tonight," I told her as I stepped through her door.

"I thought you needed me every night," she said.

"Every night I want you. That's different."

"I like 'want' better. My husband needs me. He's got needs. My daughter has needs. They're constant." She wrapped her arms around me. "But go ahead," she said. "This one time. I talk to Jeremy every day. I visit every chance I get. Cry, if that'll help."

"I don't know." I was hollowed out, distant from my own body.

"It's okay."

"I don't know what I need."

"He called me from the hospital after you left. He wanted me to tell you something he told me years ago. He said you wouldn't believe him because his mind is off, but you might believe it coming from me. So here's a story for you. Six years ago Jeremy was walking through the garment district when a little piece of pipe, maybe an inch-and-a-half long, fell from a building, who knows how many stories up, and it hit him in the head. Knocked out a piece of his skull. His brain was literally exposed to the air as he lay on the pavement. And he died. That was his experience anyway. He looked down and there was his body beneath him, just like everyone says happens, then he floated up and saw all these lights, and he knew it was all okay. Everything was, for the first time ever, right. But then something shifted in the lights, and they told him he had to go back. And so he fell to his body. He didn't want to go." She looked into my eyes. "This is his gift to you. He doesn't tell many people."

"What do you think about all that?"

"I don't know. He says people who've experienced this die quicker than others. They want to go back, so they check out, first chance they get." A sound started up from the other part of the apartment—Carina crying softly in her bedroom. Alena sighed. "She's been a real bother tonight." She patted me on my shoulder and stepped back. "All better?"

"I guess."

"We only have three weeks left. I don't want to be sad. I'll be sad when it's time to be sad. Okay?"

I nodded. "He gave me a picture of you."

"The one at the window?"

"Yes."

"I like that picture," she said walking from me down the dark hallway. I looked out the windows to the clocktower standing over Brooklyn. I took a seat on the couch and waited.

~

As soon as I stepped into the office the following Monday I knew something was wrong. No one looked up from their computers. Alena sat quietly at her desk scratching at papers. I turned on my machine, let it crank and rattle to life. There was a message from Jeremy waiting inside, sent to us all.

Dear friends,

I'm afraid my condition has taken a turn for the worse and by the time you are reading this I will have already left New York to join my family in Minneapolis. The Mayo Clinic in nearby Rochester is one of the best hospitals in the world so I'll be in good hands. I'll keep in touch regarding my condition through Alena.

Forgive me for not finding a way to say goodbye to you in person, but trust me, I did you a favor. I wouldn't visit this place unless I had to.

Until our paths cross again,

Jeremy

The light was too white in the room. My hands were unwilling to move to the keyboard. I looked up to see Carla from proofreading standing to the side of my desk watching me. "He was trying to be brave," she said. "He didn't want us to see him like this."

I nodded. She returned the nod somberly and knowingly, then walked back to her desk. I opened my desk drawer and found inside a single, tiny violet. So this would be the violets week. I carefully turned it between my thumb and forefinger, then looked through the glass wall of Alena's office to see her typing away on her computer. She surely knew I was at my desk by now. I wanted her to look up, to catch my eye and acknowledge me, felt I must talk to her if only for a moment. But she kept her head down. When at three o'clock she left gripping her purse, I nearly called out. She didn't look back, just awkwardly said over her shoulder, "I'm leaving early. Goodnight."

I came apart at her exit, didn't know how I would get through the next hour, let alone make it till the following night when I'd see her again. I had no assigned work to distract me, and the emptiness of the desk behind me was growing, spilling over. Thankfully an analyst appeared with an un-scheduled job, a small, perky young man in a new suit. Maybe he was twenty-four, fresh out of Wharton Business School, or Harvard, or Stanford. He looked shamefully young and his smile too earnest, as if by force of his intelligence and will and positive outlook he was certain he could control his future, make everything work out. I took the stack of work from him like a lifeline.

Once everyone left at five o'clock Carla came by again and began to prattle about how things wouldn't be the same without Jeremy, how much she'd miss him, how maybe out of everyone here she'd felt the closest to him. Marjorie remained silent at her desk across the room.

At 7:40 my phone rang. "I need you," Alena said.

~

I waited in front of the elevator in her lobby holding a small bouquet of violets. I had to call a half-dozen florists to find them, but as the doors opened and I stepped inside I considered how foolish I was to have carried them into her building. Few things made a man more conspicuous than flowers. This was how you get caught, I told myself. You get emotional and sloppy. You go for the sentimental gesture and take your eye off the ball for one moment. I reached to push 7, but the elevator bucked, and instead of going up it started dropping down. Something was wrong. What if there was a malfunction and I got stuck? Then I realized it was dropping down to the basement. Who would be down in the basement so late at night? The car settled with a thunk, like a lead hammer dropped to concrete, and I realized how trapped I would be if someone was waiting outside the doors for me. But when they opened, no one was there. I heard the rumble of the building and its machinery.

But as the doors started to shut again there was a sudden shout and flurry of movement, then a man leapt to the doors, slapped one of them, and they opened. He stood staring at me with dark eyes, dark hair, tanned skin, a prominent nose. He was muscular, an inch shorter than me in a white Izod shirt, shorts, and tennis shoes. Her husband, it dawned on me, was taller.

"I said," he told me slowly, as if I were an idiot, "Hold the door." He spotted the violets in my hand, then looked up and smirked.

"Sorry," I said.

"How's it going? Listen. I'll be right back. Hold the door, alright?" I nodded and he disappeared, then dragged four full plastic laundry baskets, one after the next, onto the elevator. "Christ," he said, "I hate doing laundry. I bought four weeks of underwear and socks just so I don't gotta do laundry but once a month. But then, you know. It's a long night."

To my relief, he pushed 5 and the elevator began to rise. It stopped at the first floor and the doors opened to the empty lobby. "C'mon," he said to the elevator, pressing the number 5 over and over. At last the doors closed again. He looked my way, then back ahead and grinned. "Nice flowers," he said.

"Thanks."

"Fight with the wife?"

"No. Girlfriend," I said, taking his cue.

He nodded. "What floor?"

My heart froze. I didn't know what to say. Was he serious?

He looked over at me. "What floor do you want to stop at?" he said, gesturing to the panel of elevator buttons with his thumb.

I realized I'd never even pushed her floor. That was lucky. "Nine," I said. I started breathing again. I didn't know I'd stopped.

He nodded, pushed 9, then leaned back against the wall until the elevator stopped and its doors opened on 5.

"Can you hold that?" he asked, and dragged the first two baskets to an apartment a few feet away. I blocked the elevator door with my back and set the third clothes basket in the hall, then the fourth. "Thanks," he said as he fumbled with his keys. "That's good. That's fine." This was no trick; he really did live here.

"Good luck," he told me with a wink as the doors closed. The elevator carried me up to the ninth floor where I stepped into the nearest stairwell and followed it down to 7. I peered through the stairwell door window to make sure the hall was empty, then looked down at the bouquet of tiny purple flowers. Now I'd been spotted and would no doubt be remembered. The guy was just a tenant, but we were one step closer to getting caught.

I stepped into her hallway, my heart starting to race, my feet making too much noise. I reached for her door, pulled it open, and slipped inside.

She fell into my arms before the door swung shut, weeping like she was breaking, holding me so tightly it frightened me. "Jeremy's gone. He's really gone," she said. I didn't know what to do except be a mooring and not tear loose in the emotions buffeting her. With my left hand I reached back blindly, found the lock on the door, and turned it. Now we were safe. We were safe until it was time for me to leave again. I wanted to tell her about the man who spotted me, but I'd wait till later. What difference did it make? There was no ending this until it ended itself. From now on I'd ride the elevator up to 9, walk down two floors to 7, and scan her hall before stepping in. I should've thought of that before. Still, there was no way I could be certain of protecting her, and for the first time I accepted that. This was who we were together. We were counting on luck, and the nights left us to run out.

I led her to our sheet on the carpet, and for the first time we lay together fully clothed. She fell asleep within minutes, her head on my chest, her tears soaked through my shirt. Her breathing deepened and lengthened, and each breath seemed to sink into me and find home. My arm began to go numb under her. "Alena," I said trying to wake her, but she didn't respond. When I lifted her she protested and gripped me tighter. "Just get to your feet." She muttered more protest, but I hooked my arm around her waist and led her to the bedroom. There I removed the white robe and guided her into her bed. She managed to keep hold of my arm and pulled me in with her, frowning and murmuring burbles of words in what language I couldn't tell. I kicked off my shoes, pulled the sheet over us.

As we held each other I watched the shadows on the ceiling again. They were particularly active tonight because of the wind through the trees outside. The shadows didn't belong to her husband, I decided, only the ceiling they played upon. They belonged to no one, but perhaps they favored me as I was more like them. They swept and danced and jittered, and I considered this man whose home I desecrated, wondered what he was doing at that moment, and where. Earlier I was afraid he'd set me up for a hit in his basement. I'd seen too many Mafia movies. Still, I couldn't say I would blame him. I couldn't say I wouldn't want to do the same if I were in his shoes. It dawned on me I didn't know his name. I didn't want to know his name.

I kept an eye on the bedside clock and was careful to not get lulled to sleep. Her body, as always, felt like it belonged against mine. I breathed in her scent, absorbed her almost narcotic warmth until the clock read 2:30. Then carefully I disentangled from her. I walked into the living room where the violets I'd brought her ended up loose on the coffee table. I found a small vase in the kitchen and set the flowers inside with a little water, then carried it into her bedroom and placed it on her nightstand. I pulled the sheet up around her shoulders, kissed her softly, and let myself out the door.

~

I woke the next morning, still half in dream, with the idea of letting her take my life. It seemed correct somehow. Right. Something in me wanted it. I imagined her astride me, maybe holding an ice pick. I closed my eyes for a moment, then opened them, fully awake, the image fading.

That night she was in a hurry. She took me inside her before she was ready and flinched at the brief pain. Afterward I couldn't seem to give it to her hard enough to satisfy her. She drew me faster into her, more insistently until I was pounding her, when she said plaintively, "You're hurting me."

I stopped, horrified at myself. "I'm sorry," I said. "I'm so sorry."

"It's okay. Don't stop."

I began moving again, slowly, like rocking a cradle. "I love you," I told her.

"Don't say that."

"I just wanted you to know."

"I know. Now hush. Do what you do."

Afterward as I lay beside her I asked, "Why did you put me in you before you were ready?"

"So it'd hurt."

"Why did you want it to hurt?"

"It makes more sense that way."

"What do you mean?"

"How many nights do we have left together?"

"Seven. We've got seven nights left."

She took a quick intake of air, then let it out slowly. "See?"

35

Austin, Texas, 1984

Kyro has thrown a costume party and as usual refuses to play anything other than local music. The Big Boys are thrashing through his stereo speakers with their funk backbeat hardcore speed-punk, complete with horn section. It's 10:30, and fifty or so people are spilling from his house into the backyard where a keg floats in a plastic garbage can filled with ice. Some neighbors stand about with plastic cups in their hands, but most are musicians and people associated with the scene.

When The Big Boys song ends, Jimmie Dale Gilmore's acoustic "Tonight I Think I'm Gonna Go Downtown" starts up to a chorus of dismay, less because of Gilmore than the abrupt change in style and rhythm. Folks are in a jumping-and-dancing state of mind, but Kyro loves to throw curve-balls onto the party tapes he makes just to rattle people. He spends hours painstakingly designing them.

His costume consists of a charcoal-gray second-hand "Hef"-style smoking jacket with silk lapels from which his bare, pale legs extend into fuzzy pink slippers, and a navy-blue pillbox hat perched at a rakish angle on top of his head. He's smoking a joint torqued into the end of a seven-inch-long black cigarette holder and using the device to punctuate his rantings, which at the moment sounds like a spirited defense of Jimmie Dale Gilmore. With his hat, recently dyed blond hair, and black eyeliner, I decide he looks like Marlene Dietrich. From the neck up at least, and I tell him.

"Thanks," he says. He looks me over. "I see you put a lot of thought into your costume, John."

I only wear a cheap Zorro mask I picked up at a drugstore. "I try to do my part," I say, but Kyro doesn't hear me. He's staring over my head toward the open door where an unattended blond stands at the threshold, lost in a white, hand-stitched wedding cake of a dress that looks like it's been passed from mother to daughter for generations. She's small, delicate, and can't be older than twenty-two. Her "raccoon" eyes are blackened by mascara, and two dark perfect tear lines trail down her face. The sorrowful bride incarnate. It's such an amazing costume, and she looks so great in it, I hurry to the doorway where she's still standing to introduce myself. When I ask what I can get her to drink, she looks at me as if she'd been expecting me.

"Tequila," she says, finally taking a step into the house.

"In what form?" She stares at me like I'm a moron. I try again. "What would be your delivery medium of choice?" She crosses her arms, glances back out the door at the night. I'm losing her. "How about a shot?" I say.

"Make it a double."

So that's the game. She wants to misbehave and needs a boy to help her. I turn and push my way through the bodies blocking the door into the kitchen. Not seeing anything resembling a shot glass, I grab a juice glass and a coffee cup out of the dish rack and estimate a double from an unclaimed bottle of Cuervo on the counter, then quickly cut two wedges of lime and pour a small pile of salt onto a chipped but clean yellow coffee saucer I find in the cupboard. I carry the works back into the living room and am a little surprised to find her still alone, as if the circumference of her wedding dress has created some sort of force field excluding everyone but me. She stares at the twinkling lights on Kyro's plastic Christmas tree. She takes a deep breath, then releases it. Her guard has dropped. She looks a little lost, seeking something in those Christmas lights. "Your drink," I say, stepping up to her.

As she turns to me her mask—her disaffected expression—falls back into place. What is she thinking? What kind of girl would wear such a costume? And I feel the gears moving beneath us, the machinery bringing us together so long as I don't misstep, so long as she doesn't spook. She sees the plate I've brought her and studies the glassware. "Lovely," she says. She picks the coffee cup as it holds the most tequila and, ignoring the salt and lime, knocks the contents back. By her response the liquor might have been tea. Not wanting to be shown up, I also gulp mine without biting the lime, but I shudder as the tequila goes down. When it hits my belly my forehead breaks out in a sweat. I yank off my mask.

"I hate masks," I say, trying to recover. "Can't see through the damn things." I see she's studying me. I feel my stomach settle, the color returning to my face.

"I like your eyes," she tells me.

On impulse I touch my finger to the beginning of the mascara trail at the corner of her right eye. It feels wet and my finger comes away damp and darkened. I touch the same finger to the edge of her left eye and brush down its trail, follow the moisture past where the mascara ends, to her jawline. Fresh tears. I put my finger to my mouth, taste a trace of salt mixed with inky mascara. Her black pupils expand into her gold-brown irises.

"I'm sorry you've been crying," I say.

"Hi," she says.

I reach down and take her left hand in my right, finger her wedding ring while I keep my eyes on hers. The ring feels dense. I look down at the gold band.

"This feels real," I say.

"Bite it to make sure," she tells me, "if that'll speed things up."

~

There are no streetlights where we walk along this small, curving lane. She'd asked if there was a park nearby, "or something like that." The music from Kyro's party, which now sounds like it has switched back to punk, recedes like clatterings from a toybox. The shale-blue pavement reflects light from the high half-moon and the random porch lights shining from the houses we pass. Tap-tap, tap-tap, go our shoes, like small markers against the silence. Tap-tap. Live oaks and their broad limbs reach across the road over us, dark against the blue-black sky.

The moment begins to feel strained—our footsteps sounding against the pavement, our hands now gripping each other's. I decide to speak, to be casual, to cool off my mind and hers to the situation, to behave as if this stranger, this woman in a wedding dress and I, weren't specifically scouting out a location to have sex.

"So," I begin. "How long have you known Kyro?"

"Who's Kyro?"

"The guy who threw the party."

"Never met him."

"How'd you get an invitation?"

"I didn't."

Best to shut up, I decide. We walk about ten more steps before she speaks again.

"Tonight's my wedding night," she tells me quietly.

"It's a great costume."

"No, really. I got married about five hours ago to my loser ex-boyfriend. You were right. The ring is real."

My fantasy of her morphs into reality and the image of some crazed new husband combing the streets in a pick-up truck flashes through my head. Her white wedding dress glows in the dark like a second moon. "Where is he?" I ask as casually as I can manage.

"Passed out on the bed. There's a bed-and-breakfast two blocks from your party. It was supposed to be our pre-honeymoon suite. We were supposed to fly to Bermuda tomorrow. But instead of being with me on our wedding night the son-of-a-bitch goes out with his drinking buddies and gets shitfaced. Then he finally shows up after I've been waiting three hours and passes out cold on the bed. I left him there and started walking. I saw the party lights." She shakes her head. "Why would he not want . . ." she says and breaks away from me. She starts crying, standing there in the middle of the street.

"He's a boy," I tell her.

She suddenly laughs. "You're not even my type."

"Then what are we doing here?"

She wipes her face with her free hand. "Okay. Tonight you're my perfect type. You're small and artsy, and you enjoy being smart. You think it's fun. And you'll never have money. You're everything he isn't."

"That's good?"

"Tonight it's good." She shrugs. "You have kind eyes. I wasn't expecting that."

"In who?"

"In who I chose to fuck me." She pauses to let me take that in, as if proud of her daring to say such a thing.

"Are you sure about this?"

She takes a step toward me. "It's my *wedding* night. You know? I'm having sex, whether my . . . so-called husband does or not. That is . . . I mean . . ." She hesitates, weakening. "If you're . . ."

"Interested?" I say the word quickly so she won't have to. "You're kidding, right?"

"Because if you're not I'm sure someone at the party . . ."

"Hush. You're a walking talking fantasy."

She smiles faintly. What I said was enough. She reaches out to take my hand, and for a moment I almost feel sorry for the jerk she's cheating on. But if a guy does what he did he's not just asking for it, he's demanding it.

We soon turn onto a side street, and the park opens up before us. We set off across the grass and open space. I wonder how odd we would appear to someone passing by—a young man in jeans and a dark shirt beside his bride in white floating across the open moonlit field. The scene might be strangely pastoral, something from another century. Ahead a live oak that has to be seventy years old stands against the horizon, its broad limbs reaching out, curving and bending over the slope of the hillside it seems to own. We stop for a moment, staring at it. She looks my way.

"Your dress is beautiful," I say.

"It was my great-grandmother's."

"We'll have to be careful not to ruin it."

"It's too late," she tells me. "It's a burden. Let's wreck it."

She smiles. She insists. So we do it, under the tree, ripping the dress, smearing grass stains on her skirt, forcing runs in her stockings. We are in cahoots, we are in league, we are pals, and afterward we're laughing, lying back in each other's arms and staring up through the empty branches at the dark sky and its stars. It is such a joy to be chosen by this girl, used even. It's a gift, and only a fool would not acknowledge it.

～

We walk side-by-side back toward the party. Soon we hear the tinny clatter from Kyro's party and begin to slow. She stops, grips my hand.

"You gonna be alright?" I ask.

"I haven't been alright since six o'clock. Longer really. Maybe six months. Maybe a year. He cheated on me four months ago, by the way. With a friend. The wedding was already set. I thought we worked through it."

"Maybe you're better finding out sooner than later."

"That it was a mistake?"

"Maybe you can get it annulled."

"God," she says, sinking as if an enormous weight has landed onto her small frame. "Returning gifts . . . my family . . . it's all going to be so humiliating." She shakes her head. "Fuck it. Fuck it all."

"That's right," I say.

She slides her hand into my back pocket, and we begin walking toward the lights of the party again. I feel her fingers claiming me.

"You coming inside?" I ask as we approach the house.

"My husband is waiting for me in bed, my love. I need to climb in beside him like the good little wife that I am."

I consider what her groom would be waking to. "Do you need a place to stay?"

"I have a place to stay."

Through Kyro's blinds I see shadows of people jumping up and down to the raucous music. The tiny wood frame house seems to be shaking.

"I'm just thinking," I tell her, "it might be wise for you to spend the night elsewhere."

She pulls away from me and turns a full circle. "After I got all dressed up for him?"

In the streetlight I see the ruined dress covered with stems and leaves. Add to that the grass stains, the muss of her hair, the smeared lipstick and mascara, the torn white stockings. Which is the look she wanted, the look I was more than willing to help her achieve, the look that would greet her jerkoff boyfriend-husband-whatever come morning along with his hang-over. It's all come together. I've helped it all come together.

"But really," I say. "His reaction might be pretty strong. Irrational."

She laughs. "Maybe that's the idea."

"You can stay at my place tonight. Start fresh tomorrow."

She puts her hand on the back of my neck and looks up at me. The corners of her mouth lift, then she pulls me to her and kisses me. It is a long, slow, deep kiss. "You're yummy," she says when she breaks it off, "but it's time for us to part."

She's acting, getting into her role again, but when she pulls away I grab her hand. "Then go home," I tell her. "Go someplace else. To a girlfriend's house." A trace of doubt flickers across her face. I've helped propel her toward a precipice. "I'll drive you wherever you want," I say.

She wrenches her hand free from mine. "But . . ."

"But what?"

Her mouth twists in anger. "I want him to *see*."

We stare at each other. In Kyro's yard a few people mill about. From the house, Butch Hancock softly and raggedly sings "If You Were a Bluebird." I see where she's headed. I reach for her hand again, but she pulls it away.

"I thought you understood," she says.

Her lips tremble, and then she's crying, her small shoulders shaking. I know I can move to her if I move slowly. So I do, then take her in my arms. "He's not worth it," I tell her. "He's just a fool who doesn't deserve you."

"I know, but . . ."

"Walk away. Spend the night with me or a friend. Don't crawl into bed with him. Please. Please don't do that." She tips her forehead to my chest. "You're gorgeous and wild," I tell her, trying to say the right things, things she wants to hear that are also true. "He did you a favor. Did you really want to be married to this guy? This is the luckiest night of your life, when you slipped out of the noose. There are better guys out there. Better for you."

She looks up at me. "You've been a surprise."

"So have you."

"But we could never date. Because of how we met. Cheating. It would bring bad luck."

"What are you going to do?"

She shrugs. "Okay. I'll go to a friend's."

"Do you want me to drive you? Or call a cab?"

"I'm parked on the street."

As we walk to her car I put my arm around her waist, and she sags against me. We stop less than a block away in front of her dark Chrysler. She looks toward the two-story bed-and-breakfast she parked in front of, a light still lit in the right upper window where her husband is sleeping stupidly, naively, unconscious to how his future has just been rewritten. She turns to me. "I want to give you something," she says.

"You already have."

"No. I mean something to keep. They took my veil and garter. I'd give you my ring but it's toxic."

"You should give it back to him anyway. To break the cycle."

She hesitates, then reaches down to a rip at the bottom of her skirt and peels off a strip of fabric. She rolls it up and hands it to me.

"Thank you," I say, taking it. Her hair shimmers in the streetlight, as blond and light as Kari's. As I reach out and touch it, she leans up to kiss me on my cheek, then steps back and slides into her car. She rolls down her window and looks up at me. "Adios, amigo. Compadre," she says. "Whatever you are."

"Buena suerte."

"It all sounds so much prettier in Spanish," she says, and pulls away. I'm overcome with a sudden urge to run after her. Then she turns a corner and is gone. I look at the fabric in my hand, when a woman's arm suddenly loops through my own. I jump at the contact before realizing it's Zoe.

"What was that all about?" she asks. I clench the fabric in my fist to hide it. Zoe's guiding me toward her house. "Come back to the party," she tells me.

Car lights hit us from behind, then a taxi rolls by. "I think I'm partied out for the night," I say. I wonder if Zoe was watching us, if the girl's scent is on me, if Zoe will catch it. If she knows what I'm holding in my hand.

"But it's early," she says. There's an irritation in her voice I've never heard before. "You haven't danced with me yet."

"I'm pooped."

"What have you been up to, John, that you're so pooped? And who was that girl?"

"I don't know."

"You don't know?" She steps in front of me and studies my face in the light from her porch, then begins wiping at my cheek with a finger. "What's this? What's this stuff?" She rolls a stain of mascara between her finger and thumb, then looks at my mouth. "Have you started wearing lipstick, John?" she says. She reaches up and plucks a small, round leaf from my hair. "Did you just pick up some random girl? And have sex with her? Like in someone's front yard?"

"No. We went to the park."

"The park?" Her voice is so loud it seems to echo. She glances around, then whispers, "The park?"

"She wasn't random."

"Who was she then?"

"A girl with . . ."

"What? A girl with what? And her name, John? Did you catch it?"

I have no answer. It's true—I don't know her name. What does that mean? What does that say? If anything. Zoe drops the leaf. "This is . . . I don't know," she says. "Disappointing, I guess." She turns and walks away from me and up the concrete steps to her house where she pulls open the screen door, then looks back at me for one long moment before disappearing inside, the screen door banging behind her. Gone in an instant, like a deer into a forest.

36

When I come into work I see Zoe smiling and talking to a cashier. She looks happy. For a moment it seems like an ordinary day. "Hi," I say, and in an instant she turns to give me the most chilling look I've ever received. And it's as if the ground has given way beneath my feet. She begins talking to the cashier again, laughing casually, cheerfully.

For the rest of the day she looks straight through me if she looks at me at all, and at each instance I am exiled. She takes her cigarette breaks alone. I'm as confused by the intensity of my reaction as I am at hers. I see Kyro in the bulk aisle and approach him carefully. It feels odd, enlisting him to help resolve the relationship between me and his girlfriend. Especially after that kiss at her—and his—door earlier in the summer. I worried after the kiss she and I might be awkward working together. Instead it seemed to make us closer. It was our secret, and our not going farther that night allowed it to stand. I've often thought she told Kyro about the kiss, that he understood and let it go, though I could be imagining this. He may know nothing. He probably knows nothing and prefers it that way. The thought does cross my mind, though, when I'm alone with him. On one hand, I kissed his girl; on the other, I took care of her, as well as him. I did not cross the line when she was drunk and I had the chance. I've been proud of this, but of course I've never brought it up.

Kyro's standing on a stepstool emptying a sack of brown rice into a bin. He replies before I've said a word, without even turning to look at me. "I'm sympathetic, but I can't help you."

"What should I do?"

He glances down the aisle for Zoe, then back at the bin. "Give her time. She takes time. I tried to tell her you were a free agent, that she had no stake, but she didn't like hearing it so I shut up. She's slow to anger, but once she gets there it's not pretty."

"All because of that girl?"

"She says there's more to it."

"I don't understand."

"Honestly, John. I don't either. But . . ." He frowns.

"What?"

"I've never seen you put moves on a girl like that."

"Like what?"

"Like someone who knows how to put moves on a girl."

I hesitate. This makes no sense. "She was interesting."

"She was. Don't get me wrong, I always wished I could do it. I was always so self-conscious. Now I don't need to, of course. Anyway, if I can help you out I will. For now, I recommend letting it rest."

I struggle through the rest of my shift. As the hours pass I begin to get angry, as much at me as her for allowing myself to be so easily manipulated, for being weak, small, devastated, frightened. Haven't I earned her friendship? Don't I, and our relationship, deserve better? Finally I get enough of it. She doesn't understand what happened between me and the girl. Neither do I really, but I know it mattered, and even if I was selfish or wrong, I still believe I somehow helped her and I'm not going to be ashamed of it. However you slice it, it's none of Zoe's business. And I wonder if the bride's okay, if she's through the worst of it, if she thinks of me. I remember the strip from her wedding dress she gave me, how her hair looked like Kari's under the streetlight.

And that's all it takes. In my mind I'm reaching out to touch Kari's hair. Then I'm setting a brush into it. Preparing her for that brutal boy. And I'm falling and the world is falling with me.

Suddenly a child careens into my knees and falls at my feet in front of the carrots and the eggplants. He'd been running. I have some vague sense of him having run from his mother laughing. He hesitates, as if deciding what to do, then begins bawling.

"I'm so sorry," I tell his mother.

She's thick waisted and wearing a flowing, beige skirt. She picks him up and holds him to her chest as she rolls her eyes at me. "There's always the drama with this one." She turns to the boy and begins to bounce him. "Isn't that right, baby?" she says, carrying him away.

I realize I'm so bent out of shape at Zoe's reaction that I'm knocking over children. I'm embarrassed and sick of it all. Nothing sounds better than getting away from her, from Austin for a few days. And I consider that Kari never saw me when she checked into rehab. I showed up afterward when it was safe and the worst was over. Does she even know I was there? Amanda said she told her, but does she remember? Maybe she could use a visitor. Maybe she's due that much from her brother. I could apologize. I could begin there.

I talk to my manager and arrange a few days off from work, then call the airlines and buy a ticket on a flight to Tucson. As soon as it's done it feels like I've stepped out of a harness, like I've claimed back a piece of my life. I manage the string of workdays till I leave. When I pass Zoe I don't bother to look at her.

~

"Hello, little brother," Kari says when she meets me in the lobby. Her face is drained, dry, washed out. She wears no makeup, and her pale features disappear beneath her chopped, dyed, jet-black hair. Its color unnerves me. She's thinner than I've ever seen her, and her subtle curves have straightened into lines. I try not to appear shocked at her appearance, at the fact that she now looks older than either Amanda or Catherine.

"Aren't you all grown up and sexy," she says. "When did that happen?"

"You look good, Kari."

"No I don't." She turns and I follow her through the lobby outside to the clinic grounds in back where we sit on a bench. I think of how we once sat beside each other on the swings at home and the way the breeze nudged us as we'd sway over the ground. She offers me a Marlboro from a pack, which I decline, then lights it for herself.

"I'm sorry," I tell her.

"For what?

"I wasn't here for you. When they checked you in."

She laughs. "Don't worry about it, honey. I wasn't here for me either." She's never called me "honey" before. The word doesn't fit her. "Besides, you're the first one to see me since. You drive all the way out?"

"I flew."

"You're sweet. Still in Austin?"

"Yeah."

"How's that working out?"

"Good. I mean it was good."

"Till when?"

"It's fine."

"Girl trouble?"

"It's complicated."

"No kidding."

In the sunlight I see fine lines fanning from the edges of her eyes. Then I notice a tiny scar over her left cheekbone. From a . . . man's ring? I picture the hit and hear the awful sound of it, and am panicked, helpless, grasping for any foothold as I try to cover, to hide any trace of my reaction. How did she come to such circumstances? How do we fall so far? What have I come here to do? I don't know.

I hear the words, "How are you doing?" leave my mouth stiffly, forced. If she notices she doesn't care. She takes a puff.

"It's boring. It's awful. It's hour after hour. I can't get a drink. I can't get a man." She waves the cigarette in the air. "We're not supposed to, anyway. You know . . . fraternize." She shakes her head. "Good thing, good thing," she says. "Because it's always the same men."

Or the same man, I think. It's always Gary Phillips. She puffs on her cigarette and looks at me, then turns her gaze to the expanse of bright green grass over the clinic grounds. This, in a desert. The sky is blue and cloudless. Her skin looks so pale as to almost be translucent. Before I realize it I've taken her right hand in my left. It feels small, like a little bird. I haven't held her hand since I was a child, and mine has never before felt larger than hers. Who is she, this girl, this woman, this burnout, my sister?

She puffs on the cigarette in her free hand. "For the record, Amanda calls. All the time, in fact. When did she become Miss Do-Good? Mother, not much. As usual, she's all 'front.' No calls from Catherine, of course." She shakes her head. "I was not like them, you know. I was never like them, and it's taken me this long to figure it out." She looks up at me. "I was like *you*," she says. But she blinks, angles her head. "Although . . . my god, do you know who you look like? You look like Amanda." She withdraws her hand from mine, and with it plucks the cigarette from her left. She puffs away. "Is this a recent development?"

"I don't know."

"Say 'thank you.' It's a compliment."

"Thank you."

She shrugs. "I guess I let you down."

"I was twelve. What did I know?" But another part responds that yes, she did let me down. She came up short and everything broke. And I'm a sixth grader with no place to put my confusion. Then I'm a seventh grader and know I should never have pushed her to go away to college. She wasn't ready. She should've taken a year or two, gone to a school nearby. She was never strong. But I pushed her anyway. Like I wanted her gone. Then she was. They all were gone. Kari has turned toward me. She's watching me. And I see myself as an eighth grader trying not to think about it anymore, trying to be a normal kid, trying to blend in, glad my sisters hardly ever call.

She leans toward me. "What the hell are you still doing in Texas?"

I'm surprised by her question. "I don't know," I say.

"Take it from me, it's time to start knowing. And another thing I always wondered. Why did you go to UT? Just an hour from the house? Why didn't you try to get the hell out like the rest of us?"

"Mother said Daddy's money was running low so I'd need to go to college in-state."

Kari's lips curl in the beginning of a smile, one that's ironic, trained to accept pain as comical, whether given or received. And I know what she's going to say before she says it. I want to stop her, but now there's no point.

"And you believed her?" she says. She holds the look, cuts me with it, then turns back to the clinic grounds, the smile stuck to her face. "She used that money like a champ, didn't she? To get us out of the house and, it seems, to keep you nearby."

So Mother lied to me. Did I just accept it without thinking? Worse, beneath it all did I always know? My grades were good. My test scores exceptional. I could've gone anywhere. Duke, Berkeley, USC, Boston College . . .

"There's plenty of money," she says, taking a puff. "Always has been."

My head's spinning with what she's told me, with what choices I could've made, and didn't. "Austin's a great town," I tell her.

"I'm sure. How often do you see her?"

"Every three months or so. I drive down and have dinner with them, then leave. Because I'm just up the road I don't have to spend the night."

"I've thought how lucky it was for you that Aunt Phyllis moved in and got all codependent with Mother," she says. "Took you off the hook." She glances my way again, takes a puff. She's enjoying this. "You should've left town though. Shoulda got outta Dodge." She lights another cigarette from the butt of the first, then stomps the butt out. She shrugs, lets out a breath. "Amanda tells me you've got this art thing you do."

It's hard to speak. It's hard to respond naturally. I can't remember what I told Amanda about my art. I can't remember I told her anything. "Typography," I say.

"What?"

"It's design," I tell her. "Posters and stuff."

"Then where would you go for that?" she asks. "Where do people like you find that kind of work?" She raises her head to meet my eyes. Hers are pale green with light flecks of brown. Have they always been that color? Or is it the light? "I mean," she says, her voice softening for the first time, "where would you go to find people like yourself?"

"Los Angeles, San Francisco," I tell her. "New York City." The answers come surprisingly easily. They've been there all along.

"Then what are you waiting for? Go, little brother. Go go go go go. While you can. Don't be like me. Don't do what I did."

"What was that?"

She looks away. "I dunno."

"But, Kari. You left home. You left Texas."

"No I didn't. Not really."

37

It is such a long, slow walk with Kari back through the clinic lobby. No one here meets your eyes, and it smells as sterile as death. I have trouble finding air to sustain me. We have nothing more to say. I can't wait to get away from her, something inside me already starting to buck, to panic, as if she's contagious and I'll become like her if I'm exposed to her for long, as if I will collapse as she collapsed. She drifts in front of me. Her hand carries her cigarette to her mouth, back to her hip, then to her mouth again. Finally we step out the front doors, glance at each other a moment, exchange a brief, brittle hug.

As I walk toward the parking lot I look back up the slope to see her watching me. It dawns on me this is the first time any of my sisters stayed behind and *I* left. Her figure forms a straight line. Like a matchstick. She doesn't wave before turning to go back inside. As the door closes behind her I take a breath. I can breathe, and it all seems miraculous, this knowledge I now carry, and all I want to do is run with it. I want to run to my rental car, speed back to the airport, get on a plane and fly away from her. From my long-lost sister. From her failure and mine. Down to Austin. Where I'll empty my meager savings. I will leave the state, finally. Finally, I will move away. I will move to New York City.

～

When I call Mother to tell her, she starts crying. "Now I'll be all alone," she says.

"No you won't."

"Your sisters never visit."

I begin to strangle at her words, at the sound of her voice. "You've got Aunt Phyllis," I say. She's sobbing now, unable to speak. Every moment I remain on the line weakens me. But maybe it weakens her too. At last she grows quiet.

"Do you need money?" she asks.

"No," I tell her, and she begins crying again.

~

The next day I give notice to Whole Foods, and that quickly it is done. I'll be taking the money I have in the bank and betting it all that I can find a way to survive in New York City before it all runs out. I surprise Zoe in the back room, catch her alone for a moment, and tell her I'm leaving. She looks down at the ground. She sighs, then puts her arms around my neck. I feel their weight. Then she touches her forehead to mine before walking away.

On my final workday they throw a small party for me in the break room complete with a big white cake from the bakery. At the end of my shift I shake hands, exchange phone numbers, promise to keep in touch. I search the store for Zoe but can't find her. I grab my backpack, figuring I'll call her later to try and set a time to see her and Kyro before I leave. I step out the back door for the last time. There Zoe sits on the concrete ledge, smoking a cigarette and pretending not to notice me. Heat rises from the asphalt as I walk across it to sit beside her. Insects buzz in the trees. She sighs. She looks beaten.

"How's it going?" I ask.

She shrugs. "When do you fly out?"

"Day after tomorrow."

"You must be pretty excited." There's a bitter edge to her voice.

"Aren't we past this yet?"

"I wish, but . . ."

"But what? Will you please talk to me?"

She shakes her head, her anger flaring even as she tries to control it. "Back door man," she mutters.

"What?"

"The blues song by Howlin' Wolf. About the man a gal slips around with when she's in a slipping-around mood. That's cheating, John. In case you didn't know." She focuses her dark eyes on mine. "It's lying. Whichever end of the stick you're on."

"What the hell are you talking about?"

"Just tell me. How many girls have you cheated with?"

"Since when?"

"Since you came to Whole Foods. Let's start there."

I think back, all the way from New Braunfels till now. Of course I think of Laura. I was seventeen, shy, invisible to my classmates and felt blessed by her, chosen. But none since the night I flew back from Tucson and met Marsha at The Continental Club. And the one girl after her, a small, muscled, punk rock girl with dyed red hair named Marlene. But there was another girl too, a sweet young waitress at a coffeeshop where I'd dropped in for years late at night. She said she liked how I listened to her. She liked my touch, and she was bored with her boyfriend but didn't know how to break up with him. All in all, it doesn't seem that bad, that egregious, that awful.

"Three," I tell Zoe. I refuse to apologize for it. "Besides the girl at your party."

"She was cheating?"

"Yes. She was done with her . . ." I don't want to say the word "husband." The word carries too much weight. It doesn't feel accurate. They were never married; they just went through a ceremony. "So that makes four, I guess." It's more than I would've thought, though I've never really considered it. Still, it's not that many. We're young, and people find themselves locked into relationships they shouldn't be in. They get out however they can.

Zoe looks surprised, maybe even disappointed. "Are you sure that's all?" she asks.

"No. I'm lying."

She turns away. "But I heard . . ."

"What did you hear? And from who?"

She shakes her head. "A rumor. I guess. Girls talk."

I wonder who started the rumor and what they knew, or thought they knew. "And you believed it."

"It's still too many, John. It's not right or smart."

"Fine. But for what it's worth, I liked those girls. Scratch that, I *like* them. A lot. And they were sweet to me, generous, and they were all with real assholes for boyfriends."

"So you helped them."

"I'm not going to feel bad about it. It was their call, by the way. They approached me." Except for the bride, I consider. But she definitely came to the party dead-set on picking someone up. And what did she do afterward? She kissed my cheek. She gave me a piece of her wedding dress. I start to tell Zoe about it but stop myself. It's too personal. I don't want to share it. "Zoe," I say, "when did it become your business?"

She looks down at the asphalt. "Four? Four girls?"

"Over three years."

She shrugs. "It still seems like a pattern. But I thought it was worse. I suppose it's not my business. Kyro told me it wasn't. It was, just, humiliating. Finding out . . . why didn't you tell me?"

"You want me to kiss and tell?"

"I guess. For me, anyway. Do you think you'll ever come back?"

"I don't know."

"Remember that night . . . when we drank too much? Correction, when I drank too much. Anyway, I remember it. And I remember I asked you if you wanted coffee. And then I kissed you. And the next day I was so grateful, you know, that you did the right thing. I mean, I thought what a stand-up guy you were. Because . . . I mean, if you'd come in . . ." She trails off, shakes her head. "And then . . . I heard about you and supposedly all these girls. So I thought, you know, you didn't come in that night because . . . maybe you didn't want to."

It hurts to hear the words. "You thought I was this slut for everyone but you? If I wasn't sure Kyro was the right guy for you we would've never made it to your house. We wouldn't have gotten out of the parking lot."

"I'd started thinking before all this . . . that maybe that's why you don't have a girlfriend. Because of . . . me? Because we hang out so much? Maybe if you weren't with me you would've found a girl? And stuck around?"

"It's just time I left. I feel it, you know? In my bones. Like I can't be . . . completed here." I lean toward her. "You're so important to me. Do you have any idea? It killed me when you hated me. It crippled me."

She nods and looks down at the asphalt. A tear runs down her cheek. "I never hated you, John. Hate was never the problem with you."

38

The airplane tilts its wings, and through the tiny window the broad, green expanse of Central Park opens up through a summer haze. My heart pounds in my chest so rapidly I wonder for a moment if I'm having a heart attack. I don't know if it's ever beaten so. But as I realize there's no physical pain I figure it's simply terror, and then it slows, just a little. The plane straightens its wings, and we begin our descent. I touch the cross beneath my shirt, press it against my chest.

Whose idea was this? It feels as if I got talked into it by some part of myself who's run off to party and cause more trouble elsewhere, who's left me alone to manage the details, everything I own wedged into an airplane about to land in New York City, and only $3,200 in cash and travelers checks, and a friend's couch to sleep on for a week. Two, maybe, if I start begging him, a buddy from high school. He's some sort of business guy in New York and living with a roommate who owns the lease, so I can't wear out my welcome. And I wonder if this is how Kari felt when she arrived at Florida State, or every mile along the way. Terrified. And she was never strong. She just wasn't, we all knew it. And so she broke. Maybe she was always broken.

The plane bounces off an air pocket and I fumble for the barf bag in the seat pocket. But I stabilize, and we go down lower and lower until suddenly we're hurtling mere feet over the water. I can see individual waves, white-caps, but can't see land at all. Has the pilot lost his mind? Is there engine trouble and we're crash landing in the East River? But at the last second a landing strip appears under our wheels, and we touch. We touch ground.

A cab drops me off at my friend's ground-floor apartment on the Upper West Side, and the doorman gives me a key to his apartment. Soon I'm sitting alone on the couch that is going to be my bed for the next week. It's only two in the afternoon. And my friend won't be home until six at the earliest. I'm so restless I can't imagine waiting till then, so I dare myself to foray out. To attempt my first ride on an actual subway train down to Times Square, where the ball falls, where the New Year begins.

I walk to the corner, descend the stairs, and buy a handful of tokens from the subway booth operator. I drop one into a turnstile and pass through just as a train comes barreling into the station. I'm about to sit as the train takes off, and I lose my balance and nearly end up in the lap of a woman who catches me. I take a seat beside her and grip the handrail. The racket and noise from the subway is overwhelming as the train rockets downtown. I try to relax, to appear natural and blend in, though I know I'm failing. The faces, races around me are different from any I've ever encountered. I'm as foreign here as any of them. I feel my heart beating in my chest again, though I can't hear it over the clatter of the subway.

At 42nd Street Station I step off and am quickly lost in this concrete bunker with no windows and dizzying displays of colored signs—a white 1, 2, 3 in a red circle, an A, C, E in a blue, a black B, Q, E in a tan circle. . . . Pedestrians flow in confident streams, and I force myself into one in the hope it'll lead me to the street. At last I climb up a set of stairs above ground to find myself dead center in Times Square. I pull myself out of the stream and quickly step back against the station wall. A one-legged panhandler sits on a cardboard box shaking a can. "Vietnam vet," he says. "Vietnam vet." I look down 42nd Street at the row of old movie houses now showing porn or horror or martial art movies. I look up toward the heavy, dusty sky, but the messages below it capture me first; the 100-year-old signs, the 50-year-old signs, the cutting-edge designs put up only yesterday, all of their flares and colors and neon trills and gyrations. Old logos, modern logos, but most dominant, the semi-nude bodies, male and female, their faces shameless, fatalistic, draped across billboards over the skyline. There's a drum beating somewhere. Someone rapping somewhere. Someone preaching.

It all seems too much. It seems too much to take in. Once again my heart is beating with such force I think I feel a pain in my chest. I wonder if something has gone wrong with it. No, it's just my imagination, I think. I hope. But how do people live here? How do they bear it, all this harshness and beauty?

39

New York City

I rode the elevator down to the lobby after work. My affair with Alena, whose impact I couldn't afford to consider, was nearly over even as its intensity continued to build. As it would no doubt until our final night. Still, we'd nearly survived it. Only three more nights. One part of me was relieved. Another part spiraled into terror at the thought we could be caught at the last moment. Still another was wedded to my feelings for her, but I couldn't afford to give it voice. I could hardly sleep nights anymore, could hardly lie down. My wanderings through the city were extending later and later. Exhausted as I was, as emotionally compromised, I knew I was increasingly likely to make a mistake. Such as bringing her flowers. It was a special night, yes. She needed flowers, but still it was foolish, and to another degree, selfish. I wanted to be the hero and save her, to take away her pain. So what would it be like when I could no longer touch her? Stop, I told myself. Shut up. Listen, you will rest. You will sleep for days, weeks, months. Doesn't that sound nice? Don't think about anything else. You can't lose focus. All that matters is seeing it through, getting her, all of them, to the other side safely, as she asked.

I walked past the security desk, stepped onto the escalator, and it carried me down the two flights to the ground floor. A few men and women in business suits floated down with me. As it was eight in the evening, the shops downstairs were closed. Everyone was leaving the building, going home. Two sparrows darted past my head, cut their wings and angled toward the constantly green domesticated trees, where they shot over a woman with dark hair standing motionless. People passed on either side of her as she watched the escalator intently, tracking each of us from the bottom to the top. Her eyes locked on me. And for a moment I didn't know who it was because it made no sense. She was in the wrong place. She'd stepped out of a dream and stared at me, as if both sure and unsure it was me. But of course it was me, and it was her. Without realizing it I backed up and stepped on the man's shoes behind me. I turned to apologize, then faced forward again toward my sister. I lifted my hand and that extraordinary smile broke across her face. Amanda. Who I hadn't seen since we put Kari into Windom.

There was nothing to do but be ferried down. When I stepped off I hesitated at the landing before realizing I was about to be run over by those behind me, so I quickly moved ahead toward my sister. Her hair was shorter. I saw no streaks of gray and wondered if she was dying it. She wore a charcoal business suit, would look at home in the office I just stepped out of, except she looked more real, more human than most of the upper-level women there did. There was a sense of her body beneath the restrictive clothes, movement implied in the way she stood, like a dancer. Like Alena, I realized. She wrung her black leather purse in her hands.

"John?" she said. I stopped a few feet away. For a moment I thought she might cry. "I can't believe how . . . good you look."

I took her in my arms and she buried her head against my chest. "You're beautiful, Amanda. Of course."

"You look different."

"Different good?" I asked, wondering if what she saw in me was because of Alena. Or New York. Or both.

"Absolutely."

She looked up at me, and I saw the fine lines at the corners of her eyes, the two faint vertical furrows between her eyebrows. For her, it all added depth. "How?" I asked. "How do I look different?"

She touched my face. "Want to get a drink?"

We walked down the darkening street to a nearby hotel. She talked quickly, her hands fluttering. Her company had flown a number of management teams to New York for a big meeting. She'd been unsure whether to contact me because she'd be tied up during the day, and her company had every moment of their evenings planned out—they were seeing *Phantom of the Opera* the next night, then flying home Sunday. But she was thinking of staying an extra day. She'd never been in New York. And maybe we could get together for dinner Sunday?

"Sure," I told her. "But why were you in my lobby? How did you know I'd be there?"

"I didn't. But I remembered Mother saying you worked till eight. So I looked up the company address and sneaked away from our dinner hoping to surprise you. I can't believe I found you!" She put her arm around my waist.

When we sat down at the bar she showed me her card. "Amanda Morel— VP Human Resources. Macklin and Sons." A big law firm out of Atlanta. The font was Palatino and appeared a bit stodgy. Probably the idea. Conservative. Solid, serif type. Letters braced by tiny feet.

"A promotion."

She smiled. "Yeah."

"Looks like a big promotion."

"Pretty big." She reached across and squeezed my hand. "Anyway . . . I really would love to see you."

"Definitely. We're on. Sunday dinner."

"The thing is, I won't be able to stay at my hotel Sunday night. They're booked solid. I mean, if you wouldn't mind me crashing at your place—I could sleep on your couch—then I'd change my flight to Monday morning."

She saw the reaction on my face before I could mute it. She released my hand. "Wait," I said. "Hold on."

"It's okay . . ." She looked embarrassed.

"No. Wait. Let me think for a minute."

"I've just thrown myself into your lap. I can't expect you to . . ."

I couldn't tell her to leave. What could I tell her, though? Something close to the truth? I looked in her eyes. "Amanda. I want you stay. You can sleep in my bed. I'll take the couch. Because I'll be coming in late that night. Or more accurately, early in the morning, and there's no point in waking you. I will have to go out Sunday night. A little after ten o'clock. And if that's good for you, that's good for me. So stay. We can have dinner and catch up before I leave."

She hesitated. "Are you sure?"

"I insist."

"Then I insist on sleeping on the couch. I won't hear any argument." She lifted her glass of white wine and took a sip as she studied me. "It's a woman?" she asked.

"Yes."

"Are you in love?"

"Probably."

She frowned. "Men. You're never sure of anything, are you?"

"I'm sure of absolutely nothing."

She nodded. "It's true. Even you. The best of them all."

"I'm not the best."

She reached across and touched my hand, then sipped her wine and changed the subject, filled me in on Catherine and her two boys and her bicycle shop that she and Charlie owned and operated. She told me about her own little boy and girl, how it's been tough with her new responsibilities at work, but they'd hired a nanny and that helped. And I realized I'd never seen her youngest, Sarah, in person, only pictures. Mark, Amanda's husband, was fine, she told me. Kari was hanging on. She'd been sober almost six months this time and cashiered in a grocery store in Little Rock. Which she said she liked.

Amanda paid for our drinks—she only had time for one—out of her expense account, then we walked out. It was dark outside, and I held open the door to a cab as she slid in. She reached through the window to squeeze my hand. "Thank you, John."

"Don't thank me. You're my sister." I watched as the cab took her away, fighting an odd urge to run after it.

I began walking downtown, amped up. I considered walking all the way home to burn off energy. But I was too restless, it wouldn't be enough, so I turned west at the next block and headed toward 8th Avenue and its Irish bars, its prostitutes who now, in the thick humid summer nights, would openly approach you. And their pimps, or guys pretending to be their pimps, pretending to be players, who razzed you as you walked by. "Hey Chuck, don't you think she's pretty? Don't you think my lady's pretty?" Sure, you said, she's pretty. She's a beaut. "Then why don't you . . ." but you kept moving and the pimp, or the pimp's minion, moved on to the next rube.

I ducked into the first Irish bar I came to, Rosie's on 7th, but it felt too upscale. So after a pint I headed another block west and stopped in McCann's, where I ordered another one. I joked with the waitress. She was rangy, tough, her face a bit rugged. You could see sweat stains under the sleeves of her T-shirt. She didn't care and nobody else did either. I liked her. It was hot in the bar even with the AC, which consisted of a couple of window units rumbling in the wall. She called me *darlin'* as I left, and I tipped her well, thanked her in my Texas accent.

The sidewalk was crowded. Couples of all races, all classes brushed by one another, their spirits high, their accents and languages swirling in the air. It was Friday night. The homeless lay against buildings on the hot concrete as they held out their cups. If you dropped in a coin you'd smell them. I held my breath and dropped in a coin. The porn houses were dimly lit and ridiculous, bizarre, irrelevant to someone not involved. The prostitutes maintained their presence, and one was wise to pay attention, out of respect, if nothing else. "Smoke smoke, coke coke," I heard from the shadows, but only a fool or a tourist would buy dope on Times Square.

I reached McHale's and dove in. I loved the bar, but it irritated me the only stout they carried was Murphy's, so after a beer I headed farther south. A block below Port Authority I spotted a bar with its name lit in green neon across its window—O'Donnell's. The jukebox inside blasted The Pogues' "If I Should Fall from Grace With God," and Shane McGowan's voice, along with the band's bass, drum, accordion, banjo, tin whistle, and god knew what else tumbled out the doorway like a drunken brawl.

Then I was inside and had a Guinness in my hand, and the waiter had an Irish accent, as seemingly did everyone else in the place. It was filled with Irish girls, as Times Square seemed to be then, and I wondered if they came over with the band, U2, or because of them. And they were cute and brassy and smart and literate, and I could listen to the sound of their voices all night. One girl with short dark hair was dancing a jig in the middle of the floor, kicking, whirling about, and I found myself dancing with her, our arms interlocked, bouncing to the Pogues and laughing. And I so liked what I saw in her eyes, the intelligence, the matter-of-factness and the guts it took to cross the water. All here on a Friday night less than a stone's throw from old Hell's Kitchen, the last stand of the Irish in Manhattan, a place the real estate developers had renamed Clinton as it was more image-friendly and easier to sell to the rich once they'd torn down or gutted and refurbished it all. Then the girl slipped away from me, was elsewhere, but she glanced back, smiled, and held the smile. I thought, I should buy this girl a drink. This girl needed a boy to play with in New York City, a boy to kiss and dance with. And why shouldn't she? But with a sinking in my gut I knew—I could go no further. I was spoken for. It was simply who I was. Then at least get her name, a voice inside told me. She was lovely, she was fun. Get a phone number for later. Later? I answered. There was no later. There was only who I loved. And why did I hedge admitting it to Amanda? Perhaps I just didn't want to hear myself say the words: "Yes, I'm in love." Or maybe I didn't want to have to explain it.

And so I began to make my way out the door. I glanced back to see the girl watching me. She looked a little disappointed, slightly puzzled, but shrugged it off quickly, made a point of laughing and beginning to dance again. I walked out into the hot night, not ready to go home, but as the bartenders say at closing time, I couldn't stay here.

40

We lay naked on the sheets on the floor. Her left hand rested in my right. There was just enough breeze outside to cause the shadows from the street-lights to shift across the ceiling. Her air conditioner rumbled in her win-dow. I loved the sound of it. I loved to hear the compressor kick in. It was midnight. Maybe three more hours with her. My sister was waiting in my apartment. Alena ran her foot along my shin.

"How long has it been since you've seen your sister? What's her name?"

"Amanda."

"Years?"

"Yes."

"Why?"

"She's there. I'm here. How long has it been since you've seen your family?"

"When Carina was born my mother flew over along with one of my sisters." She sighed. "I guess you had to tell Amanda about me."

"I didn't tell her much. She just knows there's a woman."

"She's the successful one. And the middle one is . . ."

"Catherine. The happy one. The one who got away."

"Didn't Amanda get away?"

"Yes, but . . . I dunno. She's been much more involved, more responsi-ble. She's helped out Kari."

"The lost one."

"Yeah."

She rolled over to look at me. "How is Kari?"

"Amanda said she's been sober six months. She's been sober six months before, though."

She put her hand on my chest. "You're far away tonight."

"Seeing Amanda. It made me remember things."

"You can't save people, baby. People have to save themselves."

"I pushed her to go to college, to get as far from home as she could, like Amanda and Catherine."

"You were a little kid."

"I had influence."

"She was six years older than you. You shouldn't have had influence."

"But I did."

"It's not your responsibility."

"She didn't even make it through her first year." I turned to look at Alena, but it was hard to hold her gaze. I looked past her out the window at the clocktower. "Have I ever told you . . ." I hesitated. "I used to do Kari's makeup."

"No." Alena raised up to see me better. "I never knew."

"So she'd look pretty for that guy I hated."

"The one whose ear you bit off?"

"Yes. Kari's face was delicate. It was fun to work with. Like . . ." I reached up to touch Alena's face. She shifted and the blue light from the street illuminated a plane of her cheek, darkened the eye above it.

"Like . . . *me*?"

My heart sped up in terror at the thought. I studied her face, examined it to make sure. "No," I said, and I heard a sigh of relief roll out from deep in my chest. "Thank god, no. Your lines are stronger." I took her chin in my thumb and forefinger, shifted her face from side to side. "Your bone structure . . . the lines of your face, the angles they make and planes they form. . . . They're extraordinary."

"Your sisters are the ones who taught you to draw. To see."

"I didn't start drawing until I was almost out of college."

"You didn't draw or paint or anything in school?"

"No. It seemed wrong."

"Wrong?"

"I mean . . ." But I didn't know what I meant. "I just didn't want to, I guess."

"There were no girls to put makeup on anymore? And the last one, that didn't go so well? How old were you when Kari left?"

"Twelve."

She stared at me, then after a moment lay on her back, looked up at the ceiling. "John. Touch me."

"What?"

"Tell me something that's not about your sisters."

I sat up to see her better. "The lines of your body match the lines of your face. The symmetry . . . from head to toe . . . it's . . . it's why I couldn't take my eyes off you. It's why men stare at you on the street. Women too."

"But . . . John . . . you're still seeing me . . . from seeing them."

"What?"

"I don't want you to see. I'm tired of you seeing. I don't want to hear about your sisters. I just want you to smell me, to feel me, like an animal. I want you to want *me*."

I rolled on top of her. "I've never wanted anyone like I want you." She covered my eyes with a hand, and I was in her. "But without them . . ." I said.

"What?"

She started to struggle out of my grasp, but I held her tightly. "Without them . . . you have to know this . . . I never would've found you."

"I don't care," she said. "Close your eyes. Make it about the sex again. Make it about us."

⁓

Wrung out, exhausted, I walked down the hallway to my apartment. When I unlocked my door and pushed it open, Amanda answered from the dark, awake as I feared she would be. "John?"

"It's me," I said, and clicked on a lamp.

"These posters on the wall are great. Yours?"

"Yeah."

Amanda sat in sweatpants and a T-shirt on top of the couch. She'd been looking out my window at the buildings and the lights. She didn't mention my two charcoal drawings that followed the one I gave Alena—I'd pinned them to my bedroom wall. Which meant she hadn't seen them. I was glad. I didn't know what to think about the drawings. I needed to keep them private. It was almost 4:00 a.m. I only wanted to get inside my bedroom.

"What time does your plane leave?" I asked her.

"10:30. Approx. I'll let myself out in the morning. I just couldn't sleep. I guess I'll sleep on the plane. This view is something." She'd turned off the air conditioner and opened the windows.

"That's why the couch faces it."

"You don't have screens on your windows. Anything could tumble out. Or in."

"That's the way it is here. Hardly anyone has screens."

"There's no separation between you and the city. How do you sleep? I feel like I'm inside this living *thing*. I feel it breathing in and out."

"You get used to it."

"I don't see that. Maybe you become part of it and can sleep. But still."

"You're really okay on the couch?"

"Yes. I think I'll probably be up awhile. How was your . . . uh . . ." She hesitated as we looked at each other. "Sorry."

"It's okay. I don't know what to say about it."

"It's alright." She shrugged. "John?"

"Yes?" She wanted to tell me something. I sat beside her.

"It was really great to see you for dinner."

"Yeah. It was."

"We should . . . see each other more often. Don't you think?" There was a hesitancy. She was afraid I'd reject her.

"I'd like that," I said.

"Really?"

"Yes."

"John," she said, then looked out the window. "I'm getting divorced."

So there it was. My most successful sister, the smartest, the most responsible of us all. Even she couldn't make her world safe. "Amanda, I'm so sorry."

"Me too."

I reached across and took her hand. She squeezed it, then turned my way.

"You know, when you were a little boy you were the cutest thing there ever was. Remember how you'd brush our hair? You'd sit on that stool behind us holding your brush. Watching us so intently. I don't know I've ever felt as loved by anyone."

"Even Daddy?"

"Maybe Daddy."

"I can hardly remember him. I wish I remembered him."

"And then I was gone. Off to college. Blew out of town. I tried to visit though. Do you remember?"

"Sure," I said. But truthfully it was vague.

"I mean, Christ. Mother. She'd trot you out in front of me like you were her pet. She called you Joujou. In front of us. Made a point of it. Do you remember?"

"No."

"I couldn't bear it. And you looked different. Acted different. I know you were just surviving as well as you could. I mean, it's not like she beat us or anything, and there was always money, and that matters. But still, to be part of a family means having something to belong to. Mother belonged to her bottle. Remember how she'd pass out on her bed and Daddy would read to us. You were so little then. You don't remember that, do you?"

"No."

"He called you 'little man.'"

"You did too."

"Then when he died, *we* were the family. Me, Catherine, Kari, you. Until I'm eighteen and gone, finally, just like I always dreamed. But you still had Catherine and Kari, and then Kari. Right? Until she left. And by then at least you were older. And Aunt Phyllis was there to help manage Mother and Grandmother. What was I supposed to do, try to get custody?" She laughed. "And here you are now, this gorgeous man, a stranger I know. Just . . . honestly, just radiating life. I can't take my eyes off you. And you're out in this city at night, god knows where, till dawn. With god knows who." She looked into my eyes. "I wouldn't judge you. I couldn't. I just . . ."

"What?"

"I wish I knew you."

I hesitated. "She's married."

My words hit her like a shot. She looked down at the floor. Whatever she thought she might hear from me, this wasn't it. I wondered if it was another woman who broke up her marriage, or another man. "God, we're all fucked up, aren't we?" she said.

"What about Catherine?"

"She was always practical. She and Charlie and her kids and her bike shop. Cut herself off from us and stayed cut off."

"I appreciate you did what you could to save Kari."

She shook her head. "There's no saving Kari."

"I blame that guy," I said. And I knew it wasn't right, or at least not entirely right. Nothing's ever so simple, but something in me believed it anyway. Something gripped it.

"What guy?" Amanda asked.

"Gary Phillips."

"Who?"

It made no sense to me that she didn't know the name. Something in me quaked at it. "You know," I said. "That guy in high school."

"The football player?"

"Right. Gary Phillips." Something twisted inside me just from saying his name. "He beat her, you know."

"I never . . . no. I mean, I knew he was a lousy guy, but . . ."

"Regularly. As far as I could tell." I was amazed this surprised her. How could she not know?

"Oh John."

"I put makeup on Kari. She was so hopeless she begged me to do it, and so I did. And I liked it. It felt like I'd found some special part of me. And it had power." Did I like the contact too, I wondered. Of course. I liked holding her face in my hands, seeing what was hidden, drawing out her secrets. "Amanda, did you know this? I've never told you this. I've never told anyone this, except for . . ." I almost said her name—Alena—but I stopped myself. "I brought out Kari's beauty for . . . for *him*. And she's been looking for him ever since."

"I'm sorry."

"There's no fixing her."

"No, John. I'm sorry for *you*."

Her words sank into me with such weight I couldn't move. I needed to get to my feet. I needed to sleep. I was exhausted, irrational, saying odd things. I stood. "Don't feel sorry for me. I just spent the night with the woman of my dreams." I leaned down and hugged her. "It's true. Listen, I've got to get up in about five hours."

She nodded. "Go get some sleep."

"We'll stay in touch."

Walking to my bedroom I felt naked and raw from what I told her, as well as ashamed at how I'd swept the conversation from her when she should've been the one talking. She was the one whose marriage was breaking up. At my door I turned back. "Amanda, I really hate hearing about . . . you and Mark." I didn't want to say the word "divorce."

She nodded. "I'm glad we talked."

In my bedroom I turned out the lights and stripped down to my underwear. Why did I tell Amanda about Kari and the makeup, something I'd hardly thought about until I told Alena? Something I'd hardly remembered. We were just kids, and it was all so long ago. And it's not like anything radical happened. It's nothing compared to a lot of families.

I sat at the edge of my bed and looked out at the same buildings, the same dark and lit windows that Amanda was watching, the same silhouettes of water towers against the same dark sky. And I felt a release in it as I always had, at the shapes of the structures and their lights and their shadows, at the way we were all public and private here, known and unknown, exposed and hidden, alone and part of it all. Amanda was right. The city was a living thing. You felt the presence of those who had lived here in its structures. It was formed out of us as much as brick and steel and light.

I breathed again. It was as if I could breathe. I got in bed. I slipped under the sheets.

~

Someone was in my room, and I was dreaming. I dreamed I was riding the subway. It swayed, it raced. I looked out a window to see another train shooting along the next track. A woman with dark hair stared out its windows and met my eyes. Who was in my room? I sat up in bed so fast my heart felt like it would leave my body. And she stood in the doorway like a dark ghost. And what did it want?

"John," she said, and she was crying, moving toward me, and I was scared but I didn't do anything because I knew it was Amanda. As she reached my bed I saw her clearly, I recognized her. "Joujou," she said, and wrapped her arms around me. I was only in my underwear. I hadn't showered and Alena's scent was on me. Amanda pulled me into her, and there was nothing to do but go. She cried like she was breaking, like she was coming apart, her head tucked into my chest. It felt so strange to hold her. She was smaller than me.

"We left you," she said. "We all left you behind."

"It's alright."

"I loved you so much. I loved you more than anything. And I abandoned you, there in that house, to be alone."

"I abandoned Karl."

She looked up. "No. No you didn't."

"Over and over."

She stared up at me. And I saw the answer to the question I could never bear to ask: How did we all lose each other? Amanda and Catherine felt they failed me by leaving me, and I knew I failed Kari. We all did. She stood between us as testament, as the wreckage of everything once beautiful in her. And who would think about that if they didn't have to? Who would stay in contact with something so crippling?

"There was nothing you could do, Amanda," I said. "What could you do?"

She began to cry again. I looked out the dark windows at all the buildings and the dark sky behind them. I held my sister.

41

I opened the door to Alena's apartment. We did what we did. I didn't mention my sisters, and she didn't ask. Afterward we lay beside each other on our sheet. It was our last week. The red roses week.

"I can't believe . . ." she began. She turned to look at me, then away. "I can't believe I will only see you two more times." She seemed more puzzled by it than saddened. She squinted at the ceiling. "Maybe instead of offing my husband I should off you," she said softly, almost to herself. "Maybe that would be the easiest way."

"Maybe it would," I said. "I woke up one morning last week thinking about that."

"What?"

"You were on top of me. You had this ice pick . . ."

"Stop. It's not funny."

"It didn't feel like a bad thing. I was okay with it."

"Please stop."

"Sorry."

She sighed. "I chipped a tooth today. It's nothing serious, but I was on the bus when it jolted forward and I hit my tooth on a handrail."

"Let me see."

"No. It's okay. But it made me think. We're going to run out of luck."

"We're tired. We're both tired."

"I know. It's time it ended. Before something bad happens."

"Your husband flies in Monday."

"Yes. Monday. After Sunday. Our last Sunday. He lands at two o'clock that afternoon. I'm taking the day off from work so I can . . . you know. Get ready."

It hit me that I'd have to see her at work the following Tuesday. She'd have to see me. I couldn't imagine what that would be like. What if there was trouble between them? What if there wasn't? "If you need me for any reason," I told her, "you know, on Monday or whenever, call. Don't hesitate."

"Thanks."

I didn't like how this was all going. It felt like we were closing up shop. Like we'd already said goodbye. She turned her head my way. "Is there anything you'd like to do . . . I mean, that we haven't done yet?" She smiled, and it felt better. She was making it manageable, about the sex again. We were fellow libertines again, searching each other out between the cracks, in the empty spaces others didn't see, or didn't want to see. We'd both move on.

"Anything?" I asked.

"Anything," she answered flatly.

"That's a generous offer."

"So?"

I looked out the window. The clocktower stood against the clear black night. "The only thing," I said, "is there any way you could come to my apartment? Could you get a babysitter? So I didn't have to worry about running this gauntlet to reach you. Or that guy on the fifth floor or one of your neighbors seeing me. Or Carina walking in on us. And we could meet at six. Five o'clock. Take our time, this last time. You know? Breathe easier?"

She smiled as she watched me. "That would really make you happy, wouldn't it?"

"Yes."

"I thought maybe you'd want to tie me up and whip me or something."

"It's late in the game to be leaving marks."

~

She closed the door behind me as I moved silently, my head down, toward the stairwell. I didn't know her husband's name. I didn't want to know his name. If it was only Alena and this man, things would've been different. I could have separated them. Justified it. She and I could've tried to be together. But there was the daughter. And there was the father. Without his involvement would the affair have even happened? No. Someone else would've snapped her up long before I met her. Without him there would've been no "us." He and I were stuck with one another, as if in opposite orbits around the moon, until it ended. He made me possible, and it was oddly possible I was part of what saved his marriage. If it was saved. Another man might've tried to wreck the family. Another would've been careless in his comings and goings. Another might've blown up in the office and created a scandal that would find its way back to him. And a casual affair might not have been enough for her. She might have repeated. I'll never know. But because we'd put so much at risk, carried it so much farther than we'd planned to, or should have . . . maybe she would turn back to her family. At least for a long time. Not that such an outcome would've made what I did good, forgivable. If I was good I would have ended it earlier. If I was good I never would have begun.

Down the path of right angles and concrete under the harsh lights of her white stairwell, three in the morning, the clattering echo of my footfalls familiar now, almost comforting. There'd be one more night risking Alena, her family, and myself at her home. Then once at my apartment, where the risk would be so much less. Then it would be done. We'd walk away.

At the bottom of the stairwell I pushed open the metal door and stopped at the sudden darkness. No jealous husband awaited me. Nothing but the thick and humid night.

~

Wednesday night I headed out into the city again. As I stepped onto 43rd Street from the Times Square subway station I felt a hand on my ass. I spun around to see who'd just copped a feel. He was my size, with my coloring. He didn't look friendly. "Want some dick?" he asked.

I stared him down. "You must've come in from Jersey," I told him. We were a hair's twitch from swinging at each other when, as if cued by a dog whistle, we both turned and darted away. That was too close. You never wanted to get into a fight in this city. You either knew this or quickly learned it. You had no idea who you'd be hitting, what they were capable of or what disease they carried in their blood, and the last place you wanted to find yourself was the city lockup.

I headed west toward 8th Avenue and thought of a short, stocky female stage manager I knew who rented a one-bedroom on 47th and 10th and befriended a group of prostitutes working her block. She struck a deal with them saying she'd watch their back if they'd watch hers when she came home late at night from running shows. She knew how to dress down, how to walk so she didn't draw attention.

A foolish blond girl I met with Billy at McHale's, an actress wannabe from Missouri who was neither smart enough, tough enough, or "street" enough, moved foolishly deep into the Lower East Side. After her apartment was broken into for the third time in six months the guys at the local bodega told her because she'd been friendly and given them regular business they'd talked the most recent burglars out of staking out her place and raping her. Maybe they were shining her on. Still, the little fool wasn't planning to move. I don't know what she was thinking or trying to prove. You need to know to get out of the water when you're drowning.

Sometimes at night I spotted people shooting up in basement stairwells off the street. Scattered crack vials over the sidewalk were just part of the landscape on the Lower East Side as you headed to clubs, to bars, to a late-night snack. Last week along a narrow street below Houston in Tribeca, I stepped over a Keith Haring "Baby" drawn in chalk by the artist on the sidewalk just for fun. It was round and buoyant and distinct and so very cute, and Haring's signature beams of light radiated from its body. The street was cobblestoned and empty, and the wind whipped through the dark neighborhood taking claim. The next rain would wash the drawing away.

The music that poured out of the bars I passed or entered, the music that lodged in me, was the Gipsy Kings, Tom Waits, Prince, Leonard Cohen, Los Lobos, the Pretenders, U2, Sinatra. Alena loved Sade. One night she called me at work to play "Is It a Crime" into the receiver. Yes, it was cornball, absolutely, but it touched me. On television, MTV played Eurythmics, Run-D.M.C., Peter Gabriel, Public Enemy, Michael Jackson, the Beastie Boys, the Bangles, Siouxsie and the Banshees, Depeche Mode, Talking Heads, Madonna Madonna Madonna. . . . It all blurred together, and I walked past, I walked through. I walked. I rode the subway.

I walked through Washington Square Park where the Dutch gave the land to black slaves as a reward for protecting the area from Indian attacks and named it "The Land of the Blacks." In the 1800s it became a potter's field, and no one knew how many bodies were still buried here beneath our feet, or which of this boneyard's trees was the legendary "hanging tree." In the 1950s the Beats ruled the park. In the 1960s, the hippies.

I thought of an entire underground culture of gays meeting on benches here, decade after decade standing beside landmarked trees before anyone knew they did such things, signaling each other in subtle, desperate codes. Putting their lives at risk in hopes of encountering one of their kind. I felt a kinship, how they met under cover of night to break taboos and become themselves. I had an urge to touch the trees: oak, elm, maple, sycamore. I wondered how many people who'd come to this city had touched the same trees in the same manner, and over how many years. As I laid my hands on the trunks, felt the bark, rough or smooth beneath my fingers, I wondered if those people, those ghosts, knew my touch because we'd touched the same living thing, and if I would feel the touch of those who followed me.

42

"Then tell me. What about me is like them. Specifically."

We lay on the sheet facing the window. Curled behind her, my arm draped over her side. It was our last time to meet in her apartment.

"You're sure?"

"Yes. I want to know."

"Not as much as I feared. I've been studying you."

"You're always studying me. So what do you see?"

"There's the way you stand in a dress. You don't use a dress to hide in or as a kind of armor, you know, like many businesswomen. You can tell you're . . . well, very much present in your body. That's like Amanda. I didn't know it till the other night when I saw her. You both stand like dancers. Move like dancers. Your feet though, those are like Catherine's."

"You look at my feet?"

"They're the feet of an athlete. They're overtly muscular. In Catherine's case they match the rest of her body. In yours they give away a secret about your physicality. How you're rough and ready, all other nuances aside. Like you could shock everyone, sprint fifty yards in an instant and vanish. You look less like Kari than the other two. Though there's a delicacy of line that's related. Not the same though. Your bone structure is more pronounced, less fragile. Your hair is entirely different from Kari's—hers is light and blond. Yours is thick and dark, more like Amanda's used to be."

"When you were a boy."

"Your coloring is more like Amanda's, except your skin turns olive at the first touch of sun. It just shifts. I've never seen that before. Amanda only tans, and it takes some effort. And your hair has a different quality. Maybe it's thicker, with a subtle curl throughout that seems natural. Do you do anything to your hair for that?"

"I take care of it. That's all. So . . . when you were a little boy did you brush their hair?"

I hesitated at her question. It was hard to speak.

"John," she said. "Who cares? Who cares if you brushed their hair, or what it meant, or how it marked you. Do you think I care? Just tell me you brushed their hair."

"I brushed their hair."

"You loved it, didn't you? You loved them."

"Of course."

She sighed. "Now tell me more. About them. About me. Go on."

I took a breath. "My sisters look American. But you look like you're from somewhere else. Another country. Another time, even. Maybe that's it as much as anything. It's subtle, but things about you, the shape of your eyes, the length of your neck, the proportions of your body . . . I could see you in Italy a thousand years ago."

"Or in Crete, two thousand?"

It was easy to talk again. The story was telling itself. "Yes. And the color of your lips is a darker, deeper red than I've ever seen on a woman. Almost blood red. As are your aureoles, your nipples." I placed my hand between her legs. "Here. The same. Your color." She turned to look at me, brushed my lips with a finger.

"There's one more thing," I said.

She stiffened, as if bracing. "Go on," she told me.

"Your makeup."

"What?"

"How you apply it. How you know your face so well. How you see. Like . . ." I hesitated.

"Amanda."

"Yes."

She turned away, stared at the ceiling. "I truly hate her," she said softly. "I've never hated anyone so much."

"But Alena, if you see like Amanda, that means you see like me. That means you and I are . . . of a kind."

She turned back to me, her hand taking mine as she looked into my eyes. "No one sees like you, John." She held my gaze, then turned away.

"You know the truth? I could never be with a man who knew me so well. Who watched me so closely. I wouldn't be able to hide anywhere."

"It was okay for awhile though."

She shut her eyes and took a breath, then pulled my hand to her belly. "Tell me the story, John. About the girl on the statue."

"You know it already."

"Tell me anyway."

I thought of the cars and buses flying down the hill a half-block away, the subways beneath them rattling toward Manhattan, the trees shifting below us from the summer wind and their patterns of leaves playing across our ceiling, and outside her window in the distance, the clocktower.

"I found a picture of a bronze statue," I said, "made by an artist in Crete, before Rome was Rome, before Greece was Greece. Some artist we'll never know. I found it when I was looking up Crete in the library."

"Why were you looking up Crete?"

"I wanted to understand you."

"Why did you want to understand me?"

"You know why."

"And the statue was . . ."

"A bull jumper. A female bull jumper and a bull."

"Female?"

"Yes. In Crete as a sport and spectacle they lined up their finest youth, female as well as male, and set a charging bull upon them. The bull would pick one of them as a target. But instead of running away, that target would run toward the charging animal, and at the last possible second leap or somersault over the creature. This was before either the Coliseum at Rome or the Olympic games."

"So who was this girl in the statue?"

"We don't know. She was just a bull jumper."

"What does she look like?"

"She's thin. She's lithe, elegant. A young woman stretched out in midair over the beast, her back to its back . . ." I hesitated, realizing this might be the last time I ever told this story.

"Go on," she said.

". . . her back to its back . . . the back of her head to its head, her arms held out, her body curved over it as she faces the sun. She's golden. She forms a perfect arc. Like a crescent moon. She must have put her hands to the horns of the bull and pushed off, then flipped in the air to stretch out. How else could she have arrived at that position?"

"It sounds dangerous."

"It would be."

"What's going to happen to her?"

"She lands on her feet behind the bull. She bows to the crowd. They applaud wildly."

"And the bull?"

"It's okay. It's implied by the statue."

"So she gets away with it. Nobody gets hurt."

"If the statue is right, yes."

～

Saturday night before my last night with Alena, my legs, though heavy with exhaustion, carried me even faster and farther than usual. I'd given over to them in an attempt to burn off energy, but it made little difference to the edge I felt. My wanderings took me back to the Lower East Side. Loisada. Tompkins Square Park, specifically. Even more specifically, the same bar and barstool I visited several weeks ago, where through grimy windows I watched the festivities in the park. Tonight the bar was playing the entire Ramones ragged and jagged first album through its speakers, and people from the park wandered in and out for a quick beer.

Mayor Koch had placed a midnight curfew on the park and a few protesters were arrested. Still, no one moved out and the park had been buzzing since, even more than before. I stared out the window at the white makeshift structures in the park. A group paraded by carrying a long banner that read: "Gentrification Is Class War." Bystanders on the street applauded and waved. People were grinning, laughing, walking around carrying boomboxes. I knocked back the rest of my beer and wandered out the doors into the hot night. Deep inside the park I heard someone speaking through a bullhorn and the ever-present African drums thrumming from at least three different directions. Someone started up a snare, rat-a-tat-tat. The park was turning into a big party. I decided to step in for a few minutes.

I wandered past a group formed around a guitar and bongos next to a sign reading "No Park Curfew!" Beyond them four Latino old-timers played dominoes on a card table like they'd probably been doing every

Saturday night for decades. The mostly white spiked-hair and tattoo crowd mixed with Latinos and black people. A girl walked past with a shaved head and a white pet rat riding her shoulder. I heard more firecrackers and wandered toward a small fire. People danced at its edges, and beside them another sign read "Stop the War on the Poor."

As I wondered how the police expected to enforce their curfew, I felt a sudden shift, like a brief wind. I turned and looked behind me without knowing why, when I realized other people were looking that way too. An animal response rippled through the park, and I knew I'd made a mistake. I didn't check the time before coming in, and it was now midnight. A sound I'd never heard before evoked a fear as ancient and deep as my bones, dug from a cultural memory of terror—the sound of horses charging, their hooves clattering across pavement, then a deeper sound as the hooves reached dirt. I turned and began running from it, hearing shouts behind me and bottles breaking, cursing myself as I realized what I'd put at risk—if I got caught in this police action, which increasingly looked like a police-state action, I could be in jail for days before I got out. Which would mean Alena and I would not have our last time together. At my home. Just the two of us. We would not get to say goodbye and end it on our own terms. When I got out her husband would be back. I would never be with her again.

Helicopters battered the air overhead. I ran faster toward the back of the park hoping to escape before the net closed but pulled up short seeing a wall of police officers in riot gear pouring through the north gate. When I heard horse hooves to my back I ducked behind a tree and hunkered low to the ground where I froze. A horse raced past chasing a man in rags, forcing him into the phalanx of riot police who took him to the ground. I looked back toward the center of the park to see the police tearing down the barricades and tents the homeless set up. One cop on horseback at the west end pulled a man out of a tree who then crashed to the ground. Another mounted cop thundered by who, I saw, had removed his badge. I heard more bottles breaking, and people outside and inside the park were screaming. Now the cops spilled back into the street, crashing through the crowds on the sidewalks. One pulled a man off his bicycle and began beating him with a nightstick. Two cops raced past on their horses. They'd taped over their badge numbers. I watched them riding toward the wrecked tents where several bodies lay face down against the dirt, handcuffed behind

228

their backs. Beyond them on the sidewalk lay another body, motionless, like garbage to be picked up.

I heard footsteps approaching and nearly bolted but saw it was two pro-testers running toward me and the wall of cops beyond me at the north end. The two didn't see me any more than the cops did. It was as if by being still—or maybe it was more than that, maybe it was something I simply knew—I'd found the one invisible spot in the whole park. Until they ran by, then pulled up ten yards in front of me. The nearest one was bald and had been hit on the back of his head. Blood ran down past his neck into his shirt. The other was long haired and scraggly. At the same moment both threw beer bottles high into the air toward the cops before turning back to run. As they shot by, the cops finally spotted me. Their eyes fixed, and all I could think of was Alena and that I had to escape. That if I didn't the affair was already ended. It was over now, as I squatted on the ground.

Three cops began to run toward me. I looked toward the fence at the east edge of the park. It was taller than my head but the only way out, so I dashed toward it, hearing the footsteps of the police behind me, hoping my natural speed and the weight of their gear would slow them enough. I ran so fast I felt like I was flying, like I was hardly touching ground, and before I even reached the fence I leapt up toward the iron spikes rimming the top and grabbed one in each hand, pulled myself above the fence, then over where I released and turned in midair. I landed on my feet. I glanced back to see the cops inside already pulling up, turning back toward the melee and slower game.

I took off sprinting down the sidewalk past an old, bearded homeless guy standing on the curb cheering and applauding me. "Get out of here!" I yelled as I ran by him, then turned east down one of the dark, treacherous streets no one in their right mind would turn down. The beaten path was dangerous enough in this neighborhood, but off the path, god knew what you'd run across. But I only knew what I was running from, which was capture. I only knew I was running toward Alena. I turned right at the first block, then left at the next toward the river again. The street was dimly lit and empty, its tenement windows dark and broken out. The noise from the riot behind me had become distant, trivial, like the tinny clatterings of a child's toy in another room. My footsteps slapped the pavement, echoed from the walls of the silent buildings, trembled against and through me, as familiar as my skin.

43

Waiting for the hours to pass I watched the daylight streaming through the windows into my apartment. I watched the clock even as I tried not to. Finally I went out for lunch at a diner. I sat in my booth long after I finished eating and watched people pass, outside, through the glass. I studied them, wondered at their lovers, the shapes of their lovers' bodies, their religions, races, genders. Every lover, no matter how public or private the affair, remained a secret to all but their partner. To what degree were we built from such secrets, such relationships? If so, what was I?

I walked up the eighteen blocks to Bryant Park where I sat on the wall beside the stone lions in front of the New York Public Library. It was a nice day, in the mid-eighties with a clear blue sky. Finally I headed back to my apartment. There I nodded to Eddie, my doorman. I realized, with some pride, he would see Alena when he sent her up. He would be the only one besides Jeremy to know we were connected.

My bedroom dresser was set against the east wall and my bed floated in the room's center over the wood parquet floor. I'd recently positioned the bed sideways so at night I could turn to either face the city or away from it. My two drawings were on the wall to the right. But the room was much too bright from sunlight, as it would be later when Alena came over. I rummaged through the closet looking for the colored sheets the actress I subleased from didn't bother to pack and found the dark purple set on the floor. When I hung them across the windows, the room softened to violet.

I walked out, closed the door, then looked over my living room. The gray second-hand couch Billy gave me when I moved into this apartment, the taupe armchair the actress left behind along with her small fold-out dining table. Only my drafting table, my art supplies, my stereo, and my bed were really mine. Everything else was hand-me-downs or stuff I'd picked up off the street. The walls were bare except for my posters and my drawings in the bedroom. My eighteen-month sublease was up in two months and I'd need to find a new place to live.

I put my art table in order, then cleaned the bathroom and washed the dishes. I showered, then examined the poster I was designing for another small theater company. I couldn't focus on it. I paced the floor. I sat. I rose. I sat again and a sob broke from my throat. I laughed in surprise, which sounded as unexpected as the sob. I couldn't come apart now, I told myself. She'd have no patience for it. And lucky me, really, when it was all said and done, soon the worries and stress of the past months would be over, and what I'd literally prayed for every night, that we'd make it safely through to the end without being caught, without her family being destroyed, would be won. I would have honored my part, and we would have escaped, survived, cheated disaster, got what we wanted, and slipped away into the night like thieves. This evening should be a celebration. A wash of relief rolled through me. I began to chuckle, and that turned into laughter. I lay back on the couch and looked at the ceiling. I would sound crazy, I guess, a guy laughing by himself alone in his apartment. I rolled over on my side to look out my windows at those across the way. I loved the city so much, the shapes of its buildings, the way the light fell between them. I closed my eyes for just a moment.

The buzzer sounded and I leapt up from the couch, my heart pounding. Had I actually dozed off? I hurried to push the intercom button. "Yes?"

Eddie the doorman's voice crackled through the speakers. "It's Alena."

"Send her up," I said.

My heart quickened as I tried to shake off the sleep. I poured a glass of water and downed it as I pictured her walking past Eddie in his cap and long coat from another era he wore even in summer, her heels clicking against the linoleum as she continued to the elevator past the sporadic, generic furniture no one used that only served to make the lobby appear less empty—a cheap white loveseat, a plastic cushioned chair, plastic flowers in a plastic vase on a coffee table between the two elevators. What did she think at seeing the plastic flowers? What kind of flowers were they supposed to be? I didn't know. I'd never bothered to wonder. They were lifeless, ridiculous. I hurried to the bathroom and quickly brushed my teeth, then checked myself in the mirror, practiced a smile. Were doubts creeping in on her, indistinct fears, a sense of exposure, sinning, risk, a feeling of being lost in this disembodied space with only my voice, vague with sleep, crackling through the intercom to hold onto as an anchor. Her beauty would make her conspicuous. She would have dressed well. Anyone passing would turn their eyes on her. How could they not? How could they not know she was meeting a man?

Now she'd be pushing the round white buttons to the elevator, watching the numbers' descent. 10 . . . 9 . . . 8 . . . It would seem to take forever. Didn't I know this? Hadn't I felt it these many nights standing in her apartment lobby under its harsh lights? Finally, through her feet she would feel the carriage stop, and see the doors mercifully open. If someone stepped off from inside it might catch her off guard. Suppose it was a mother and child. Would Alena turn her head away in shame, then slip inside the metal box as she tried to will the doors to quickly close? Would that mother, whose body had not snapped back into form, glance at Alena and catch her eye? Would the eye contact inform the mother, woman-to-woman, that a transgression was about to occur? Would she look at Alena with disdain, jealousy, concern as the metal doors shut?

By now the elevator would be rising. She'd be watching its numbers change from light to dark. Unless it stopped along the way. Unless someone stepped into the elevator with her, looked at her, then with some effort, turned away. If it was a man he would try to come up with a line, something casual just so he could hear her voice. But his line would come out wrong. She'd hesitate, then take pity, respond politely, save him.

I couldn't bear to wait inside my apartment any longer. I stepped into the hallway just as the elevator chimed and the door opened. And there she stood framed inside. She stepped out looking lost for a moment, then saw me. She smiled, relieved, found, grateful, then moved toward me across the thin brown carpet.

Only then did I notice the red rose in her hand. I took it from her as we stepped inside. I locked the door behind us.

"I'm going to be so relieved," she said, "when this is over."

"I know."

"It's exhausting." We both began to laugh. I pulled her to me, felt her body shaking from her laughter. She looked in my eyes. "Please let's make this fun."

"Of course," I said.

When I placed the flower into a vase, she untucked my T-shirt from behind and pulled it over my head. As I turned around to face her she gasped, "John."

"What?"

"This." She touched her finger to the long red mark beneath my ribs. "You're cut."

"Scraped. It's nothing. It happened last night."

"Where were you?"

"Tompkins Square."

She stepped back. "At the riot? What were you doing there?"

"I was watching," I told her. "Just watching."

"Why?"

"It was interesting. It was like this huge party. I wanted to see what was happening, then the cops showed up."

"How did you get cut?"

"I don't know. The cops taped over their badge numbers or took them off so they couldn't be identified. They charged them . . . us . . . with horses." She ran her finger along the length of the cut and I flinched at the tenderness. "I ran. The only thing I could think about was that they'd catch me and I'd go to jail and wouldn't see you tonight. I'd lose my last chance to see you. You know?"

She took my hand and guided me toward the bedroom. When she opened the door she stopped, took a breath at the soft purple light infusing the room. "So you'd be comfortable," I told her. "So it wouldn't be too bright." I was suddenly embarrassed by it, by the shabby fuss with the sheets, then the empty room, how the only things in it were a bed and a dresser.

"Thank you," she said. When she saw the two charcoal drawings pinned to the wall, she sucked in her breath before moving to them. Her fingers hovered over one figure, then followed the lines on the other. "John," she said.

"You know who it is." It almost made me angry to say it. "I'd never drawn this way until I drew you. And so."

"It comes from you. It's all you."

"I don't know what I'm doing. I haven't a clue. It's like I've ripped the skin off something."

She shook her head. "It unhinges me a little, truth be told."

"It's just lines. Lines on paper. I'll take them down."

"No. Let's not soften the edges. I wanted this to be perfect tonight. But that's, you know, a silly dream. And I feel distant. I can't believe my husband comes back tomorrow. Or that you and I'll go on at work like none of this happened. How could we ever do that?"

"We'll work it out. We'll talk and get through it."

"And I don't want to think like this. Tonight it's the last way I want to think."

"Then stop thinking. Just be here, okay?"

She nodded but didn't move.

"What is it?" I asked.

She shrugged, her body suddenly tense. "My time of the month," she said. "Can you believe it? Just this afternoon I felt it begin. But it's light, if at all. I dunno. I feel off."

"It's okay. Feel how you feel."

"I wanted everything to be perfect."

"I don't want perfect. We're not perfect."

She nodded. "I'll be right back," she said, then left. I heard the bathroom door close. I felt conspicuous standing by myself in the middle of my room, but soon she walked through the doorway again and closed it behind her. She turned to step out of her shoes and began unbuttoning her dress. She looked from her buttons to me. "What are you doing?"

"Watching you undress. I've never seen you undress before."

"It makes me feel naked."

"Good. The dress is beautiful, by the way."

She let it drop to the floor and stepped out of it. "I know. All that trouble and expense and you only see it for ten minutes." She was feeling bold again, standing in black lingerie she'd picked out and probably bought just for this. But I was less turned on by the sight, the gesture, than touched. Which moved me more toward tenderness than desire. Which I couldn't allow to rule.

Her hips shifted, and my eyes were pulled to them. Good, I thought, grateful for her instincts, as I felt the blood draw toward my center. This was who we were. This was what we were about. "I wanted to wear white," she said.

"Black suits you better."

234

"You remember I asked if there was anything else you wanted to do with me? Or to me?"

"That would be hard to forget."

She unhooked her bra, let it fall to the ground. "The offer's still good." She gave me a moment to take her in, then stepped out of her panties and stood before me. Her nakedness would be intimidating if I let it. So I scanned her body, down then back up, memorizing it, every curve, every angle. Her hips shifted again, drawing my focus.

"No one will ever again look at me like you do," she said.

"Don't think about it."

"No. I'm glad. I couldn't take it. Last chance on that offer. Going once, twice . . ."

"What I want is what we do. If I wanted something different I would've told you already."

"Take off your pants."

She was trying to be tough. If we could make it just about the sex we'd be okay. We'd get through it. It'd be fun. When I stepped out of my underwear she stared me up and down as I just did her. But she dropped her guard, bit her lip.

"There is something I want you to do for me," she said. "John."

At the sound of my name I hurried my answer. "Okay."

"You look afraid."

And I was. I didn't know why. "Does it matter?" I asked.

She hesitated, then said quietly, "What I want is . . . John, I want you to brush my hair." I inhaled sharply at her words. I heard the intake, and she did too. Without looking my way she walked to pick up the dark wooden brush she'd spotted on my dresser. She turned it in her hand examining it, then walked to the far side of the bed where she sat facing the windows. "I'm sorry. It's asking a lot. But it is what I want."

I climbed onto the bed behind her and took the brush from her hand. It was "the brush." The brush I'd kept all these years. She knew, and it didn't matter anymore, and yes, I would brush her hair.

And so, just as my sisters led me to Alena, she brought me back to them, while beyond her, beyond the thin, colored sheets I'd hung over my windows, stood the buildings that had stood in this city over a hundred years, buildings I'd seen every day, every night, their windows lit and curtains open, familiar strangers passing before them, living their lives apart yet connected to mine, as was the way in this city. And past them, more buildings, row after row in browns and whites and grays; darkening, shifting silhouettes, patterned by tiny window lights, set farther and farther into this aging cityscape, the old water towers on their rooftops like sentinels, the sky behind it all deepening in shades of blue. The streetlights would come on soon, and a few stars would appear through the haze. Alena sat exquisitely upright, like a dancer, waiting. What did her hair smell like? It smelled like rainwater.

When I set the brush into her hair something tore inside me. Still, I ran the brush down her hair's long length, lifted it, then ran it down again. The brush slipped, it curled, it slid, it possessed and released. Her hair was silk, it was velvet. Heat rose from her neck, a faint smell of cardamom. I didn't want to stop no matter how much it hurt. I did it over and over.

～

Holding hands, we rode the elevator down to the lobby. We didn't separate even as we passed Eddie the doorman and walked through the glass doors outside where it was summer. A summer night in New York. Then she and I were beneath the trees, her high heels tapping the sidewalk alongside me down 24th Street. I wanted to point her out to people we passed. To strangers. To the young Asian couple, to the little old Jewish lady walking her terrier, to the three frat boys become businessmen headed to the bars. Look, I wanted to tell them. Do you see her? Look at her. Please.

At 2nd Avenue we stopped at the corner. It was time to finish it. We would return to our lives. The cars streaked by racing downtown. We turned to each other. She smiled faintly, and I knew it was a cue. We were risking standing there too long. She wanted me to end the moment, to finish it and not make her ask me to. So I stepped into the street and flagged a cab. One pulled over immediately and I opened its door. We stared at each other.

The word, "Well," slipped from my mouth. I shook my head. I had to do or say something. I reached behind my neck and unclasped the chain that held my cross. "Lift up your hair," I said.

"No. It's too much," she told me. But her hands were already moving toward her hair, and mine drew the chain around her neck and connected it behind her. Her hair tumbled over it. The cross rested against her skin.

"Thank you," she said, taking my face in her hands. "John," she said, and kissed me. It was a long kiss, a kiss on a New York City street corner, proudly displayed, asking to be seen by the world. Then, without looking back she slipped into the cab. It pulled away down the dark avenue and quickly blended into the river of other cabs and cars and lights, was swallowed, and was gone.

44

I woke staring at the ceiling. Morning light filled the room. I stretched my legs, my feet, my arms, my hands. I thought this: We made it.

I sat up and looked out the window at the buildings across the street, not sure how I should feel. I knew I was exhausted, emotionally, physically, every possible way. Numb more than anything. I was glad Alena wasn't coming in to work today. Glad for both of us.

I walked into the kitchen and poured myself a glass of water. I held it up to the light in the windows and stared at it for too long. I set it down. I took a shower. When I came back into my bedroom I found the sheets on the bed faintly stained in a few spots. I lifted the top sheet to my face, breathed it in, and for a moment was lost. I stripped the sheets off and tossed them into my laundry basket.

Instead of taking the subway to work I decided to walk the thirty blocks uptown. It was a gentle, lovely, late August morning. Fall, my favorite season, was on its way. You could feel it in the air, see it in how the clouds feathered the sky.

When I stepped into the workroom I noticed Jeremy's empty desk two seats behind mine. I had an impulse to send him a note that Alena and I survived, that it was finished and he didn't need to worry. I opened my drawer at my desk expecting to see a flower inside, but of course there was none. I began working on the stack of charts waiting on my tray stand. But it was hard to focus. I considered it'd be a good day to go outside and have a smoke, except I didn't smoke. A couple of hours later I knew I needed a break. I called across the room to let Marjorie know. Outside I leaned against the building and watched people streaming by. Four in the afternoon and some were already heading home. Soon I began to feel restless as well as slightly foolish standing there, so I went back upstairs. By six I saw my hands were trembling. I could hardly sit still. The stress, I figured. Worse than expected. I didn't know how I could manage two more hours at my desk. What I needed was a beer. I needed to sit in a dark bar, watch the game on TV, have a conversation or two with strangers. Since I'd finished my assigned work, I told Marjorie I didn't feel well and she offered to cover the rest of the shift.

I hit the street and headed toward 42nd Street. The steady pace of my footsteps, the flow of all the bodies around me, helped steady my nerves. Soon I took a seat at the bar at McHales, and after a couple beers and watching the Yankees on the TV for awhile I felt like myself again and headed home.

When I stepped into my apartment the number 1 was flashing on my answering machine. I hesitated, then pushed the button. "John," Alena said, her voice ravaged, alarming in its despair. "I . . ." She stopped herself. I heard an intake of air. "He's in the shower. I just wanted to hear your voice again." She paused. "But you're not there."

I stared at the machine. The wall of numbness I'd encased myself in, probably the moment she disappeared into traffic, shattered. Every impulse demanded I pick up the phone and call her. How could I have not been home? How could I have missed her call? I had to hear her voice. I had to call her back. But no matter how I tried to justify it, to tell myself it would be proper to risk it, a better part of me overrode, grabbed me as a stern father takes a hysterical child by the hand, and dragged me away.

I was outside in the hallway. I was going down in the elevator. I was charging down 24th Street to 2nd Avenue where I turned into the first bar I stumbled across. I ordered a beer and a shot of whisky, followed by a second. I looked around, surrounded by young loud men in suits and ties. They seemed such an affront I wanted to strike out, start a fight, make someone bleed even if it was me. Instead I walked out and headed south. I started laughing. Yes, I was in love. Entirely. What a horrible, horrible thing.

Pedestrians avoided making eye contact, stepped off the sidewalk to let me pass. I'd become one of those ranters I'd dodged before on the street. Which struck me as funny, so I laughed some more before spotting the garish green paneling and neon shamrock of an Irish bar, O'Something or other's, and turned in and ordered a Guinness and a shot of Jameson. The rage in me quietened just a little. I managed to look around, preferring the clientele here, locals and a few prepsters slumming. I glanced at the clock on the wall. 10:45 it said, and it hit me. She was now in bed with him.

My shot glass fired from my hand before I knew what I'd done, and it hit the brick wall behind the bar where it shattered. I slid off my stool and faced the small crowd staring at me in shocked silence. An old Madonna song played on the jukebox. "Lucky Star." My lips started to move. I sang along quietly.

The bartender took a step forward to reach under the register. For a bat, probably. Still mouthing Madonna's words, I laid some bills on the counter and slipped out. I turned south, criss-crossing through the pedestrians floating around me while cars zipped down the avenue. I glanced over my shoulder to make sure I wasn't being followed, then merged with the moving bodies, the shifting crowd.

I wandered through a string of bars, trying to manage my emotions with more alcohol, but I couldn't get drunk enough. Finally on Houston Street I slowed down. Cars fired off the ramp from the Williamsburg Bridge and flew past, their wind whipping at my body. How easy it would be to step into the street and take the hit. I'd probably hardly feel it. I stood at the curb considering this, judging if they were traveling fast enough to finish the job, but before I could decide one of them pulled over in front of me. A yellow cab. The driver thought I wanted a ride, which seemed funny too. I started laughing again. Alright, then, I thought. Alright.

~

The exhaustion and hangover were allies, they numbed me as I rode the 6 to work the next morning, and I began to imagine that Alena and I would somehow work through this together, help each other and preserve some of the tenderness. I stepped out of the subway car, then took the stairs to the street where I headed west toward my building. I stepped inside. Rode the elevator. I heard the sound of her voice again, its broken timbre on my message machine. I shook my head trying to clear it. I needed to be calm. I needed to be prepared for anything. But as I walked down the hallway I panicked. What if she wasn't there? What if she told her husband and he hurt her? And I wanted to kill him. I literally, truly wanted to kill this man. I even saw it: shooting him on the street. His body dropping. My stomach turned. I might throw up. I stepped into the workroom, then stopped as I looked out across the space. It was so quiet. Strangely quiet. Even my mind was now quiet. Everyone at their desk just like on a normal day. No one even bothered to look up. Good, I thought. Okay.

I took my seat and turned on my computer. After a moment I lifted my eyes from the screen and peered through the glass wall into her office. When I saw her on the phone my heart stopped, then doubled its normal pace. I looked back at my computer screen and, trying to slow my heart rate, put my hand to my belly and breathed into it. Seeing Alena on the phone seemed odd, out of place, though I couldn't say why. But thank god she was there, she was okay. My heart rate slowed. I knew I must see her. If I could only see her and hear her voice it would steady me. Just her voice, some acknowledgment of who we were, then I'd be okay. I gave her a moment after she hung up, then walked toward her office trying to not move too quickly or look too desperate, even as I felt myself flushing, the blood coursing through my skin, and how red was my face? What happened to her last night? What did the sound of her voice on the machine mean? I wasn't home to take the call. What would've happened if I'd been home? I turned the corner and stepped into her doorway. She looked up, dressed impeccably, her makeup perfect. Which seemed odd. I stared at her. I couldn't make sense of the way she looked.

"Yes?" she said.

Her tone of voice communicated I could've been anyone. I could've been a delivery boy. My cross, of course, was absent from her throat. From behind me a tiny figure pushed past, brushing my leg. Carina. Alena rolled her chair to the side of her desk and gathered her into her lap. Their beauty together, once again, undid me.

"My sitter called in sick today," Alena explained flatly. The little girl looked at me, then past me. She didn't recognize, remember me. Thankfully, but I realized I was in love with her too. I wanted them both. And I saw Alena was using her daughter as a shield. "Did you need something?" she continued. I shook my head but couldn't find it in me to move. Then I spotted it—a tremor in her right hand. She followed my eyes to it, then quickly tucked it under her desk. She turned to smile at Marjorie who'd come up behind me. I walked back to my desk and sat, my skin burning. I put my hand to my belly.

I tried not to look up from my computer or my paperwork the rest of the afternoon. I hid behind my screen and tray stand, lost myself, as if in meditation, in my work and its precise placement of text and lines and shapes and colors. I focused on this to block everything else out, pull imaginary walls around me. All of which worked fairly well, to my surprise, except for when I heard Alena's voice. Then I had to start all over again, focusing on the triangles, the colors, the fonts. Pulling in the walls, picturing them in amber. Alena left precisely at five o'clock carrying her child. "Goodnight, everyone," she called over her shoulder, her voice cool and relaxed. At her words I lost control, a mutter spilling from my mouth, my skin like ants swarming me. I bit down to stop it as I worked to steady my breathing and turn myself into a machine again. Then I was drawing the charts. Connecting lines, shapes, text.

As I took a seat on the subway and it pulled away from the station headed downtown, I began weeping openly. I didn't even try to stop. The other passengers, for the most part, kindly ignored me, as was the custom in New York.

~

I suffered through the next two weeks at work trying not to look at her, unsuccessfully trying to hate her or cheapen her and the affair. Several times she brought in Carina for a few hours, which might've provided Alena protection, but the sound of her child's small footsteps as she ran by my desk cut through any stability I'd managed.

Finally I attempted to handle it in a manner that seemed rational. I slipped into Alena's office during a slow moment and took the seat across from her. I remembered when she interviewed me in that same seat three years earlier and her beauty struck me so I could hardly speak.

"Hi, John," she said in that neutral business tone she'd perfected. I honestly thought its coldness could've drawn suspicion. What would Jeremy have thought if he'd heard it? I felt unmoored without him here. We never did go out after work to have that drink, that conversation, and I found myself missing him dearly.

"I'd love a chance to talk about my future with the company," I told her, no longer sure what I expected from her. Except . . . maybe some degree of kindness. I expected that she would do something to help. "I was wondering if it'd be possible to set up a private meeting to discuss it with you." The words sounded ridiculous as they left my mouth, even as we both knew I was speaking in code. I just wanted to talk. Would you talk with me? Would you do that much?

Her face blanched, and I saw the muscles ripple along her jaw. "I do all my meetings here, John."

"You won't even meet with me?" I whispered.

She pulled back in her chair. "No."

"You have no idea . . ."

Her face flared. "Do you really think we could talk this out?"

We were speaking too loudly, but I couldn't stop. "We could try."

She stared across her desk at me. "You know nothing," she said.

I stood, thinking she deserved the scene I could make. And for the first time I grasped the power of my knowledge. I liked how it felt. I could ruin her reputation, destroy her marriage in a single stroke. For a moment it seemed warranted. She glared back as if daring me. The ground seemed so thin beneath our feet, scarcely able to sustain us. Out of the corner of my eye I saw a figure approaching. Her daughter, leading Millie, the teletypist, by a finger toward her mother. Again, I thought. Again she brings the daughter to work. There was no daycare here. It didn't look good for the boss to be dragging her child in to the office day after day. Carina darted past my leg and hopped into her mother's lap. Alena gripped Carina tightly even as she started joking with Millie, even as the little girl began to struggle to get down but couldn't quite wriggle out of her mother's arms. And it became clear. The madness lifted, and I finally knew who I was, who I had been all along—the bad guy in the story. The dangerous guy who was out of control, a threat to her family, to her little girl. A man Alena was . . . I saw it in her eyes now . . . afraid of.

I turned. I turned and walked back to my desk.

That night when I stepped into my bedroom I stood in the darkness for a moment. As I clicked on the light, my eyes caught something on the wall between my drawings, something I hadn't noticed before—two faint red-brown marks about a foot apart, roughly five feet off the ground. The one on the right streaked upward. As I approached I realized they were handprints, like petroglyphs on a cave wall. Then I realized they were hers. A pale layer of stain on her hands from touching me where I touched her. The position we took left the mark. Yes, it had been her time. It had just begun. I could make out her fingermarks on the left, and the edge of the heel of that hand. The right was indistinct, having been driven upward from the force behind her body. Which had been me. Impossibly, it seemed, only yesterday. I tentatively placed my hands on her imprints, as if it might be a way to contact her. Then I followed the movement of the stain upward, wondering at the force behind her that sent it there. Wondering what it was to be her.

I found myself in the bathroom in front of the mirror. I watched the scissors in my hand. Their blades trailing across my throat felt cool. They withdrew, closed, then the point found its way behind my ear and scratched downward where, at the carotid artery, it pulsed in response to that central vein, that motherlode of blood that can rarely be stopped once it's breached and running. The scissors pressed more firmly. I liked how it felt. It steadied me. With a small push the vein would open. A simple puncture might even be enough. But the scissors drifted away and opened like bird wings. I tilted my head to the side, exposed my neck. They traveled toward me and snipped off a lock of hair. My eyes followed it as it fluttered downward. When I looked up at myself in the mirror I was twelve. My sisters were gone. I'd cut my hair and my scalp was bleeding.

I stopped. I put the scissors away.

45

Now, a part of me counseled, take care of yourself. Even if that meant bearing another week or two in the office while you looked for a job. You don't win by burning bridges. You win by positioning yourself to move on. So, unless you plan on killing yourself or someone else, suck it up. Get a handle. Think how nice it will feel when you give notice. Let that be your reward.

First thing Monday morning I set up an appointment with a top employment agency. They seemed genuinely interested in me, which lifted my spirits. Had I stayed at SR&G this long only because of Alena? Even our boss, David, had hinted I should move on to find a job matching my talents. As I rode the 6 to work I felt more in control than I had in some time. When I logged into my computer I found this note waiting for me.

Dear Colleagues:

It saddens me to inform you that our dear friend and coworker, Jeremy Regan, passed away on Sunday due to HIV complications. The family has requested that in lieu of any gift you make a donation to the Gay Men's Health Crisis of New York.

SR&G has reserved the small downtown chapel at St. Antony's Church on the West Side for a private memorial service this Wednesday at 5:30 for anyone who wishes to come.

Best,
Alena

I stared at the screen, blinked, and reread the note. I knew this was coming. We all did. I thought I was prepared for it. I had to remind myself to take a breath. Standing seemed more than I could manage. I glanced into Alena's office. A young dark-haired female analyst in a business suit stepped to her desk. Alena seemed perfectly composed. I looked back at the message, then hit "close." Movement to my right drew my focus, and I saw the analyst walking toward me smiling. She was pretty in that thin, fast-track way. She continued to insistently smile as she stood by my desk.

"Just a half dozen charts," she chirped. "Pretty straightforward. Alena said you're available."

"Did you know Jeremy?" I asked.

"No," she said. "I'm new."

I took the pages from her. "He used to work here."

~

It was generous of SR&G to arrange and pay for a memorial service. Still, Jeremy always made an impression on people, as was evidenced by the turnout. Everyone from our department was there, along with many secretaries I did not know clustered in pockets in the small, gold-brown chapel, and a number of scattered analysts. Five executives walked through the doorway buffeting a full-fledged partner, and they took seats together toward the back. I'd heard Jeremy's brother would be in attendance and spotted him flanking Alena, his hair a shade darker than Jeremy's. On the other side of her sat her husband in his dark business suit, his dark hair, dark eyes. She stared ahead rigidly. He took her hand. The gesture surprised me. I was surprised I approved of it, of him. Then I saw a trace of Carina's face in his.

A minister stepped to the podium and addressed us with a short, fairly decent stock sermon. Afterward a string of us stepped to the microphone to speak, everyone focusing on how much fun Jeremy was until Marjorie, of all people, broke down blubbering and had to be led away. Following her, Alena lost her words. She looked out at us. Her face blanched. "I . . ." she began, then stopped. She looked down at the podium blankly, then back up. "I miss him," she managed to get out, then turned and walked unsteadily back to her husband.

The minister made a few final comments and released us. People congregated near the podium close to Jeremy's brother. He was tall and quite handsome, of course. Alena appeared brittle in her high heels, a blank expression frozen on her face. Her husband stood awkwardly a few feet away as if to give her some space, a gesture which, again, I approved of. I grabbed Berne Mason at the edge of the throng and gave him a hug, then began to move down the line of women, hugging each in turn. First were Sondra and Gloria from proofreading, then Millie, then Marjorie who started crying again on contact, wrapping her arms around me and not letting go. "I'm sorry," she whispered, "I'm so sorry."

I patted her on her back. "It's okay, Marjorie," I said, and realized I was forgiving her. So did she. I saw it in her eyes.

I pulled away from her to hug the next woman, then the next, making my way toward Alena. She didn't see me until I released Katy Matthews, a supervisor from the twenty-first floor. Alena's eyes widened and her mouth opened in surprise. And for the last time I took Alena Marino in my arms. She was all twigs and branches. She was covered in ice. If I wasn't careful it seemed likely she would shatter, but I would not give up this last chance to touch her.

"I'll go away," I whispered. "I'll do that for you."

At my words her body became flesh and sank into mine, and again I marveled at how well we fit. Then she started to slip from my grasp, and I let her go. I hugged the next body in line—I had no idea who it was—and heard Alena sobbing. I turned to see a circle of women around her, comforting her as she clung to her husband.

I slipped out the side door unnoticed. Outside, the late afternoon sun poured down 45th Street, blinding me. I turned east and began walking past the 8th Avenue hustlers, the Broadway theaters with their lit marquees and rave-filled posters, to the dirty glitz of Times Square. I stopped for a moment, looking uptown at the TKTS booth, then turned in circles like a tourist as I stared up at the brightly colored buildings, and letters, and lights. And I knew: I would never live here again. This city, my city, would always reflect her. Every building and shadow. Every accent, uptown or downtown. I would never stop thinking of her here. And I had to let her go. I had let them all go.

I put my head down and trudged toward 5th Avenue and the building where we all worked. I rode the elevator up to the eighteenth floor, used my pass key to enter the corridors of SR&G, and followed them down to the empty, spacious, beige workroom with its many cubicles, its thin carpet, to do what I should have already done. I typed out a memo stating my youngest sister had suffered a terrible fall the previous evening and broken her leg and hip, and since my mother was in marginal health I had no choice but to go home immediately to help care for her.

I wondered if my officemates would believe this story, or if they'd think my leaving had something to do with Jeremy. I gathered my few personal belongings from my desk and laid the memo, along with my pass key, on Alena's chair in her office.

Was it worth it, a voice inside me asked. The path that took me here? What I was going through and would no doubt continue to go through? Was it worth it, losing my city over her, this place where I became myself, which I'd loved like no other? It was a ridiculous question. Its irrelevance shamed itself. Regardless of what I'd lost or gained, for better or for worse, whether I hated her or loved her. . . . Actually, that was an easy one. I loved her. And I would never have chosen against encountering her in this life.

46

I packed, was down to fitting small stuff into boxes: photographs, some seashells I picked up on Jones Beach, a snow globe someone gave me of Times Square. Tonight I would take down my posters and my drawings. The brush, my sisters' brush, rested on the windowsill where I would leave it. My windows were open. The light was diffused outside and in, cloudy in the moist air.

It was the fourth day since I quit SR&G. I wanted to leave sooner but there was no way to arrange it all. I called the actress I'd subleased my apartment from and told her to use my deposit to cover the remaining month's rent on the lease. She wasn't pleased. Tomorrow morning some friends would come by to help me load the van I rented, and I'd be gone, on the road toward San Francisco. It was as good a place as any to start over. Better really, by a long shot. The skyline was gorgeous and unique there too, and the city was old in its own way. I'd get work as a graphic artist. I'd commit to my talent. Because of my sisters and Alena, or in spite of them, or both, I would draw. I would begin to paint again.

I went out to grab a slice of pizza for lunch. When I came back Eddy stopped me. "John," he said, "this came for you yesterday."

He held a brown package. An 8½-by-11-inch box, its return address stamped with SR&G's logo, sent out through their mailroom. As I headed toward the elevator I broke into a sweat. I was pretty certain I knew what was inside. The cross. She sent it back. It was what people did. Why would she want to keep it? How would she explain it to her husband if he found it?

But my hands shook as I tried to fit my key into the lock and open the door to my apartment, and once inside I tore at the paper, afraid I'd see the cross inside, expecting it. And how would I ever wear it again? How would I be able to do anything other than drop it out the window? Or give it to a homeless person on the street, which seemed a better fate. Yes, that was what I'd do. How stupid I was to give her something so irreplaceable.

The package was so well wrapped it took a moment to reach the white box beneath the paper. I sliced through the tape on its edges with my fingernails, hesitated, then lifted the lid. And I saw what she'd done. There, braided perfectly and curled inside, was her hair, which she had cut off.

I sank to the carpet, leaned against the wall, and after a moment lifted it out. It was such a long braid she must've cut it flush at her jawline. I smelled the cardamom, the rainwater. The light in the room picked up individual threads of colors weaving through it: bronze, auburn, chestnut, burgundy, mahogany . . . all of which appeared as a single shade from a distance, but a single shade would've never vibrated like this, would've never shown such life. Her hair was, by far, the most beautiful I ever saw on a woman.

I let the braid rest in my lap, felt its weight there as my fingers lightly stroked it. I couldn't take it with me, though a part of me wanted to bury it so deeply in a closet it would pull on me forever, even as its colors faded and I grew old. Which would be foolish. Which would be wrong.

No. Soon I would take it to the window instead. I'd unwind it strand by strand, let it dissolve in the air. I was ahead on my packing. I could take my time. I could wait till the sun was going down and the light outside was at its most vibrant. I would wait until then.

Acknowledgments

I'd like to thank the University of Wisconsin Press and its entire staff, especially my editor, Dennis Lloyd, for selecting, believing in, and shepherding this book to publication, his general insight into the material, and one particularly terrific idea he tossed off casually while we were talking. At the press I'd also like to specifically thank Jackie Teoh, Janie Chan, Jackie Krass, Adam Mehring, Ann Klefstad, Terry Emmrich, Jen Conn, Jeremy John Parker, Casey LaVela, Julia Knecht, Anne McKenna, and my publicists, Allie Shay and Mary Bisbee-Beek, for all their hard work and support. I should also thank the Center for Brooklyn History for providing research about their amazing city. On a personal note, and with much gratitude, I want to acknowledge my dear readers and friends, those who came to my aid with this book both early and late: Miranda Train, Karen Bjorneby, Michael Greer, Scott Zesch, Meg Pokrass, Erin Pounder, Eric Schnall, Steve Ball, Peter Drake, Janice Faber, Jessica Heimberg, Steve Paul, Chris Moyer, and my sister, Tamara Woodruff, who, when I thought the book was dead years ago, gave me the key perspective that turned the whole thing around.

I wandered the New York City streets in the 1980s, the 1990s, and the 2000s, and I not only found a city but I believe my truest self. Those wanderings over those miles are a primary source for my setting. I would also like to credit the book *And the Band Played On* by Randy Shilts and the documentary *Gay Sex in the 70s* (Joseph Lovett, director) for information about the AIDS crisis leading up to this period. Dr. Ramon Torres, whom I discovered while researching this, is such a fascinating character, he needs his own book. And though the famous St. Vincent's Hospital where he worked, which was ground zero for AIDS, is now gone, it does live on in literature and history (although it deserves to have more written about it). For information about typography, design, poster art, and graffiti I used the books *Typography* by Friedl, Ott, and Stein; *Subway Art* by Cooper and Chalfant; *Street Art* by Victor Burleigh; the essay "The Faith of Graffiti" by Norman Mailer; and a terrific class I took on typography at the School of Visual Arts in New York City in 2007. For my understanding of makeup, I credit the very difficult makeup class I took as an undergrad acting major at the University of Texas. I was amazed at how well I did in it, much better than in my acting classes, as if, like my protagonist, I'd uncovered one of my own secrets.

I'd also like to thank the Jentel Artist Residency, the Cuttyhunk Island Writers' Residency, and the Norman Mailer Writers Colony for giving me time, space, and inspiration to develop the ideas in this novel.

Last, I have to mention that it was, and still is, a great comfort I was able to tell my mother (who is most definitely *not* the mother depicted in this novel) two weeks before she died unexpectedly that the University of Wisconsin Press would be publishing my novel. She'd seen the ups and downs of my fighting to get this book into the world and was the best cheerleader and advisor I've ever had. I could hear the relief in her voice, as well as mine, at this very good news.